# About the Au

JJ FRANKLIN comes from a mental health and counselling background. She wrote scripts for the BBC before penning her first novel, *Urge to Kill*, a psychological police thriller featuring DI Turrell, set in and around Stratford-upon-Avon, where she runs a crime-writing group.

A DI MATT TURRELL INVESTIGATION

# ECHOES OF JUSTICE

## JJ FRANKLIN

SilverWood

Published in 2016 by SilverWood Books

SilverWood Books Ltd
14 Small Street, Bristol, BS1 1DE, United Kingdom
www.silverwoodbooks.co.uk

ISBN 978-1-78132-482-0 (paperback)
ISBN 978-0-95719-353-6 (ebook)

British Library Cataloguing in Publication Data
A CIP catalogue record for this book is available from
the British Library

Set in Sabon by SilverWood Books
Printed on responsibly sourced paper

# Acknowledgements

Special thanks go to my beta readers: Janet Williams, Maureen Hill, Barbara Speake, and my police advisors, Paul Taberner for Warwickshire and Kevin Robinson for overall police procedure.

I would like to thank Marina Zain, Head of Legal for The Royal Shakespeare Company and Jackie Handy of Stratford-upon-Avon College.

Also Rodney Bright at Wootten Wawen Marina who gave me a lot of help and information regarding narrowboats.

Thanks to Jann Tracey, my editor, for her eagle eye and Jane Dixon-Smith for her work on the cover. Also, for excellent advice given on my first draft, the Hilary Johnson Authors' Advisory Service.

I'm extremely grateful for the help and advice of Rowena Ball of SilverWood Books in bringing this book to print.

# Chapter 1

The first one was easy.

Kathy turned the corner and began the long walk past the row of dark shops, grilled and shuttered against the world, towards the off-licence that spilled its beacon across the gloom.

Caught within the circle of light, she could see him slouched against the wall, drinking from a can while several young men lounged about him.

Moving towards the group, she began the old woman shuffle she'd practised, aware that glances passed between them, and they watched her, as she guessed they would.

Inside the off-licence, Kathy kept up the masquerade, bending to hide her face from the CCTV and checking that her unruly curls remained tucked under her old gardening hat.

Behind the grille a middle-aged man rose, resigned, putting down his racing paper. 'Yes?'

It was important she remained in character and gave him nothing to remember her by. Kathy hesitated, as if still deciding, before pointing to a half bottle of the cheapest whisky.

He reached for the bottle and plonked it down in front of her. 'Four fifty-two,' he said, holding out his hand.

While he sighed with impatience and rested his elbow on the counter, Kathy counted out the change as if each penny were her last. When she had the exact amount, she dropped the coins into his hand, waiting as he placed the denominations into the correct sections of the cash register.

Banging shut the register, he picked up the whisky, intent on wrapping it in the fragile pink tissue paper that served as an empty semblance of customer service.

'No.' Kathy waved her hand to stop him and indicated that he should pass it to her and he glared at her in disgust as if she had contravened some deeply ingrained customer rule. She took the whisky and he turned away, shaking his head.

Taking slow steps towards the door, she stopped to tuck the bottle in a side pocket of her shopping bag, away from where the prepared bottle lay ready in its plain plastic bag. Hearing a rustle, she risked glancing around, but the man was ignoring her and had returned to his paper.

Now came the most terrifying part. Kathy moved to the door and took a deep breath, standing for a moment before stepping down and away from the protective pool of light. She sensed their eyes on her. The moment had come.

Kathy forced herself to take two steps, before stopping as if to begin an anxious search through her bag. To aid her search, she removed the plastic bag with the whisky, placing it on the wall of a neglected flowerbed where a tired brown twig poked up through the cigarette butts and empty beer cans.

The gang moved behind her as one, thinking they were silent, but she heard them and waited. It was just as she imagined.

'Can we help you, Gran?'

'No. No, thank you.' Kathy tried to make her voice sound frightened while the fear inside turned to triumph.

'Here, let me help you with your bags.' He reached out a hand to pick up the bag.

She made a tentative gesture to take it back from him. 'I can manage.' Kathy paused, taking a step backwards to look up into his face, directly into the eyes of one of her son's killers.

Jonathan Bernard James smiled, just as he had done in court when the judge pronounced the sentence, but his eyes remained narrowed and suspicious. His mother had spoken up for him, told the judge she'd tried to do her best, but he had turned into a bully like his father and she couldn't control him. Kathy had felt sorry for the woman. Would she cry when her son was dead?

Satisfied, she looked down and moved from one foot to the other. He would have one last chance of redemption. 'That's for my Albert,' she said, making sure her voice quivered.

'Well, guess what, Gran. Your Albert's going on the wagon.'

He lifted the whisky high and his companions dutifully laughed. Her job done, she gave a small cry and hobbled away, pausing only at the corner to turn and watch as Jonathan pulled out the bottle. The discarded bag fluttered across the windswept concrete to join with the other rubbish in the gutter, while Jonathan unscrewed the cap and put it to his lips. He hadn't noticed the broken seal. Kathy didn't think he would. Likewise, she guessed he wouldn't share much of his prize with the others.

# Chapter 2

DI Matt Turrell grinned as he entered the CID office. DC Jane Meadows was in full flow. At last, everything was back to normal.

'Don't you dare start, Sam. I'd forgotten what a bloody pain you are.' She sat down at her desk and noticed a small vase of flowers. 'Oh very funny. I hate cut flowers.'

'Would I?' DS Sam Withers held up his hands but his tell-tale grin gave him away.

As Matt walked down the office, she turned on him. 'No fuss, I said, and you promised.'

'Hey, I can't control this lot. I'm only the DI.'

A pile of cards, two boxes of chocolates and three other packages covered all available space on her desk, testament to the team's relief she had survived.

Two months ago, Matt thought the serial killer Clive Draper had claimed another victim. The team had tracked him to Heath End luxury spa and Jane had been first on the scene. Although ordered by Matt to wait for backup, she had no option when the killer put others in danger. When Matt found her, so white and still, he thought at first she was dead. No one imagined she would survive, never mind return to work.

'Anyway, I've got you chocolates as well.' Sam produced a large expensive box and held them out.

'Flowers as well as chocolates. Shouldn't you be plying some poor unsuspecting girl with these, Sam? Oh, sorry, I forgot, no one's interested.'

DCI McRay came to the door of his office, or lair, as the team called it, and rescued Matt from the familiar bickering. As McRay beckoned to him, Matt prayed nothing too heavy would come up with Christmas just a few weeks away, his first with Eppie. Funny to think that this time last year they hadn't even met.

McRay held open the door for him. 'Come in, Matt. I've been thinking we'll need to keep DC Meadows busy but not overload her, at least for a while. See how she goes.'

'She would hate sitting about, sir.'

'That's what I thought.'

'Not much going on.'

'Think all our local criminals must be wintering in Spain.' As McRay laughed heartily at his own joke, Matt joined in.

'Here's something.' McRay picked up a file from his desk. 'This might ease her in gently. A lowlife got hold of some dodgy gear. One less for us to worry about but we'd better be seen to be doing our duty.'

Matt took the file from McRay. The name, Jonathan Bernard James, was familiar. 'I knew this lad, sir.'

'Always in trouble I suppose?'

'I arrested him, and four others, for murder. Remember Jack Wylde, about two years ago – kicked to death?'

'Didn't the little buggers get off?'

'Charges reduced to manslaughter.'

'So now he's got what he deserved.'

'Maybe.' Matt knew it wasn't worth arguing with McRay whose opinions were set in concrete. He thought of Jonathan's mother. At the trial, she appeared a bewildered, soft little woman, baffled as to how her boy had come to this. She couldn't understand that Jonathan, tempered in his father's punches, had sought his own self-destructive way forward.

'He wasn't known as a dealer, or even a user.'

'Then I guess he's moved on. We need formal ID so I'd start with the mother. Slim should be doing the PM tomorrow.'

'Will do, sir.' Matt left McRay's office, stopping on the way to speak to Jane, who had pushed all the presents and cards into an untidy pile at the side of her desk.

Matt bent to whisper in her ear. 'Open all of those, and say thank you, nicely, and I might have a case for us.' He indicated the file and her eyes lit up.

'That's more like it.' She stood.

'First.' Matt pointed to the jumble. 'Ten minutes.' He glanced at his watch as he made his way to his own small office. Skimming through the file, he looked up to watch her open the gifts and give thanks with a pasted smile. The pile diminished and he went towards her. 'Right, let's see if the brain still works.'

'One more.' She tore open the last card and stopped.

Matt noticed the card was from DI Grant and guessed how hard it must have been for him. Always difficult, even surly to work with, but thank God, Grant had put himself on the line when needed.

Clive Draper came close to destroying both the team and Matt's world when Eppie, his wife of only a few weeks, became a target. Though Grant had minor injuries compared to Jane, Matt would always be grateful to him for helping to save Eppie's life.

She stood and turned towards him. 'Thank you, Grant. It's a lovely card.'

'Just following the official line,' he grunted, not looking up.

Trust Grant to spoil the moment, Matt thought.

Jane didn't react, but smiled, tossing her long blonde hair as she reached for her plain black woollen coat. She'd learnt fast that the fluffy angora jacket she'd worn on her first day in CID wouldn't do. The team had teased her unmercifully before dubbing her with the nickname of Fluff. But, when he'd visited her in hospital, she'd requested that he and the rest of the team now start calling her Jane. Despite sending a memo to the team about the change, he, and the rest of them, were finding it hard after years of calling her Fluff. He knew he must set an example, although he wondered what had prompted her request.

Nevertheless, Matt relied on Jane's instinct to know when the smallest thing was out of place or when a witness was lying, and it felt good to have her back.

# Chapter 3

Matt strode out of the office, surprised that Jane was not keeping pace with him. Not wanting to bring it to attention, he slowed until she was beside him.

'Got more work to do at physio. Sorry I'm slowing you down. Maybe you should have brought Sam instead.'

He might have known she would pick up he was making an allowance for her. No one could fool her for long. 'What and leave you malingering in the office eating all those chocolates?'

'So this is get the invalid back to work, is it?'

'You bet. It's been like half the team were missing.' As they reached the car, Matt resisted opening the passenger door for her.

Once they were on their way, she glanced at him. 'You look great. I'm not surprised. Eppie rustled up some great meals when she stayed at my place.'

'I can't believe I was lucky enough to marry a woman who likes cooking. Beauty, brains and a cook – what more could a man want?' Although he was trying for lightness, he couldn't help thinking back to the danger Clive Draper had put Eppie in. In an attempt to keep her safe, she'd gone to stay with Jane.

'You're a lucky man, Matt.'

Noting a hint of wistfulness, Matt wondered if her relationship with Jenny was still on the cards. He had seen DI Jenny Hadden at her bedside during those first few critical weeks but once the painful path back to normality had begun, he hadn't caught a glimpse of her at all. Still, Jane would tell him when she was ready and now they had a job to do.

The mortuary was not one of Matt's favourite places and he was always keen to leave as soon as possible. He waited as Jane brought Mrs James down the corridor towards him. Mary James looked smaller, as if shrunken with grief. She still appeared bewildered, but then who wouldn't in this cold, clinical place where you were forced to view and own your dead. Matt was glad Jonathan had received no visible physical injuries and it crossed his mind that if he had been murdered, his killer may be squeamish. He filed this away for further examination later.

Jane guided Mary to the window behind which her son lay covered in a sheet, but dead all the same. 'I want you to tell me when you're ready, Mrs James. There's no rush and everything is up to you.'

'Thank you.'

'When you're ready I will signal for these curtains to be drawn. Jonathan will be lying just inside.'

Mary took a big breath and nodded, 'Now, please.'

Jane pressed a bell and the curtains drew apart. As Mary stepped forward, Matt moved behind her in case she fainted.

Mary looked long and hard at her son before taking a step back, treading on Matt's toes. 'Yes. That is my son.'

This calm, almost cold reaction was unexpected and Matt and Jane exchanged glances of surprise.

'My son, Jonathan Bernard James. Bernard after his grandfather. I'm glad he's not here to see this.' Mary pressed closer to the glass again as if taking in every aspect of her son's face before turning to begin a dignified walk back down the corridor.

Jane hurried to catch up with her. 'If you feel able, we would like you to stay and have a cup of tea with us, Mrs James. There are one or two formalities we should go through.'

Mary stopped and seemed confused. Matt could see then the effort she was putting into holding herself together.

'No rush. Let's have some tea for now shall we?' Jane added.

Matt passed them both and held open the door to the relatives' room, a bland, soulless place, enlivened only by a small pot of bronze chrysanthemums in need of watering. He was embarrassed this was all they could offer.

Mary stood in the doorway and glanced at the green walls, the supposedly tasteful but nondescript print on the wall that blended well with the nothingness of the room. She turned to Matt. 'Please, can I just go home?'

Matt hesitated. There was no way he wanted to sit in that room and ask her questions about her dead son. He nodded and closed the door, aware that Jane had given a faint sigh at his capitulation. Matt avoided her eyes and turned to Mary, ushering her away from the room. 'Come on, we'll drive you home, Mrs James.'

# Chapter 4

Kathy expected the sense of triumph to last but, except for those first few moments, she felt flat, depressed. Maybe turning yourself into a cold-blooded killer wasn't that easy. Stunned to realise that is what she had become, she sat down at the kitchen table. In front of her was the list she had made of each of the gang members. She had been gathering information about them since the trial. If they had received realistic punishments instead of the light sentences handed out because of their ages, Kathy felt she could have accepted it and moved on.

This wasn't the first time she felt cheated of justice. Losing Bill had been bad enough, but the driver who left her husband bleeding to death had never been caught. For years she experienced moments of rage when she saw a speeding or careless driver. Jack's murder brought all that anger flooding back. In the early days after her son's death, she couldn't grieve, not in any of the recognised ways, unlike Pam, Jack's wife, who drew her children close and tried to shut out the reality of the world, including Kathy.

In her own efforts to block out the terrible truth, Kathy wandered the streets at night, hopeful the physical action would somehow alleviate the great pain and knowing she couldn't risk meeting anyone who would say something kind or trite. During those midnight walks, she seemed to have acquired a blanket of protection. Maybe the horror of identifying her son's body, left battered and bruised by the thugs, showed on her face. She could pass through the drunken crowds pouring out of nightclubs and they would part without saying a word. On the dark recreation ground, she passed the distorted silhouette of the bandstand, alongside the shadowy, silent river, disturbing ducks and lovers alike. At Lucy's Mill Bridge, she often stood in the middle, looking down at the swirling waters of the Avon below and wanting to throw herself in. Throughout those night meanderings, Kathy came to realise that justice must be done or she wouldn't be able to go on.

Pushing aside the list, she drew her granddaughter Zoe's birthday present forward and got out the wrapping paper. The doll came with several changes of clothing so she wrapped each separately before writing the card. She'd last seen Zoe on her fourth birthday, a year ago, but only for a few minutes, as Pam hadn't invited her in. She seemed ill at ease and not liking to force the issue, Kathy had left, consoling herself that all three children looked well cared for, in a physical way, at least.

Today she was determined to enter what had been her son's house to see her grandchildren. Kathy waited until after school, knowing they would be home, as Pam never took them anywhere.

As she walked up the path, the small lilac bush, planted by Jack when they had moved in several years ago, brushed against her face. It was now a tree, overgrown like everything around it and in need of cutting back. Pushing it aside, she held onto the twigs for a moment as if they could bring her closer to Jack, could give her courage.

A small shadow appeared behind the coloured glass when she rang the doorbell, until a taller, darker shadow took its place. The tall shadow stood still. Guessing Pam was hoping she would go away, Kathy rang again, keeping her finger on the bell for just a second or two longer than necessary to let Pam know she was serious.

The door, secured by a chain, opened a crack and Pam peered out. She seemed frightened, like after Jack died. Maybe she imagined the gang that killed Jack would come for her. Kathy often tried to imagine how horrendous it must have been for her watching, screaming and helpless to do anything.

After the court cases and sentencing, Kathy hoped Pam would be reassured, but it hadn't helped. Everyone was suspect, including her. At first, she'd tried to be supportive, given her time, offered to help look after the children, her granddaughters after all, but Pam always seemed apprehensive. She had wondered if she reminded her too much of Jack. Then, when Kathy suggested Pam talk to her doctor, she found herself shut out.

This had gone on long enough and Kathy had to think of the girls. Okay, they went to school, but she'd heard that Phoebe had dropped her music lessons and Amy the Brownies. She had to get Pam to let her in, see for herself what was going on.

She'd seen Phoebe one day in the school playground all alone, head down, instead of surrounded by her friends. Kathy tried to talk to her through the railings, but sensed she was holding back, maybe out of loyalty to her mum. If Pam's state of mind was rubbing off on the children, she had to do something. Would she feel safer now that Jonathan James was dead? Would she have heard?

'Pam, it's only me,' she said to the crack in the door. 'I've brought Zoe's birthday present.' She held up the parcels in proof.

The crack widened.

'Can I come in?'

Kathy waited as the smaller shadow came close and she heard a soft voice.

'Please, Mum.'

There was a pause before the chain rattled and the door opened. Pam peered out, around and past Kathy before she ushered her in.

Zoe took Kathy's hand and led her towards the kitchen. 'Stay at the edge, Gran. We mustn't make a mess.'

Bewildered, she followed Zoe's example, keeping to the wood at the side of the rug that ran down the hallway to the kitchen. Pam followed, also walking at the edge. Once in the kitchen Pam stood as if unsure of what to do.

Kathy placed Zoe's presents on the kitchen table and turned to her. 'Any chance of a cup of tea, Pam? I'm parched.'

Pam seemed reluctant but moved towards the kettle. The kitchen was operating-room clean and seemed unused.

As Pam filled the kettle, Kathy turned to Zoe. 'Happy birthday, Zoe. So how's my little pudding then? I swear you've grown ten inches since I last saw you.'

'I'm in Miss Turner's class now.'

'And how do you like school?'

'I like it. And, and I got a star for my drawing.'

'Brilliant. I always knew you were a clever girl. Can I see your picture?'

'It's at school. On the wall.'

'Well, when you bring it home you can put it on the wall here.'

Zoe shook her head and glanced at her mum as if betraying a trust. Something wasn't right in this house, Kathy was sure. Pam plugged in the kettle and returned to the sink to wipe up the splashes before moving to the cupboard to get mugs. Kathy was surprised to see them lined up in a complete regimented fashion, all the handles pointing in the same direction. Pam hesitated before removing one mug. She appeared thinner, tired, and Kathy had the urge to go to her and give her a big hug, to hold her and tell her it would be alright, except she wasn't sure how Pam would react. There was an invisible barrier around her, holding all the sting of barbed wire.

Instead, she went forward and took the mug out of her hand. 'Why don't I make us both a brew while you sit down with Zoe and open her presents?'

Pam hesitated until Zoe piped up. 'Can I open them, Mum? Can I?'

With an echo of the old Pam and a faint smile, she gave in and went to her daughter. 'Yes. Open your presents.'

As Pam sat down to help Zoe, Kathy got down another mug and searched for the teabags. 'Where are Amy and Phoebe?' she asked, thinking how quiet the house was.

'In their rooms, chatting with friends on their computers.'

Kathy placed the two mugs of tea on the table as Zoe tore open her main present.

'Oh, thank you, Granny Kathy. I shall call her Wendy. Like in Peter Pan. I read two whole pages to the class. Miss Turner said—'

'Zoe, please stop bothering Granny and go and fetch your sisters.'

Her face dropped but she slipped down and went to get Amy and Phoebe. Turning back to Pam, Kathy found she was busy carefully folding the wrapping paper into neat squares and pressing them into tidy stacks. 'How are you, Pam?'

'I'm fine – thank you.' She paused as if unused to making conversation and with great effort added, 'Are you well?'

Kathy wondered whether to mention Jonathan's death. She might be relieved. 'Yes, thanks. Have you heard that Jonathan James is dead?'

Pam shivered and stood up, wrapping her arms around herself.

'I just thought you'd like to know.' Kathy kicked herself for being selfish, as if she needed praise for accomplishing his death. 'I'm sorry, I shouldn't have mentioned it.' She reached out to Pam who backed further away, just as Zoe came back with Amy and Phoebe. Kathy noticed they all walked down the hallway in the same way, avoiding the carpet and staying on the wooden flooring.

Eight-year-old Amy came for a hug, but ten-year-old Phoebe hung back, glancing at her mother.

'Shall we go into the lounge and you can tell me what you've been up to?' Kathy suggested.

There was a silence, which hung in the air until Phoebe broke it. 'Mum keeps that room for best.'

Kathy guessed Phoebe was used to protecting Pam, even colluding with her. She appeared subdued and not at all the bright spark of a girl Kathy remembered.

Pam was wiping down the draining board and Kathy noticed her shoulders relax at Phoebe's reply. She felt a flash of anger at the responsibility being placed on Phoebe and tried to push it down, knowing getting cross wouldn't help.

Now she was adding to the pressure. If Pam knew she would only stay for a short time, maybe she would be more willing to let her in again. 'Well, I'd better get on.' Kathy went to put her mug in the sink, but Pam took it from her.

The relief was obvious. Kathy kissed Zoe and Amy and looked towards Phoebe, who had gone to stand beside her mum. It seemed as if she was blending into her mum's shield of barbed wire, so Kathy just spoke to her instead of trying for a hug. 'Goodbye, Phoebe. Do well at school, love.'

She nodded and Zoe led the way to the front door. 'You have my number don't you, Zoe? Call me whenever you want to.'

'Yes, Gran. If Mummy lets me.'

Outside Kathy felt the tears threatening to flow. Even Jack's lilac tree couldn't stop the pain. As she walked down the path, she heard the vacuum cleaner start up and her grief turned to anger.

# Chapter 5

The small front garden, deep in weeds and grass, hid several items; Matt guessed at a bike, maybe a couple of tyres with the rest unidentifiable. Mrs James led them past with a mumbled apology.

Inside was a complete contrast, for although the furniture was shabby, even Matt noticed how tidy it was. A photo of Jonathan stood on the mantelpiece, another on the sideboard and another on the bookcase, all showing a grinning boy aged about eight or nine.

'Please sit down.' She rushed to move the TV remote and straighten the cushions on the sofa, but she remained standing. She seemed unable to stay still, fidgeting about the room to flick a speck of dust from the table or straighten one of Jonathan's photos.

Matt and Jane sat on the lumpy sofa. 'Thank you. We are really sorry for your loss, Mrs James,' Matt said.

Mrs James nodded, unable to reply.

'As you know, we have yet to establish how Jonathan died.'

Again the nod, face turned away from them. Matt sent an appealing look to Jane, who was the expert in dealing with this kind of situation. She gave a brief nod and stood, moving to stand in front of Mary.

'Mrs James, we'd like you to help us to find out what happened to Jonathan and who he was with on the night he died.'

'I don't know. He didn't tell me what he was doing. And I...well, I'd given up asking. He did mention someone called Nod or Noddy once.'

'Do you know his real name?'

'Sorry, no.'

'Might Jonathan and his friends have become involved in the drug scene?'

Mrs James turned away from her, anger in her voice. 'No.'

'How can you be so certain, Mrs James?'

'He hated the stuff.'

'Hated?'

'One of his friends died from using. Poor kid was only ten. Thought my lad was done with tears, what with all the knocking about he took. But he was in bits, crying in my lap. Last time I ever saw him like that though. He hardened up after that. Became more like his dad.' Mary was still for a moment, thinking. 'That's when I really lost him.'

She moved to straighten the small statue of a spaniel on the mantelpiece. The statue appeared decrepit and had lost part of its ear, yet she handled it like a priceless work of art.

'Present. School trip when he was nine.'

'We realise this is difficult, Mrs James. But it's tough on the streets. Might Jonathan have been dragged into something you didn't know about?' Jane asked.

'No. No way. I know what you're thinking.'

Matt couldn't help asking. 'What are we thinking, Mrs James?'

Jane shot him a glance of *don't interfere.*

'He was a tearaway, getting into all sorts of trouble. I know that.'

Matt thought Jonathan James was much more than a tearaway, but kept quiet and waited.

'It's only me who can remember how he was, before.' Mrs James moved away from Jane and sat next to Matt on the sofa. 'He was a cheerful little lad. Reminded me of my dad. Then Vince said he was growing up and needed a man's hand. That's what he got. The back of his hand for as much as a word. What I got too if I tried to stop him. I watched my little lad turn sullen, resentful and then hard, like his dad.'

'Sounds like there was little you could do,' Matt agreed.

'No. But I remember how he was and I know that lad was still inside, buried under all the slaps and beatings.' Mrs James's face began to crumple and tears ran down her cheeks.

Matt put his arm around her, letting her cry on his shoulder, despite departmental policy and Jane raising her eyebrows at him. She needed someone on her side.

'Sorry.'

Mrs James pulled back and Matt offered his hankie. She began to dab at her eyes. Matt knew it was time to get back on track. 'Can you tell us where Mr James is, Mrs James?'

'I haven't seen him for years, not since he was arrested and escaped.'

'And he hasn't been in contact?'

'No. And I hope it stays that way.'

'So he doesn't know about his son's death?'

'I suppose not.'

'Will you tell us if he gets in touch?'

'Yes.'

'Thank you. Now it's important we take a look at Jonathan's room as it may give us some insight into what happened to him. While DC Meadows is doing that, why don't I put the kettle on?'

Mrs James nodded and stood to direct Jane to Jonathan's bedroom. By the time Matt had placed a steaming hot mug of tea in front of Mrs James, she had returned to say the bedroom yielded nothing but a laptop. With Mrs James happy for them to take it, Jane wrote out the receipt while Matt handed over his card, stressing Mrs James should call day or night.

Driving back to the office, Jane ran over all the information they had, plus the gaps they needed to fill in. 'She doesn't seem to know any of Jonathan's friends. Except this Noddy fellow.'

'He should be easy to track down. Uniform will know. Did you believe her when she said she didn't know where her husband is?'

'Yes, and I don't think she wants to. Sounds like she's better off without him.'

Matt agreed. He remembered reading about Vincent James when Jonathan was on trial. As far as he could remember, he was a violent career criminal. Jane interrupted his thoughts.

'Wouldn't she have known if Jonathan had been into drugs?'

'I'd have thought so. She certainly seemed convinced that he wasn't.' Even as he said it, Matt realised he would have a hard time convincing McRay.

# Chapter 6

Sam jumped up in anticipation as they walked into the office. 'What do we have, guv? Want me to start the board?'

'Best hold your horses, Sam. I've got to talk to McRay first.'

'This might help. I phoned Slim.'

'Thanks, Sam.' Matt took Sam's scribbled notes of the pathologist's preliminary thoughts, scanning them as he walked towards McRay's office. He wasn't looking forward to trying to convince the DCI something wasn't right in the death of Jonathan James.

McRay saw him coming. 'Come in, Matt.' McRay waved him to a seat while studying his face. 'I've got a feeling this isn't going to make me happy. Right?'

Matt sat down, marshalling his thoughts to get McRay onside. 'Initially, sir, I did feel, like you, that this would be a self-inflicted drugs overdose. But there are one or two things which don't add up.'

McRay gave a sigh and settled further into his seat.

'First of all we have no indications Jonathan was a drug user.'

'According to?'

'Slim found no evidence the victim...' Matt stopped as McRay gave a grunt of disgust at the word, and waited until he gave an ill-natured nod for him to carry on. Matt read from Sam's notes. 'The victim showed no indication of regular drug use. Death appears to be due to a massive overdose of a morphine-based drug. Toxicology report has been fast-tracked.'

McRay groaned.

Matt continued. 'If we wait for the full toxicology report, valuable time might be lost, sir.'

'Trying to tell me how to do my job?'

'No, sir.'

'I should hope not. What about the mother?'

'Adamant her son wasn't a user.'

'Well, she would say that, wouldn't she? Did DC Meadows believe her?'

'Yes, sir. We both did.'

'Well, there must be a lot of people happy to see the back of Jonathan James. Take a quick look. How long has he been out of custody?'

'About two months.'

'Might be worth checking with them – they would know if he was a user. And, Matt, I don't want a lot of time wasted on this but, while we haven't anything serious on the go, it won't hurt.'

'Thank you, sir.'

Matt left, giving the thumbs up sign to Sam, who moved to start the incident board. By the time Matt had called the team together, Sam had a picture of Jonathan James in place, together with a host of other details. Matt guessed Sam had been busy doing this basic work while he was out. Moving to stand in front of the board, Matt gave him a nod of approval.

Most of the team had gathered around Jane's desk, wolfing down the chocolates, so there was no need for Matt to raise his voice. Only Grant remained oblivious and was intent on his computer screen. Matt decided to ignore him.

'Jonathan James was found in an alley between Pierce and Monument Street at one twenty-five this morning by a club doorman. He called ambulance and uniform, but Jonathan was dead on arrival at Warwick Hospital. Slim is doing the post mortem tomorrow. He estimates the time of death between eleven-thirty last night and one this morning. From his initial findings, he thinks it is likely Jonathan died of a huge drug overdose, most likely morphine-based. However, he found no evidence of routine drug use. Jonathan's mother, Mary James, is adamant her son was not a user. I know, I know, that's what they all say.' Matt held up his hands at the general moan of disbelief, before continuing. 'However, we both believe her. Slim is fast-tracking the toxicology report.'

'Could he have been branching out, trying something new?' Grant drawled, finally raising his head.

'There is always that chance, but it's unlikely he would choose to start with this drug, or that he'd be able to get his hands on such a large quantity. We need to check what's on the street right now. Grant, could you have a word with the drug team?'

'If that's what you think is best, sir?'

Somehow, Grant always seemed to imply Matt's decisions might not be right, but Matt was used to the man now and didn't rise to the bait. 'Thank you. We should also check for break-ins at doctor's surgeries, pharmacies, etc., for any report that involves morphine or its derivative.'

Grant nodded and Matt moved on.

'For those of you who weren't here, or have a bad memory, two years ago, Jonathan James was one of five youths convicted of the manslaughter of Jack Wylde. He was undoubtedly the ringleader and served the longest sentence, although reduced because of his age. We need to trace his co-defendants, just in case one of them has developed a grudge, life ruined and all that.'

'I've traced one of the four, guv.'

Matt stepped back and gave the floor to Sam.

'Harry Winters, aged sixteen when the offence was committed, was sentenced to six months at a young offenders' unit. He was a model prisoner and since being released managed to get a part-time job at the Chalice...' Sam paused to review his notes. 'The Stratford Chalice Hotel in the porters' department. Not only that, but he's doing drama at Stratford College.'

As Sam turned to write Harry's name on the board, Matt stepped in. 'Thanks, Sam. Harry seems an unlikely candidate for Jonathan's death, but we'll need to see him and chase up the others, to see if they have any idea who may have killed him and to rule them out.'

'What about Jack Wylde's family?' Jane asked.

'There was only his wife and three young children. She was present at the time and was traumatized, as you can imagine. Certainly worth checking out. Think you should be the one to do that, Jane.'

'Thanks a lot,' she said, pulling a face and ignoring the titters from the others.

She appeared tired and Matt wasn't surprised when she shoved the chocolate-guzzlers aside and sat down. He'd have to make sure she didn't take too much on, at least for a while.

'What about Jack's mother?' Grant called out.

Matt wondered why it sounded like an accusation, but he replied calmly. 'True, good call, Grant. We'll add her to the list. Also, we need to trace who was with Jonathan last night. We do have a name, well, a partial, from his mother, of a Nod or Noddy. Uniform may have some idea. Have a word with them, please, Wendy. The more we know about the street scene and who Jonathan was hanging around with the better.'

Wendy nodded, embarrassed but pleased to be mentioned.

'Sam, dig up the other three involved in Jack Wylde's murder and we'll pay them a visit tomorrow.'

'I have their names but not much else, guv.'

Matt wasn't surprised Sam was way ahead of him. 'Let's have them, then, Sam.'

Sam spoke while he was writing the names on the board. 'Tom Grace, Nick Tyler and Dave Beeson.'

'Thanks, Sam. I seem to remember a girl on the scene at the time too, girlfriend of Jonathan's. Think her name was…Tilly. We'll need to dig up her file. She was interviewed, but no charges were made. Can you cover the post mortem tomorrow, Sam? I know the mortuary is your favourite place.'

Sam nodded, trying to act nonchalantly. Everyone was aware that Sam had to steel himself to visit the mortuary. Yet he would return all enthused, regaling any one of the team not fast enough to escape about the wonders of the human body. Matt had to get him to calm down just to get the basic facts.

'We also need to check with the prison services. They'll be able to tell us if Jonathan was a user. Can I add that to your list, please, Wendy?'

Wendy nodded.

'Grant, if you can check out the CCTV from Jonathan's home to where he was found. I think that's enough to be going on with. Jonathan's mobile phone and computer are currently being analysed. Let's get an early start in the morning.'

Matt waited until everyone had dispersed before going over to Jane. 'Why don't you write up the notes from today, then head home?'

'What, at three o'clock in the afternoon?'

'Yes.' Matt didn't intend to give her any room to wriggle out of his request and walked back to his office.

He'd just sat down and opened Jonathan's file when she stormed through the door, banging it behind her.

'Go home? What the hell do you mean by that?'

'Sit down.' Matt indicated a seat by the coffee table and got up to join her.

'I don't want or need any special treatment, Matt.' Refusing to sit, she stood with arms folded.

'Don't worry. I'm not treating you any different than I would anyone else injured on duty.'

Matt sank into a chair and indicated the other. Jane plonked herself down. Matt thought of going to the head's office at school and had the urge to laugh. Yet, he recognised he would have to handle her with care to get her on side.

'Look, Fluff. Sorry, Jane. We have no idea where this case is going. If it does turn out that Jonathan was murdered, and it's beginning to look that way, then we may have someone who is out there seeking their own brand of justice. That puts a lot of others in the firing line and I don't want their deaths on my conscience.'

He thought of young Gracie, whose death still haunted him, even though she had died over five years ago. After locking up the wrong man, he'd allowed the murderer free to kill young Gracie. The day they found her was a day he would never forget. It was evident what she had gone through and the horror always distressed him. Ashamed of his failure, he'd offered to resign, but McRay had talked him round. At her funeral, he had made a vow that he would do his best not to let anyone down again.

'We need the team up to full strength and you are a vital part of the team. I'm being selfish by taking care of you, easing you in gently. Besides, you look bloody awful. Now, get those notes down and go home, or go home and write them up, whatever you want, please. Just go home.'

'What a load of old tosh, Matt. Are you sure you haven't kissed the Blarney Stone?'

Matt laughed, relieved to see signs of the old Jane.

# Chapter 7

The sea was dull and sluggish with waves taking their time in a long rising and falling swell. Deep in a swirl of emotions over Jon's death, they suited Vinny's mood. He was thankful that Harold, nicknamed Ops, had maintained the right contacts and was able to let him know so quickly.

Vinny would have liked to be in the bar, planning how he would avenge Jon, but that wasn't an option while playing the part of a devoted uncle to the Swift family and their five little monsters. The smallest child tugged at his coat, demanding a story. Suppressing the urge to bat her away, he smiled and lifted her onto his knee. 'Right, Kylie, what's it to be?'

Mrs Swift passed over a picture book and went to chase the three-year-old who was scrambling over passengers' legs and belongings.

Vinny promised himself that he would make Ops pay for this hideous journey. Surely the old fool could have thought of another way to get him safely back into England. The Swifts, grateful for the money, accepted him as Uncle Vince with no questions asked. As part of their family group, he should be able to get through customs. Young Kylie had taken to him, so he would carry her. Who would suspect a devoted uncle? In his haste, Vinny had tried to alter his appearance by dyeing his hair a shade lighter, nothing too outlandish, and having a haircut he hated. He'd developed a small goatee beard over the last few months and decided that would help too.

As he read the picture book for the third time, he reminded himself it wouldn't be long until they docked. Ops had arranged for someone to meet him outside the docks and the Swifts agreed to drop him off at the designated place. Everything should run smoothly. After all, he was paying Ops enough and he was the best.

He consoled himself that his role as uncle would soon be over and he would be able to get on with his mission. Once he'd found out who killed Jon, he promised himself they would pay a heavy price.

# Chapter 8

'Matt, you're squashing me.'

'Then move your end to the left.' Matt sighed as Eppie moved to the right. 'Your left.'

He took the weight as Eppie manoeuvred backwards through the doorway to the flat. The folding table wasn't heavy, just awkward. They struggled into the small living room and leant the table against the book-case. Eppie sank onto the sofa.

'Maybe this wasn't such a good idea.'

'I told you that.'

'So we invite your parents round and then give them dinner on their laps?'

'Or take them out?'

'Like we don't want them here.'

'They wouldn't think that. Besides, Mum understands.'

'That you don't get on with your dad. So right, we'll never see them?'

'It's not like that.'

'Oh grow up, Matt.'

Eppie jumped up and went into the kitchen, easing past the table and the small Christmas tree she had insisted on putting up. Matt knocked several baubles off every time he walked past, but he hadn't the heart to say that he never bothered to decorate his flat. She was looking forward to Christmas in England, her first for many years, and Matt couldn't deny her.

This hassle was the last thing he wanted at the start of a new case. He liked to sit in his comfy old chair and let the details wash over him. It was where he got his best insights, made those important connections. There would be little chance of that this week, as Eppie had insisted they invite his parents to dinner on Friday and the preparations for that, plus the fact she had started a new job two weeks ago, were sending her into a hive of activity.

Matt's past efforts to get on with his dad had ended with each of them losing their tempers. Dad had never forgiven him for following Granddad into the police force, instead of going to university. Since his marriage two months ago, they'd seen his parents on a few occasions, admittedly with other people around. He sighed, knowing he wouldn't be able to get out of this dinner.

Eppie plonked a beer down beside him. 'I'm sorry.'

Matt pulled her onto his lap, pushing back her brown hair to kiss her. He loved the way her small body melted into his. 'It will be fine, I promise to be on my best behaviour.'

'Only while they're here, I hope?'

Matt kissed her again but she wriggled away, murmuring something about dinner. He watched her as she went back to the kitchen, walking as she always did, with that sense of purpose.

Eppie was a great cook, so she should have no worries about his parents on that score. He knew she'd never taken to his tiny flat. While he'd never noticed the lack of colour, Eppie had persuaded him – no, insisted – that the flat needed light and colour. Now bright curtains hung at the windows, and he had to admit he had accepted and even liked the matching cushions on the new modern sofa. It pulled out into a bed, ready for the occasional visitor. She'd culled his rugby trophies that graced the mantelpiece to allow room for some of her belongings, including a wedding present he wasn't particularly fond of: a small jade Buddha, a present from her father. It sat there and seemed to glare down at him.

He hadn't realised how much marriage was about sharing and thought things would stay as they were, with the addition of Eppie, of course. Although it was difficult, after nearly losing her so soon into their marriage he would do anything to keep her happy.

'Dinner's ready. Grab your tray.'

Eppie handed him a tray across the folded table. There was a pork chop, with mashed potato and tasty gravy. All smelt delicious and he congratulated himself again on his good luck.

After he had wolfed down his meal, Matt joined Eppie in the kitchen to clear up. He quite liked having his hands in the hot soapy water and the time spent together doing ordinary domestic chores. When the doorbell rang, he let Eppie answer and heard Ida Davis's voice.

'We've just received the tickets, so I thought I'd bring yours round.'

Ida and John Davis lived in a flat down the corridor. No one saw very much of John but Ida was always cheerful and friendly. Puzzled about what tickets Eppie had been buying, he picked up a tea towel and went to say hello.

'Thank you, Ida. We're looking forward to the show.'

'I think you'll enjoy it. Oh hello, Matt. I see you're getting him domesticated. That's the way.'

'How are you, Ida?'

'Very well thank you. Have you both fully recovered?'

Eppie went to Matt and circled her arm around his waist. 'Yes. Although if he forgets something he still blames that bang on the head.'

Ida laughed and Matt invited her to sit down.

'No, thank you. John's waiting for his dinner. Hope the table fits.'

After Ida left, there was silence between them as they finished tidying the kitchen. Finally, Matt spoke. 'So what am I sure to enjoy?'

Eppie hesitated. 'Ida's choir is singing at the new Royal Shakespeare Theatre. They're having an open event for all local groups to test everything out. She is so excited.'

'You want me to go with you?'

'Yes.'

'To listen to Shakespeare, musicals, stuff like that?'

'Why not?'

'Because.'

'Because what?'

'It's a girly thing.'

'God, you are old-fashioned. Why do you say that?'

'It will be all screeching and the like.'

'How do you know if you've never been?'

'Well, er...everyone knows.'

'Who? A lot of blokes sitting around in the pub?'

'No...everybody.'

'For an intelligent man, Matt Turrell, you are woefully uneducated. Listen, if I can come and enjoy your rugby matches then you can, occasionally, just occasionally, put yourself out for me. Right?'

Matt felt himself backed into a corner and decided the best option would be to comply while hoping that work or some other emergency would rescue him when the time came. He held up his hands. 'Okay, I give in. Mrs Turrell, I will be delighted to attend with you. Here is my arm, ready and waiting.'

Eppie saw he was taking the mickey and flipped him with the tea towel before moving in closer and pummelling him on the chest, forcing him to take both her hands, twisting them behind her to draw her in close.

'You might enjoy it,' she said, lifting her mouth towards his.

'Oh, I'm sure I will.' Matt bent to kiss her, fusing them together and arousing the need in both of them. He took her hand and led her into the bedroom, removing her blouse and his shirt. The doorbell rang.

'Let's ignore it,' he begged.

She nodded like a naughty schoolgirl and jumped on the bed. Matt grinned and followed her. The bell rang again and this time didn't let up. Someone was holding their finger on the buzzer.

'Bugger, I'd better find out who that is. You stay right here.' Matt grabbed his shirt and headed for the door.

It couldn't be work, as they would ring. Maybe Ida was in trouble. He couldn't imagine her holding onto the bell that long unless it was an emergency. Flinging open the door, he was surprised to see a middle-aged woman. Her hair and dress shouted expensive more than elegant. Her face, despite its expert make-up, appeared shrewish and angry. Before he had time to ask what she wanted, she pushed past him.

'About time. Suitcases in the hall.'

'I'm sorry, who are you?'

'Angela. Your mother-in-law. Unless Eppie has taken a lover already.'

'I beg your pardon?' Matt couldn't believe that this bossy, rude woman had descended on them without so much as a warning. Still, he was aware that his shirt was undone and hastened to fasten it. Now he understood why Eppie didn't want anything to do with her mother. She was supposed to be far away in Argentina, happy with her fifth husband. Angela stood glancing around the flat.

With a sniff, she turned to Matt. 'Cases.'

'You can't stay here.'

'And why not? This is my daughter's home. Such as it is.'

'Yes, but '

'Mum?'

Eppie came from the bedroom fastening her robe. She stopped, shocked at the sight of her mother. He waited for her to decide what to do.

'It's alright, Matt.'

'Right, I'll get the cases.' Matt turned and went into the hall, wondering how Eppie would deal with this. Angela, he couldn't remember her latest married name, hadn't come to their wedding or even sent a card. Eppie had been hurt. How dare the woman turn up unannounced? Seeing the number of cases waiting in the hallway, it looked like she intended staying for months. By the time he'd manoeuvred the last heavy suitcase into the flat, Angela was seated on the sofa and Eppie was standing by the bookcase trying to compose herself.

'So what are you doing here, Mum?'

'It seemed the natural place to come.'

'Why?'

'Need you ask?'

'Yes. You haven't bothered with me for years. So why turn up now?'

Angela glanced at Matt. 'A coffee would be nice, if you are able.'

Matt flushed. He didn't intend to be spoken to like a servant. 'A please would be nice, if you are able,' he snapped, regretting the words as soon as they left his lips.

Eppie gave him a stricken look and he guessed she didn't want him to make matters worse.

'I'll make coffee,' he muttered and went into the kitchen. He made a special effort to be quiet so that he could listen. There was silence for a moment.

'Why, Mum? Why now, when you couldn't even send a card for our wedding?'

'I was heartbroken about that.'

'I can imagine.'

Matt caught the sarcastic tone in Eppie's voice and hurried with the coffee. He wanted to support her.

Angela continued as if uninterrupted. 'Fernando has thrown me out. A little hussy has turned the silly man's head. He'll live to regret it. I'm sure he will.'

More likely, the poor man wished he'd done it earlier, Matt thought as he loaded the tray.

'Well, you're not going to win him back from over here are you, Mother?'

'No alternative, dear. The heartless man cut off all my credit.'

'So, what's the plan? You can't expect to live here. We have no space.'

Good on you, Eppie, thought Matt, as he carried the tray through.

'It would only be for one night. Just until I sort myself out.'

Eppie raised her eyebrows at Matt. He gave a shake of his head.

'We'd be happy to book you into a hotel or guest house for a night,' he offered.

'I just want to be close to my daughter. There is no one else I can turn to.'

Matt could see that Eppie was weakening. Angela was good at turning the screw. Maybe they'd manage for one night. The new sofa bed would have its first guest.

'Then we'd be happy to put you up for one night.' Matt noticed the relief on Eppie's face at his decision. He hoped he wouldn't live to regret it.

# Chapter 9

When Vinny said goodbye to the Swift family, little Kylie began crying. He ruffled her hair and promised he would see her soon, just in case anyone was watching. As their car drew away into the darkness, Vinny muttered a *thank God for that* into the frozen air before turning towards the small transport cafe. He hoped his pickup wouldn't be long, as he didn't fancy hanging about. Glancing around the parking lot, he could see a lot of lorries and over to one side, a few cars. The icy wind cut across the open space and sent draughts down his neck. Shivering, he went into the cafe. Maybe someone was waiting for him inside.

Vinny finished his third coffee, his foot tapping with impatience. This was bloody stupid – the longer he sat here, the more chance someone would recognise him. Maybe he'd been wrong to trust Ops. Then again, he'd been bloody brilliant in getting him away when the heat was on. He decided to give him another five minutes and spent the time planning what he intended to do to the bastard who'd murdered his son.

As Vinny contemplated ordering yet another cup of coffee, he became aware of car lights flashing on and off outside. He wiped a space on the steamed-up windows with his sleeve and peered through. Still not able to see clearly, he went outside to investigate and recognised Dan, Ops's half-witted runner. Trust the idiot to bring unnecessary attention to himself. Vinny hurried over to him. 'Stop doing that, you bloody fool. Do you want everyone to notice us?'

'Thought it was the best thing to do.'

'Well it isn't.' Vinny sighed as he opened the passenger door. 'You took your own sweet time, didn't you?' he complained, turning off the radio.

'As instructed. Ops said to use an old car and drive carefully – no going over the speed limits, do nothing to attract attention. That's what he said.'

'Meanwhile, I'm stuck here for the entire pissing world to see.'

'Ain't my fault. Don't draw attention to yourself, that's what Ops said.'

'Bugger Ops. Always was too cautious. You'd think he was up against MI5.' The warmth of the car soon soothed Vinny and reminded him how hungry he was. 'Got anything to eat?'

'Half a sandwich back there. Oh, and there's some chocolate in the glove compartment.'

Vinny didn't fancy anything that had been near Dan's mouth, so opted for the chocolate, allowing the sweet, smooth taste to comfort and re-energise him. There was a lot to do if he was to avenge Jon. He'd start with Harry. One of Jon's pals since infant school, he should have some idea who Jon was hanging about with, and who might want to harm him.

He'd made sure his lad could stand up for himself. God knows it hadn't been easy with his useless mother trying to turn him into a nancy boy. He might even pay dear Mary a visit, but he was sure the police would be keeping an eye on the house. Not that she would know anything; if she'd anything about her, his lad wouldn't be dead. In Vinny's eyes, Mary had a lot to answer for.

Dan took the M3, then the A34 and soon they were heading towards Newbury. Vinny could feel his eyes starting to shut and when he woke he didn't recognise anything. Aching for a pint, he looked longingly at the lighted windows of the pubs, but with the evening trade in full swing, he resisted making Dan stop. He probably had orders from Ops not to anyway. Although, if he'd a mind to, it would be easy to bully the pompous twerp into doing whatever he wanted. Still, he reasoned it would be best to reach his hideaway before he started throwing his weight around. Wherever it was, there'd better be a fridge full of beer waiting.

Vinny sat back enjoying the warmth and allowed Dan's careful driving to take them towards the M40.

# Chapter 10

The first one had been easy. Or should that be the second? Then, Kathy reasoned, Ken's death was a mercy killing, so maybe didn't count. He had been on the long and painful road to death and all he wanted to do was to get on with it.

Ken had unknowingly given Kathy the means to avenge her son.

Kathy had been going to sit with Ken to give her elderly friend, Maisie, a bit of a break. Maisie wasn't well herself so it gave her time to have a bath and a peaceful cup of tea. A month ago, Kathy had been sitting beside the bed, half listening to the sound of the radio from the kitchen below. She thought Ken was sleeping, exhausted after the nurse's visit, when he reached out to grasp her wrist with his white, veined hand.

'Kathy,' he whispered, his voice dry and cracked. Pausing to fill his tired lungs, he continued. 'Make it go away. Please…' his voice tapered off.

Why had he chosen her? Could he see the murderous blackness building inside?

Ken's hand tightened on her arm. He pointed his other hand to the neat tray of medicines that stood on the corner of the dressing table. Kathy had collected the prescription for Maisie the previous day, so several ampoules of diamorphine stood ready. Ken had a strict routine of doses and the next wasn't due for hours. Kathy shook her head and stood, hoping to make Ken more comfortable. With her free hand, she tried to offer him a sip of water. He moved his mouth away, lips closed tight.

'I can't give you your medicine yet, Ken. It isn't time. Shall I call Maisie?' The grip on her wrist tightened until it hurt.

'Please…please.'

Everyone should have a peaceful death, not the horrendous ones Jack and Bill had suffered, she thought. What difference would it make if Ken went a few days early? Maisie had accepted he was going to die and Kathy would be there to support her. Kathy nodded and Ken released her wrist. It had taken all his strength to cling on and from his white face, Kathy wondered if her efforts might still be needed.

Moving towards the medicine tray, she glanced back at Ken. He watched as she picked up one of the ampoules. She couldn't inject it like the nurse, so snapped the top and tipped the powder into one of the tiny medicine cups. As she stood wondering if she should add a little water, Ken's rasping voice made her jump.

'Whisky,' he said, pointing to the bottle beside the bed from which he had a small tot at bedtime.

Taking the cup over to the bed, she poured in some of the whisky, watching as the powder dissolved. When Kathy held the cup to his lips, his mouth opened eagerly as if it were communion wine. A little dribbled down the side of his mouth but he managed most of it and lay back exhausted.

Hearing Maisie coming up the stairs, she wiped Ken's mouth and put the cup into her handbag. She should be with him at the end. He would want that.

'How is he?'

'Sleeping like a baby. Come and sit down.' Kathy patted his hand in goodbye and moved back to the medicine tray to retrieve the broken ampoule and slip it into her pocket.

Maisie sank down in the chair and took Ken's hand. His face relaxed and Kathy saw a glimpse of the old Ken.

'I've left out some of Mrs May's wonderful fruit cake. You will have a cup of tea before you go, won't you?'

'Yes, I'll be here for a while.'

Picking something up in her face, Maisie turned back to Ken. 'You think…?'

Kathy moved back beside the bed. 'Well, he does seem so peaceful.'

Half an hour later, Ken gave a big sigh and died. Maisie gave a matching sigh and rose to kiss him.

After calling the doctor and making Maisie a cup of tea, Kathy spent her time tidying the bedroom. Coming to the medicine tray, she asked Maisie if she would like her to get rid of everything and she nodded.

Now she had the means as well as the motive and Kathy was certain she could create an opportunity.

# Chapter 11

Waking from another doze, Vinny noticed that Dan took the slip road sign posted Warwick before going round the island to take the A46 bypass towards Coventry. At least he was on home territory. After a short distance, Dan turned off onto the A4189 heading away from Warwick.

Peering through the pitch black, Vinny forced his eyes to stay open. It was important to know his bearings. A few miles further on, they passed through the village of Claverdon where the windows of the cottages shone out across the ice, offering warmth and comfort. Vinny watched them slide by with envy.

Reaching Henley-in-Arden, they turned left, onto the A34 to Stratford and were soon passing through Wootton Wawen. To Vinny, it seemed they were going in circles. Then, just outside Wootton Wawen, Dan turned left into the car park of the Navigation Inn. Vinny sat up in anticipation of staying in a pub.

Dan drove through the car park into the dark beyond the pub. Bumping off the tarmac, Vinny could make out the icy branches of the trees ahead and to his left, up a bank, a glimpse of narrowboats, silent and dark, grouped together like a pack of monsters waiting to attack. Deciding he was getting fanciful, Vinny gave himself a shake.

'Is this it then? Where's the house? I'm parched.' Vinny opened the car door.

'Stay where you are…please. I'll just check.' Dan got out of the car and disappeared into the dark.

Vinny itched to remind Dan just who was the boss. If he wanted to, he could smash the little shit's face into the dashboard. But he reminded himself that Dan was only following orders and didn't have the brainpower or the courage to think outside of them. Gazing over the frozen ground, he wondered what the hell they were doing here and hoped he wouldn't have to sit here for long. All he wanted was a cold beer and a warm bed.

Dan returned to the car and leaned in. 'We can go now.'

'About time.' Vinny got out of the car, already tasting his first English pint in four years. He turned away from the water, intent on going to the pub, but Dan called him back.

'This way,' Dan hissed.

Vinny couldn't believe what was happening. Dan was halfway up the slope to the canal.

'What the hell?'

'Come on. Come on.'

This better be worth putting off that pint, Vinny thought, as he altered his course to follow.

Dan led him past the narrowboats, coming to a stop at the smallest, moored alone at the end of the line. As they got nearer, Vinny could just make out the name, *Daisy Lou*, embellished with flowers, mostly daisies.

Dan stopped and ushered him aboard. Horrified, Vinny held back. He'd hated boats since a stag do on the Isle of Man. Coming back on the ferry, he'd been as sick as a dog. Dismissing the idea that it was anything to do with the amount of beer consumed, he'd made up his mind to avoid boats ever since. The ferry from France had been bad enough, but this rickety tub was a step too far.

Glancing right and left, Dan gave an impatient wave of his hand to hurry him along. Vinny took a reluctant step onto the frosty deck. To his right was a small door with yet more daisies. He assumed it led down into the cabin.

'Come in.'

He recognised Ops's voice and made his way down the narrow stairs. Ops sat at the small table. He nodded as Vinny banged his head on the deck head and stumbled into the tiny room, waiting until he recovered before indicating the seat opposite him.

'Place must be made for midgets,' Vinny cursed as he sat down.

'And certainly not a place the police will think of looking for a large, clumsy man such as yourself.'

It took a moment for the facts to fall into place. Ops expected him to stay here! It would be like living in a coffin. He'd been looking forward to some comfort.

He stared at the man. Ops always reminded Vinny of a cross between an undertaker and a solicitor and he couldn't remember him displaying any emotion. In fact, he didn't seem human at all. It was hard to tell his age, but he guessed between forty and fifty. When they'd met in prison ten years ago, Vinny, thinking this fish out of water might be useful, offered him protection.

Ops's bald head appeared pink and polished and his gold-rimmed glasses enlarged his grey eyes so that they seemed able to stare right through you. Vinny thought Ops might have a Welsh background, for there was a certain lilt in his voice.

'My sincere condolences on the loss of your son.'

Vinny nodded to acknowledge the reference to Jon, while thinking how to tackle this unexpected turn of events. Before he could marshal his thoughts, Ops spoke again.

'They will never find you here.'

'You expect me to stay here?'

Ops raised his eyebrows in surprise that his decision was up for questioning. 'Yes, I do.'

Those grey eyes focused on him and for a moment Vinny wondered if it might be best to go it alone, to tell Ops just what he could do with his disgusting idea. Yet he knew he was lucky to have Ops to sort out all the practical details. With his help, he would stay safe until he was able to take his revenge. That had to be his focus. So what if he was uncomfortable for a few days? It didn't matter as long as he got his hands on Jonathan's killer.

'Keep below the radar and you won't be noticed. Here is a mobile phone with my number in. Use each SIM card just once. I've left you an endless supply. Dan has stocked the fridge with food and drink and he will replenish it as needed.'

Vinny looked around, trying to see where a cabin this small could fit a fridge. Ops pointed to what looked like a cupboard next to the tea-cup of a sink. Vinny reached across, opened it, and was heartened to find it stacked with beers.

'That's so you don't feel the need to indulge yourself at the local hostelry. You are not to go anywhere, and I mean anywhere, without my permission. Do you understand?'

'Might be difficult. You know what I've got to do?'

'Full well.'

'Something might come up where I've got to move fast.'

Ops gave a sigh and spoke as if he were addressing a child. 'That is what the phone is for. You ring me. I will sort out the safest way for you to approach any situation that might arise.'

'So I just sit here, twiddling my thumbs? I'll go mad, stuck here in this shit hole.'

'You have all the comforts of home – food, warmth and drink, not to mention television. I know it is not your luxury villa in Spain, but neither is it permanent, just convenient to keep you safely hidden while we move forward on your agenda. I can't see the problem.'

Vinny clenched his fists, letting his fingernails cut into his flesh. He couldn't afford to use brute force on Ops as he was the one man who could keep him out of jail long enough to do what was needed.

'If you want, Dan can stay with you for company. In fact, that would be a good idea. He has been through everything about the running of the boat with the owner, so would be invaluable.'

Company, Vinny thought, more like a spy. The little rat would report everything back to Ops. He wouldn't even be able to have a shit without Ops knowing. 'No. I mean there's no room. We'd be falling over each other.'

'Not to worry, Dan will fit in anywhere. I'll have a word with him.' Ops rose to leave.

Knowing it was his last word on the matter, Vinny resigned himself. Given time, he was sure he could make the little weed, Dan, do whatever he wanted. He'd enough experience in prison in moulding men to do his bidding, so one snivelling little runt should be easy. He stood to thank Ops, intending to walk up on deck with him, but hit his head again. Ops waved him to stay inside and went up to the deck, where Dan was waiting to help him onto dry land.

Vinny could hear their murmured voices and moved around the small table to look out of the window. He was pleased to see Dan not looking too happy at the prospect of bunking in with him. That was another thing – where could you sleep in this thing? He'd better grab the best bunk. He turned to move down the narrow aisle, pausing to open a door to the bathroom, complete with shower. To Vinny, it looked like it belonged in a doll's house. Moving on, he came to a bedroom where a double bed took up most of the room. Above and around the bed were loads of cupboards. He tried the bed and found it comfortable, although the thought of sharing it with Dan made him feel sick.

Just then, he heard Dan's voice. 'Just going to pick up my things. You want anything?'

'More beer. And fish and chips, if there's anywhere still open. I've been longing for some decent ones,' he said, moving back into the main cabin. Dan gave a thumbs up and disappeared. Maybe it wouldn't be so bad after all. Dan could wait on him and fetch anything he wanted.

He resolved to make the best of it and set about investigating every cupboard. Finding the television he turned it on and taking a beer from the fridge, settled down to watch.

He had to admit, Ops was bloody brilliant. While the police were busy looking for him on the roads, he could be quietly chugging along the waterways. That's if this tub kept afloat.

# Chapter 12

Matt eased himself out of the sofa bed, trying not to wake Eppie, who had tossed and turned all night. The added complication of her mother was the last thing she needed today, as she was organising her first conference and he knew she was anxious it went well. Not that he had slept much. The sofa bed was too small for his six-foot length and his feet stuck out of the end to freeze.

Marvelling at the skill of Angela in getting her own way, he began to get ready for work. She'd never intended to sleep on the sofa bed, and while Eppie prepared her a snack the previous night, she asked if she might have a shower. The fatal mistake was saying she might change in their bedroom. Angela wheeled first one and then another suitcase into the bedroom and by then it was too late; Angela had asserted squatters' rights.

At the office, Matt snatched a few peaceful minutes to catch up with the information arriving on his desk. Slim's preliminary report added nothing to that already relayed verbally. There was little time to read on, as the rest of the team had started to arrive and it was time for the briefing.

'Good work, everyone. Now although we wanted something to occupy us, let's not have this hanging over us for Christmas. We need to work hard now, otherwise we'll be eating bacon butties instead of turkey for Christmas dinner. Personally, I want to spend Christmas with my wife.' This brought a few whistles and catcalls. Matt laughed, hoping the message hit home as he nodded to Sam to carry on.

'We now have more information about the gang who kicked Jack Wylde to death. Tom Grace went back into custody a couple of months ago for assaulting a man outside a pub in Leamington. Apparently, a general fracas broke out while Tom and his mates were drinking one Saturday night. After the general melee, Tom ran after one of the opposing crew and attacked him with a broken bottle.

Seems like he hasn't changed at all, guv.'

'No.' Matt sighed, certain they would hear more of Tom Grace over the years. 'Do we know when he's due to be released?'

'Checking on that today.'

'Good. Wendy, have you any more on Nick Tyler or Dave Beeson?'

Wendy nodded, blushing as she stood. 'Dave Beeson, nicknamed Beanie, is now nineteen and unemployed. He's had mental health issues and has been in and out of St Michael's in Warwick. His first breakdown came just a month after the trial and he went from youth custody to a mental health unit. He now lives with his married sister, Julie Pritchard, in Leamington.'

'And Nick Tyler?'

'He seems to be doing well. He has a steady job working with his father in a small building firm. They do house extensions and such. Nick has his own flat and a girlfriend who works in Boots. She's expecting their first child in two months. And, this is interesting – her name is Tilly. Tilly Rowlands.'

'Jonathan's girlfriend,' Sam noted.

'So chances are Nick was treading on Jonathan's territory. Might be a cause for friction between them,' Matt added. 'Thanks, Wendy. We'll need to follow them both up.'

'I guess two out of five going straight's not bad,' Sam interjected.

'No, and if those two can make it, maybe the other two will, in time, follow suit. There's little to add to Slim's preliminary findings, except that the stomach contents contained a mixture of cider and whisky. Jonathan may have taken, or been given the drug in this way. Grant, any news from the drugs squad about what's on the street?'

Grant took an age to stand and seemed unsteady as he flicked through his notes. 'The usual street drugs – coke, ecstasy, heroin and the rest. However, they have no knowledge of this form of opiate on their patch, or in the surrounding forces. And they have their ears pretty close to the ground, sir.'

'Thanks, Grant. It's beginning to look as if Jonathan was the target. That is, unless we hear of any similar overdoses. Any luck with chasing this Noddy fellow, Wendy?'

'Yes. Uniform says it could be a Phil Nodding, who hangs out with Jonathan. I have an address for you, guv.'

'Good. We'll get onto that straight away.'

'How about the prison service?'

'They've confirmed Jonathan was a non-user.'

'Grant, see if you can get hold of Phil, in-between looking at the CCTV.'

'Will do.'

'Jane, you're off to visit Pamela Wylde. Sam, you have your favourite, the mortuary.' Matt waited for the ripple of amusement before carrying on. 'Then, check out Harry Winters. I'll catch up with Kathy Wylde. She should be pleased at the news.'

# Chapter 13

Everything was ready. Eppie rechecked the client's instructions for the third time just to be sure. Two conference rooms, both with white boards, seating for sixty. Coffee at eleven fifteen, lunch at one thirty in the Hanover Suite and afternoon tea at three forty-five. The Tudor ballroom for the evening's major awards presentation, set out with rostrum and overhead projector.

This was the first conference she had organised for the Steller agency and, although Chris guided her through, she was in charge. Eppie expected Mrs Natasha Bellemy, vice president of Bellemy and Sheen, to arrive early and Chris warned that she was a tyrant who felt it was her duty to find fault with everything.

Eppie heard her first, clip-clopping down the corridor with a following entourage, barking orders as she went.

'No, no, Sian, I want Meredith and his team in the Croft suite. Why can't you listen?'

There was no time to see who poor Sian was as Natasha spied Eppie and swooped towards her. 'Mrs Turrell, I want a word with you.'

'Certainly, how can I help?'

'Follow me.'

Eppie had no choice but to follow the smartly suited Natasha as she led the way to the ballroom.

As they stood in the doorway, Natasha spread her hands dramatically. 'This is just not good enough. I'm sure you can see why?'

Eppie referred to the notes taken at their first meeting. 'Well, no, I'm sorry, Mrs Bellemy, it is exactly as you outlined.'

'I didn't realise what an awkward shape the room was then. You should have informed me. Have it changed.'

Mrs Bellemy went on to describe how she wanted the ballroom set out while Eppie scribbled frantically.

'I expect it to be done by coffee time.'

'Of course, Mrs Bellemy.'

As Natasha swept from the room, Eppie looked around and sighed. The layout was entirely different to her original request. Still, there was nothing to do but get on with the changes. She turned and went hunting for the conference and banqueting office. They had a team of strong men who could move everything around in a trice.

Directed from their office to the workroom, she was dismayed to find it empty, except for Harry, the spiky-haired junior. He looked at her as if she was asking for the moon. 'I'm sorry but everyone's gone across to our sister hotel to help set up for a wedding.'

'When will they be back?'

'Not sure. Bob said I was to stay 'til eleven, then get off to college.'

Eppie felt a surge of panic. 'Couldn't you call Bob and explain the situation? Please?'

Harry picked up on the urgency. 'I'll have a go.'

Eppie waited while he dialled a number. She heard the ringing going on and on until Harry gave her a rueful grin and clicked the off button.

'Sorry, they're probably right in the middle of shifting stuff.'

'Can't you help me?'

Harry referred to her notes and shook his head, reminding Eppie of a plumber condemning a washing machine. 'It's a big job. Lots of heavy stuff.'

'I don't mind helping.'

'Oh no. That wouldn't do.'

'Harry, this is my first event with Steller and if I can't get it sorted by eleven, I will have messed up. Please help me. You're the only one who can.'

She may as well have given Harry a superhero cloak. He took a deep breath. 'Alright, but I do all the heavy lifting – understood? You can rearrange the chairs. Start on that now while I get a trolley and collect the platforms from the store room.'

Eppie could have kissed him but instead she rushed back to the ballroom to start work, cursing Natasha as she went.

They both worked hard, Harry humming away to himself as he shifted the heavy blocks into position. As soon as she finished rear-ranging the chairs, Eppie moved to help him manoeuvre the last two blocks into place, before they both collapsed to view their efforts.

'I'm never going to be able to thank you enough, Harry.'

'Nothing to it. Bit like what I do at college.'

'What is that?'

'Drama, stage management, a bit of everything.'

'Are you enjoying it?'

'Yes. Never thought I'd get the chance.'

Eppie sensed there was a lot behind why Harry nearly didn't get the chance, but there was no time to ask as Natasha approached, causing them both to jump to attention.

While she paraded around the rearranged room, Eppie and Harry held their breath awaiting her verdict.

'Move the rostrum more to the left.'

Harry sprang to obey.

'Good. I suppose that will have to do.'

Natasha turned abruptly and left the room. Behind her back, Harry clicked his heels and gave a mock salute. Eppie felt like joining him but just laughed with relief instead.

'We did it.' Eppie high-fived Harry and was rewarded with the widest grin she had ever seen, changing his face to give him a little-boy look.

'Let me treat you to a coffee and cake,' she offered, intrigued to know more about him.

Harry glanced at his watch. 'No need. It was just work. Thanks though. I need to get off. Late for college.'

Harry seemed shy, as if he'd dropped the hero cloak and turned back into a gawky, awkward teenager. With a final smile and thanks, Eppie let him go while musing about him.

Eppie would have liked to avoid Mrs Bellemy for the rest of the day, but instead chose to stay close to her so she would have no excuse to say she didn't get everything she needed. By mid-afternoon, after a series of small grumbles from Natasha that she managed to sort out, Eppie was developing a tension headache. She was glad it would soon be time to go home, until she remembered her mother.

# Chapter 14

Today, lying on the slab, Jonathan looked as if he was asleep and Sam winced as Slim made the first incision. Even his fascination at the workings of the human body failed to block out that a couple of days ago the corpse was a healthy young man. By the time it was over, Sam was happy to escape into the cold air and glad that his visit to see Harry Winters would take his mind off the post mortem.

Stratford was heaving with Christmas shoppers and it took him a while to reach the college. Unable to find a space in the parking lot, he opted for the no parking zone before making his way to the main reception, where the receptionist directed him to the drama department and offered to ring ahead to say he was on his way.

Crossing the parking lot, he entered the square structure, moving from the sun into darkness. Sam stood still while waiting for his eyes to adjust and jumped at a hand on his arm. In the dimness, he could just make out a woman with a clipboard.

'Are you DS Withers?'

'Yes.'

'Shush.'

'Sorry.'

'The young man you want to speak to is there.'

Getting used to the darkness, Sam followed as she pointed out a young man waiting behind a stage flap holding a sheet of thin metal. He was listening intently to what was going on beyond. Sam guessed this must be the backstage area. Deciding it would be best to wait for a natural break in the proceedings, he went forward into the auditorium. In the stage space, several young people were moving about, scripts in hand. During a pause, while someone waited for a prompt, Sam hurried across to sit near a man who was taking notes.

The students were good and Sam found himself engaged, almost forgetting why he was there. Even the dramatic clap of thunder didn't remind him. When the note-taking man called for a break, he was disappointed, knowing that he wouldn't find out what happened at the end. Still, he'd better get on with the job. Sam approached the man who he assumed was the teacher to introduce himself, knowing there must be rules about just wandering in.

'Excuse me,' Sam ventured, warrant card already in hand as the students flopped down in groups with their cans of Coke.

He looked up, an annoyed expression on his face. 'Yes?'

'DS Withers. I was told I could have a brief word with Harry Winters.'

'Oh yes, the office rang. Don't know why it has to be in the middle of my session though. Don't keep him long. We're way behind now. I don't know how we're supposed to carry on with all these distractions. Hurry up. Hurry up.'

Although Sam thought he was being a bit precious, he nodded his thanks and moved over to where Harry was chatting with a petite blonde. He wasn't going to be at all pleased at Sam's interruption.

'Harry Winters?'

Harry barely looked up. 'Emm.'

'Could I have a word, please?'

The girl looked up at Sam and smiled, widening the prettiest blue eyes. He could understand why Harry didn't want to drag himself away. Deciding it would be a shame to upset Harry's chances with such a catch, Sam suggested they talk somewhere else.

Harry gave him an assessing look and led the way outside. Two female students were enjoying a forbidden smoke further along the wall of the building. They looked up as Harry emerged with Sam, but decided they posed no threat and turned away to indulge their habit.

'Detective Sergeant Sam Withers.'

'I could tell. Although I thought I'd left those days behind me. What is it this time, some old lady fallen over or what?'

Sam could understand his frustration. It was hard leaving the past behind once your details were on file and likely to be highlighted in the case of any similar offence. Harry was a young man who was trying to break out of the trap by getting on with his life and Sam admired him for that.

He spoke softly so they couldn't be overheard. 'It's just a routine visit, Mr Winters.'

Harry laughed. 'Mr Winters. Makes me sound about a hundred. Try Harry.'

Sam liked his smile, even if he did look as if he was auditioning for a boy band with his spiky hair. 'Thanks, Harry. Sam. I guess you've heard about the death of Jonathan James?'

'Yes.' Harry looked at the ground and scuffed his toe amongst the gravel. 'I haven't seen him since that night, except briefly in court. Now it doesn't feel like me...involved...in what we did.' Harry looked up, facing Sam. 'I don't want to hurt anyone...ever again. It was the worst time of my life.'

Sam believed him. He'd read the case file. A mixture of cheap drink and teenage bravado was the deadly combination that caused the senseless death of Jack Wylde. There was one more question to ask before he left Harry to get back to his thunder and the girl.

'When you knew Jonathan, were you or anyone else in that group using drugs of any kind?'

'Nothing heavy. Sometimes grass. We stuck to alcohol mostly as it was easier. Jon always looked older than he was.' Harry was quiet for a moment.

Sam sensed he wanted to ask something and was gathering the courage to do so. He waited.

'Is that how he died?'

'It looks very likely, but we're not sure of the exact details yet.'

'He wouldn't touch drugs. Not after Cal. Broke Jon up more than the rest of us put together.'

'That's why we're looking into his death, Harry.'

Harry nodded, understanding Sam's position. 'He was alright, at first. Lived not far from me. We'd play a bit of footie and have a laugh. His dad was a hard man, used to knock him about. He started to change, seemed to go out looking for trouble. Once he realised he could get the booze, you couldn't hold him back. Rest of us just followed along. Bloody sheep.'

Harry obviously deeply regretted that whole episode of his life. Sam doubted if he would ever come to their attention again. He'd learnt the hard way how much damage one mistake could make. Hopefully, he would be able to put it behind him eventually. Harry broke into his thoughts.

'I thought I might go to the funeral, in memory of the fun times.'

'I'm sure Mrs James would be really pleased to have you there, Harry. Thanks for talking to me. If you do think of anything else that might help us, give me a call.' Sam handed over his card and turned to make his way back to the car park thinking of the uphill battle Harry was facing.

# Chapter 15

This visit to see Jack's mother was little more than routine, as Matt didn't expect Kathy Wylde to be implicated in Jonathan's death. Although grieving relatives had, in the past, decided to pursue their own brand of justice.

Kathy Wylde's house was in a side road going out of Stratford towards Shottery. The house, a pre-war semi, was welcoming with a bay window and neat garden. Matt pushed open the garden gate and made his way to the front door, thinking what an ideal family home this would make.

A short blast on the bell brought Mrs Wylde to the door, wiping floury hands on an apron – one of those you rarely see women wearing nowadays. Although she was only in her fifties, Matt thought it suited her. He remembered her from the night Jack Wylde died. She'd remained calm as she supported her daughter-in-law. Now her blue eyes seemed wary. Maybe she associated him with bad news.

'Oh, hello. Inspector Turrell, isn't it?'

'Could I have a moment, Mrs Wylde?'

'Of course. Come in.'

Except for faint touches of grey at the temples, Matt saw little change in Kathy Wylde over the two years. If anything, she looked better, less drawn.

'Is everything alright, Inspector?'

'Yes. You may even find the news pleasing. It's about Jonathan James.'

'Oh. I'll just wash my hands.'

She ushered him inside and Matt followed her down the hallway and through to the warm kitchen. The smell of baking overwhelmed him. He sensed that Mrs Wylde was flustered at the mention of Jonathan's name. She dropped her eyes while she washed her hands and he felt she was using the time to compose herself.

'I must just check the oven, Inspector. Then you can have a hot scone with your tea if you wish.'

Matt hadn't the will to resist. 'That would be wonderful. Thank you.'

She removed a tray from the oven and began putting scones on a cooling rack. 'I usually cook a few for old Mrs Moore and the rest help raise money for the choir.'

'They look delicious.'

'Help yourself, please.' She placed a plate, knife, butter and small pot of homemade jam before him and turned to put on the kettle.

As he tucked in, Matt was aware he could become too comfortable here and decided he'd better concentrate. 'Are you aware that Jonathan James has died?'

'Yes. I heard or saw it somewhere. How did he die?'

'We're not certain at this point, Mrs Wylde.'

She turned away to fill the teapot. Without turning back to face him, she said. 'I'm not sorry.'

'I can understand that.'

'He kicked my son to death.'

'There were others involved,' Matt mumbled through a mouthful of scone.

'He led them. That was obvious in court. Yet they still didn't deal with him.'

Matt thought the word *deal* was out of place.

'How would you have liked the courts to deal with him, Mrs Wylde?'

'I would have locked him up for good.'

'So it distressed you when he only got a light sentence?'

'Yes. I felt angry and let down. How would you feel?'

Matt agreed with her completely. 'If it were my son, I would feel the same.'

Kathy looked at him, surprised at his reaction. 'Why are you here, Inspector?'

'It's a courtesy visit, Mrs Wylde. We're letting all those involved with the original murder know. One of my officers is on the way to tell Pamela Wylde.'

'She won't let anyone in.' Kathy sat down on a kitchen chair next to Matt. He thought she might be about to cry.

'Since...since Jack, Pam has shut the world out completely, including me. It's as if she's afraid, terrified that it will happen again.

54

I try not to imagine what she saw. I did at first and nearly went mad. For Pam it is always there, the terrible threat – that another innocent day will turn, become murderous for no reason.'

'The children?'

Kathy hesitated, as if it was all too painful to tell. Matt waited, nibbling, hoping she would continue.

'The oldest colludes with her mum. Protects her. The younger ones are frightened and bewildered. I don't know what to do.'

'I'm so sorry.'

'When I took Zoe her birthday present, I was lucky Pam let me in. Things are not right there and I feel so helpless. They are Jack's girls. He would expect me to do something.'

Matt, unsure of what to say, nodded.

Kathy looked up at him. 'Do you know the children can't even walk on the carpet? They have to keep everything tidy or it sends Pam off into a cleaning frenzy. Their lives must be a misery. The kitchen looks unused. I don't know what they eat. They seem to spend most of their time in their rooms. I feel so utterly useless.'

It would be terrible to see your grandchildren in such a situation, Matt agreed. This was one of those unseen, ongoing heartbreaks left behind when a family member is murdered. 'I can see how difficult it is for you. Do you think Pamela would accept professional help?'

'She's reluctant to let me in. It was only because little Zoe begged her.'

'Yet the children go to school?'

'Yes. Pam takes them in one of those big four-by-four things – looks like an armoured car. She drops them off and picks them up. The girls have no freedom.'

'Would Pamela trust the school?'

'I doubt it. She didn't want me in the house and I'm Jack's...was Jack's mother.'

Once again Matt thought Kathy might be about to cry, but she rallied and he glimpsed her inner strength.

'Maybe Mrs Wylde will relax now that Jonathan James is dead.' He detected a slight nod as if she thought of this too.

'I told her he was dead – when I took Zoe's present round. It didn't seem to make any difference.'

Matt thought she seemed disappointed by Pamela's reaction. 'When was Zoe's birthday?'

Kathy gave him an intense look before answering. 'Yesterday. Why?'

The day after Jonathan's death, too early for a press release. Even the local television hadn't picked it up until this morning. 'How did you hear about Jonathan's death?' He watched her, certain the question had thrown her though she rallied quickly.

'I'm not sure. It might have been at rehearsal or at work.'

'Well, maybe the news will make a difference once it has sunk in.'

'Yes, maybe.'

Now that his suspicions were aroused, he was sure she was relieved at his answer. This was a situation where he needed Jane's input and he cursed himself for not bringing her. At least he would be able to let her know what the situation was at Pamela Wylde's. He needed to ask one more question.

'Can I ask where you were on Monday evening?'

'Monday? I was here at home, Inspector. No, wait a minute.' She stood to consult a wall calendar. 'Sorry, it was an extra Gilbert and Sullivan rehearsal. We're involved in the concert to reopen the Royal Shakespeare Theatre. Well, we're testing it out really. It's very exciting and we want to be perfect.'

With a shock, Matt realised it must be the same concert Ida was involved in. At least he would be able to check Kathy's alibi. Something was wrong, but he decided to leave it for the moment. He could always come back.

# Chapter 16

Kathy felt unsettled after DI Turrell left. He was taller than she remembered. On the night Jack died, he'd brought a sense of composure as he took charge. When the doctors left her and Pam sitting dumbstruck in the relatives' room, he'd come to talk to them, said the usual words – I'm very sorry for your loss – but beyond the stock phrase, Kathy felt he'd meant it. He'd promised that he and his team would do everything to catch Jack's killers and all five of the boys were in custody within two days. At Jonathan's trial, he gave his evidence in a clear, authoritative manner. Kathy admired him and was glad he was on their side.

Now, she was in conflict with this dedicated detective and didn't relish lying to him. He would be working hard to find out who murdered Jonathan and to bring her to justice. Although he would treat her with civility, Kathy didn't think she could bear to see the disappointment in his eyes.

Kathy sat down at the kitchen table, overcome with apprehension. Maybe she hadn't thought it through. She'd never considered she could be arrested, just expected a sense of relief that one of Jack's killers was dead at her hand. Even Pam hadn't been impressed.

Feeling confused, Kathy decided to push it to the back of her mind and began washing the kitchen floor. Giving in to pure physical action usually helped her to get things into perspective, yet this time it wasn't enough. Pictures of Jack lying battered in the hospital kept coming into focus, followed by Pam and the girls.

At this time of year, there used to be outings to see the girls in their school Christmas shows. Afterwards, Jack would treat them to pizza and they would sit, laughing and talking. That was all gone and the disabling sense of loss and outrage swept over her.

The kitchen floor gleaming, she made a cup of tea and got out her list. She needed to carry on, owed it to Jack and his family. Next on her list was Harry Winters, now eighteen. She'd heard through Ida, who knew his family, that he was working at a hotel in Stratford while studying drama at college. Ida said he was a nice lad and his mother nearly died of shame at what he'd done.

# Chapter 17

'So what are we going to do about her?' Matt whispered in Eppie's ear.

'You wouldn't like my answer.'

'Well think of something fast.'

Easing away from the towel rail that was burning into his back, Matt thought how absurd it was that the only place they could talk was in the bathroom. Angela was now firmly ensconced in their bedroom. She was the sort of woman who was used to getting her own way, and declared it imperative that she have a good night's sleep, adding that a woman of her years couldn't possibly be expected to sleep anywhere but in a proper bed. Matt wondered why she couldn't stay in a hotel and pay for the service she wanted 'til Eppie reminded him that her husband had kicked her out without a penny. Not that Matt could blame him; he would like to do the same.

Eppie sat on the side of the bath. 'We have to think of something before tomorrow. There's no way she'll fit around that table – just the four of us will be a squash.'

'She can have my place.'

The look Eppie gave him told Matt he was condemned to attend the dinner. Mum was no problem, but his feelings towards his dad were stuck back in the time of Granddad's suspension. Dad had used it to underline how precarious a life in the police force could be in a clumsy attempt to push Matt into going to university and following in his footsteps. For a while Matt was torn, before turning his back on a history degree and opting to join the police.

'Do you think she might like to go to rehearsal with Ida? She used to like Gilbert and Sullivan. I think she was quite involved before Mike and I cramped her style.'

'Anything is worth a try.'

'Right. You keep her talking while I nip down to Ida's.'

'Oh God, what shall I talk about? Rugby's out, so is work.'

'Listen to her then. Pretend she's a suspect. Do you want me to sort this?'

'Yes.'

Eppie opened the bathroom door, forcing Matt up against the shower cubicle. She turned to kiss him. 'Good luck, Agent Turrell.'

'If we come through this, we'll meet on the other side, Agent Eppie.' Matt returned her kiss and with a laugh, followed her from the bathroom.

Angela was sitting on the sofa watching the early news. She ignored Matt as he sank into his chair. Giving a thumbs up to Eppie as she left the flat, Matt sought something to say and decided to link into one of the news stories.

'Dreadful business,' he ventured in response to a story about serious flooding. All he got back was an 'Mmm' so Matt waited until the next item about a dog saving its owner from a fire. 'Lucky fellow,' he said. Not receiving any reply, he decided to give up and opened his paper, looking up only when Eppie returned, relieved as she nodded.

Eppie moved to sit beside her mother. 'Mum?'

'Yes?'

'I wondered if you would like to go out tomorrow night with our neighbour, Ida.'

'Why on earth would I want to do that?'

'Well, she's in the Gilbert and Sullivan society.'

Matt watched Angela's eyes light up.

'I've taken so many leads in G&S. My Yum Yum was rated '

'That's why I thought you'd enjoy it. Plus, they're involved in something very exciting.'

'Such as?'

'The reopening of the RSC theatre and a movement workshop with someone from the RSC. Ida's checking to see if you could go to their rehearsal tomorrow as she's not sure they'll allow you to join at this late stage.'

Matt saw from Angela's face that she was tempted. He piled on the pressure.

'They might be very glad of any tips you could give them.'

'Yes, they might. But I thought I was needed at this dinner party to meet your parents?'

Eppie jumped in before Matt could reply.

'To tell the truth, Mum, we have a very small folding table and it's

60

going to be extremely difficult to fit four people round it. I think five would be just impossible.'

'Although, I know Mum and Dad are desperate to meet you. We thought that a pub lunch on Sunday might be a little more...er...' Matt looked to Eppie for help and she filled in.

'Relaxed.'

Matt warmed to his task. 'We could go out to the Cotswolds, to one of those historic places, all warm stone and welcoming fires.'

'That does sound rather delicious as well as more civilized. If Ida can arrange it, then I would be delighted to go.'

Behind Angela's back, Matt gave Eppie a silent high five.

# Chapter 18

Knowing they had a lot to get through, Matt started the briefing early. 'Jane, you visited Pamela Wylde. How did you get on?'

She moved to the front. 'No luck, I'm afraid. Although I'm sure someone was home as the car was in the driveway. No one would answer the door. Sorry.'

'Don't be. As you know, I went to see Kathy Wylde. According to her, Pamela Wylde has never recovered from her husband's murder and has not only become virtually agoraphobic but appears to be suffering from some obsessive-compulsive disorder. Even she has problems gaining entry. I do think it is unlikely that Pamela Wylde would be capable of killing Jonathan James. However, if we do need to see her, Kathy Wylde has agreed to visit with us. Kathy Wylde is an entirely different matter though. She remains affected, of course, by her son's death, but she, I think, is quite capable of planning and committing murder. At least, murder in this fashion. Also, she informed her daughter-in-law of Jonathan's death yesterday. I'm sure this was before it became general knowledge. Could you check on when the news came out please, Wendy? There was still a lot of anger there.'

'Surely that is to be expected, sir?' Grant spoke up from the back.

Matt noted Grant drawled more than usual, his voice almost slurred, and he made a mental note to keep an eye on him before replying, 'Yes, to some extent, I agree. But this felt like it hasn't shifted in two years. Most people begin to let go eventually. Yet Jack Wylde's death continues to have dire consequences for his family.'

'Being worried about her grandchildren must be adding to how she feels,' Jane suggested.

'Very likely. I'd like your input on this one, Jane. Could you contact Mrs Wylde senior, with a view to setting up a meeting with Pamela? It would give you a chance to assess both of them.'

'Will do.'

'Grant, any luck?'

Matt thought it unusual that Grant sat while giving his report. He usually stood. He resolved to talk to the man before the end of the day, to see what was going on.

'Nothing worthwhile on the CCTV, just Jonathan staggering along Pierce Street before disappearing into the alley where he was found. No sign of him before that. Have a couple of contacts from his mobile. No known drug dealers though.'

'Phil Nodding?'

'Not home.'

'Right, it's important we talk to him. If he was with Jonathan on Sunday night, he could be a valuable witness. Grant, will you and Sam see him later today. Sam, can you catch up with Nick Tyler while Grant is finishing off the other leads? Thanks everybody.'

Matt returned to his office knowing he needed to get everything ready to report to McRay. Jane followed him in so he went to join her at the coffee table.

'What's on your mind?' He hoped the case wasn't proving too much for her. The doc signed her back for light duties only, but she'd sabotaged his attempts to ease her in gently.

'It's a bit delicate.'

'I'm happy for you to work less hours, if you need to.'

She frowned and shook her head. 'No, I don't want that.'

'Then?'

'You know I asked you to call me Jane, instead of Fluff.'

'Yes. I did send a memo around. It's damn difficult though and I couldn't help wondering why?'

'Someone commented on it – said it sounded like a dog.'

Matt gave a snort. 'More like a cat. It wasn't Grant, was it?'

'No. I just got to thinking, no one else has a nickname around here – so why me?'

'Nicknames are reserved for the best.'

'That's crap and you know it.'

'Sam gets called Ginger sometimes.'

'Hardly ever.'

'Then there's Slim.'

'Not directly one of the team.'

'Honestly, Fl...Jane, everyone holds you in such high regard. However, if the team aren't conforming, I'll talk to them.'

'Fluff sounds like...well you know.'

'A bit of fluff?'

'Yes.'

'Has anyone around here ever treated you like that, DC Meadows?'

'They wouldn't dare.'

'No, because they all respect you and what you bring to the team. Everyone, especially me, has missed you like hell.'

'I'd still like you to have a word. Thanks, Matt.'

Mindful of the numerous memos that crossed his desk regarding respect, he stood. 'Come on then, let's do it now.' Matt led the way to stand in front of the team, wondering what he should say. Everyone was busy and it took a couple of tries for Matt to get their attention.

'I need to remind you of the memo I sent round a couple of weeks ago regarding a request from Fl...DC Meadows, that we change the way we address her. Perhaps you can tell the team how you would like to be addressed, DC Meadows.'

'From now on, I'd like to be called Jane or DC Meadows.'

There was silence at first, until Sam called out, 'You're serious?'

Noting the shocked faces and disgruntled comments, Matt thought this is how the team would react. 'Yes, Sam, this is genuine.'

'But, why? I've always thought Fluff was the lucky one. It's a sort of privilege, isn't it? I wish I had a nickname. Anything except Ginger, that is.'

'Would you feel better if everyone had a nickname?' Matt turned to Jane.

'No.'

'Right. No more discussion. We need to honour DC Meadows' decision. It's going to be difficult, I know, but we care about her, so we'll do it. Right?'

Matt looked out at the glum faces, seeing some reluctant nods, and decided to reinforce how serious he was. 'That's an order. Although I'm hoping DC Meadows will be patient with us over the next few weeks, while we get used to using her proper name.'

'Yes, of course, and thanks, I really appreciate it.'

Returning to his office, Matt speculated again on why Fluff, Jane, had suddenly found such displeasure with her nickname.

# Chapter 19

Sam could hear the sound of banging as he approached the three-storey Victorian terraced house. Following the noise, he headed for the rear of the building down a narrow entry and turned the corner to walk into a cloud of brick dust. This didn't seem to bother the burly man wielding a hammer to what looked like the remains of an outside privy. There was no doubt he was in the right place as a white van with the letters 'Tyler and Son' stood next to the skip in the untidy rear yard.

Sam waved his hand in an attempt to get the man's attention. There was no way he was going to move in closer, not with that hammer swinging.

'Hello,' he said nervously as the man stopped to glare at him.

'Yes? You from the council? We've got all the necessary from you lot.'

'No. Police.' Sam opened his warrant card as proof, noticing that the man was immediately wary.

'What now? Can't you leave the lad alone?'

Sam was relieved when he put down the hammer and began wiping his hands on his overalls. 'Just a general enquiry, Mr…?'

'Tyler. As you lot well know. The lad has learnt his lesson, I've seen to that. By the time he's done a hard day's work with me, he's no mind for mischief.'

'He's not in any trouble, Mr Tyler. This is just a routine check.'

'Suppose you'll be doing these "routine checks" until he's ninety?'

'I think that's unlikely, Mr Tyler. Especially as he seems to be turning his life around, thanks to you.'

Tyler grunted, but seemed pleased that his efforts had been recognised. 'Left to that daft mother of his, the lad had no chance. Just did what he liked, no routine at all. This is what's needed, hard work and routine.'

Sam nodded, wishing it were that simple. 'You may have heard that

Jonathan James has died. I just need to have a word with Nick about his death, Mr Tyler.'

'I'd heard. Good riddance to bad rubbish, too. But what's it got to do with my lad?'

'We're talking to all of the people who knew Jonathan in the past in an effort to find out how he died.'

'Nick's nothing to do with him since…well since you know what. I saw to that.'

'I do appreciate that, Mr Tyler, however—'

'Oh, have it your way. He's upstairs, back bedroom. Don't you go upsetting him mind. We've only got two weeks to finish this job. Time is money.'

'I'm sure it will only take a minute, thanks.' Sam stepped gingerly over the rubble of bricks to enter the shell of the house. He stood for a moment in the remains of the kitchen, to let his eyes become accustomed to the gloom, before making his way down a hallway to the front. The remains of the stairs were on his left and he climbed up with care, as there were no rails to hold onto. He could hear the juddering of a sander as he moved up and the air was thick with dust. Reaching the top, he could see a well-built young man wielding an industrial-sized sander on the floor of the back bedroom. Just as Sam stood wondering how he was going to get the young man's attention, Nick twisted the heavy machine around and saw him. Turning off the sander, he removed his mask and stepped forward.

'My dad's downstairs.'

'I've just spoken to your dad, Nick. It's about Jonathan James.' Sam watched as Nick's body slumped.

'It's never going to go away, is it?'

'Jonathan can't influence you now, Nick.'

'It was so bloody stupid.' As if to emphasise, Nick kicked out at the sander, which shuddered under the blow.

Sam couldn't help imagining how it would feel to be on the receiving end of a kick like that.

'Mind if I have a fag?'

Sam nodded his consent and was glad to follow Nick down the stairs to the front door. Outside he took some gulps of clean air as he watched Nick light up. It had only been two years since he'd given up, and the temptation was great to beg a weed from Nick. Nick visibly relaxed as he drew in the drug.

'I haven't seen Jon since… Felt pissing sick by what we'd done, afterwards, when the booze wore off. Can't blame everything on him, though. I was there, put my boot in with the others. Feels like it was someone else. Now I'm with Tilly. And, before you ask, yes, she used to go out with Jonathan. She didn't want anything to do with him afterwards.'

'When did you last see Jonathan James?'

'Not since court. When I came out Dad got me working. Didn't like it at first – he's pretty strict. Think he feels bad for buggering off and leaving me and Mum. She's alright, did her best. Guess I didn't give her much chance. Took Tilly round the other night, told her she was going to have a grandson.'

'Congratulations. When is the baby due?'

'February. Gives me time to do up the flat.'

'It certainly sounds like you have your life sorted, Nick.'

'I hope so. Can't take back what I've done and I still feel bad about his family. All I can do is make sure my kid grows up different.'

'I'm sure you will. Thanks for talking to me, Nick. All the best with the baby.' As Sam turned to walk away, he was aware of Mr Tyler standing watching from the front window. Nick Tyler was a lucky lad.

# Chapter 20

The two years had made a difference and Kathy didn't recognise Harry. In her mind, he would be hard and cold, the past etched on his face. Yet here was a young lad with an honest, open kind of face that easily broke into a smile. He worked with another young man to place the red plush chairs at the round tables. Kathy thought it looked like they were setting up for a wedding, as there was a top table and many flower arrangements waiting on the raised platform.

The other young man cracked a joke and Harry laughed. Kathy decided this couldn't be him. Then he looked up, saw Kathy and indicated to the other young man that he was coming over.

'Hello. Are you one of the family?'

Kathy looked puzzled so he tried again.

'The wedding?'

'Oh no. I was just interested in how it looked before all the finery is added.' Kathy forced a laugh. 'Actually, I was looking for the ladies', but think I must have taken a wrong turn somewhere.'

'That happens a lot. Let me show you the way.'

'No need – if you just point me in the right direction that will be fine.'

'Can't have you getting lost again. If you wandered into the kitchen, the chef would probably chop you up for lunch. Those TV chefs have nothing on him.'

As Kathy followed him along the carpeted corridors, she was sure she had the wrong youth. Harry was one of the last tried and by then Kathy just didn't have the heart to become even more disillusioned with the system. She'd only attended the one day and, seeing how it was going, couldn't bear to go back.

Reaching the lobby, he turned to grin at her. His smile was spontaneous. Kathy couldn't help smiling back.

'The ladies' is just down that corridor on the left.'

'Thank you so much and I'm sorry to have bothered you. Can I ask your name?'

'Harry.'

'You should be on reception with that smile, Harry.'

'Thanks. I have to do so long in each department so I guess I'll get there eventually. But thanks.'

As Harry walked away, Kathy's head was whirling. Harry shot all her expectations to pieces and was nothing like the boy she'd built up in her head. With *that boy*, taking revenge would have been easy, but Harry, cheerful, helpful Harry, was a very different prospect.

Kathy had persuaded herself she was a cold, hard woman but now she wondered if she could carry on with her plan. Dizzy with the shock, she decided to have a cup of coffee while waiting for Ida. She would put everything out of her mind for a while and concentrate on the upcoming concert. Today she and Ida were going to look at costumes.

By the time Ida arrived, she felt calmer. 'Shall I get you a coffee, Ida, or are you ready to order?'

'Let's order, shall we?'

Ordering over, Kathy blurted out, 'I saw him, spoke to him.'

'And?'

'He seems like a nice lad. Not the sort...well you know.'

'I told you he was a decent lad and I'm glad you've met him, as you'll be seeing more of him soon. He's coming to help us with the Open House. I wasn't sure how to tell you.'

'That's why you pushed me into this?'

'Forgive me, Kathy. I thought it would be better if you saw him, judged for yourself, before he turns up at choir. I'm sorry, dear, if that was interfering.'

'No. You were right, Ida. I needed to see for myself.'

'It was all down to that Jonathan James. He led those boys into what they did. Harry's parents were horrified. But the young man is working hard to overcome what he's done.'

Kathy felt sick. How could Harry overcome the fact that Jack was dead and three young girls were without their father?

'Oh, Kathy, I'm sorry. I know Harry can never repay you, or your daughter-in-law and the children. But rather than going from bad to worse, like so many of them do, he is making an effort. Mind you, he has good parents behind him, not like that Jonathan James. He didn't have much of a chance, did he? Not with a father like Vincent James.'

Emotions in a whirl, Kathy was confused. She could still justify what she did to Jonathan James, despite his seemingly difficult upbringing, but now she had seen Harry and liked him she wasn't sure she could carry out her vengeance. Ida knew how much anger she still held over Jack's death and Kathy realised this was her attempt to help her overcome it. However, Ida's plan did put Harry where she could observe him and, if he deserved to die, then having him at choir gave her many ways to achieve this. For now, Kathy was relieved to move on to a safer subject. 'Why, what did Mr James do?'

'Don't you remember that post office robbery, about four years ago, the one where the postmistress was shot and injured? The police said he led the gang. I've heard he's been on the run ever since.'

# Chapter 21

Matt followed Jane down the path to the neat townhouse, reminding himself he must get used to thinking and addressing her as Jane. The small communal front garden consisted of a square of lawn surrounded by bare flowerbeds. A smartly dressed young woman opened the door to Jane's knock. With her coat over her arm, she appeared harassed by the interruption. Matt observed her as Jane introduced them both, flicking open his warrant card at the required moment.

'Why do you want to see Dave? He hardly ever goes out so he can't be in any trouble.'

'It's just routine, Mrs...?'

'Pritchard...Julie. I'm Dave's sister. He's not well, you know. I don't want, or need him upset.'

'We are not here to upset him, Mrs Pritchard. We just need to ask a few questions about Jonathan James.'

'Well, that will get him going for a start.'

Matt decided it was time to enter the conversation. 'We'll be as gentle as we can. However, this does need to be done, and the sooner it's over the better, for Dave's sake.'

Recognising the voice of authority, she gave in and stood aside.

'I'll call work, tell them I'll be late,' she said, leading the way into the living room through an arch off the hallway.

'You don't have to be here, Mrs Pritchard. We can take it from here,' Jane reassured her.

'It's best I stay. He's...well...here he is.' She turned to address the lanky young man who stood at their entrance, TV remote still in his hand. 'Dave, these people are police officers. They've come to have a word with you. It's nothing to worry about and I'm going to be in the kitchen.' She turned to Matt. 'Would you like a cup of tea or coffee?'

Matt answered for both of them. 'No, thanks, we're fine.'

'Okay. Sit down, Dave and let's turn off the television.' Mrs Pritchard took the remote out of his hand and flicked the set off before leaving through another archway to the kitchen.

Dave stood for a moment then sank onto the sofa, collapsing into himself, arms locked around his knees. Matt gave a nod to Jane to start. Dave would be more likely to talk to her, as he seemed to get on with his sister. As she went to sit beside him, Matt chose the armchair near the fireplace and sat back, not wanting to appear intimidating.

Dave looked at her. 'Are you from the hospital? I don't need to go back there.'

'No, we're police officers, Dave. Is it alright if we call you Dave?'

'Yes, but I haven't done anything wrong. Not like before.'

'We know that. We just want to have a chat, see how you're getting on. Are you willing to talk to us?'

'Suppose so.' Dave refused to meet her gaze and hugged his knees harder.

'That was a bad time for you, wasn't it, Dave?'

Dave nodded.

'Do you see any of the other lads from that time?'

'No.' Dave turned his head away.

'I'm guessing you want to forget those awful memories.'

'They come back when I'm asleep, over and over again. Won't stop. The pills don't work. Nothing does.'

Matt became aware that Dave's sister was hovering in the archway, so he stood up to join her.

'Mind if I change my mind about that coffee?' he asked, turning her towards the kitchen. It was obvious that she would have preferred to stay close to her brother but Matt smiled at her, giving her no option. She nodded and led the way into the smart, bright kitchen. He watched her as she prepared the coffee, knowing that she was intent on listening to what was going on in the living room. 'You worry about your brother?'

'Yes. Can't help it. He's been in a state ever since…since that poor man died. Do you know, I don't think our Dave had much to do with…with what happened. He was always easily led by the likes of that James lad. It's played on his mind, made him ill. Here in his head.'

She put a finger up to her forehead and Matt could see the tears in her eyes before she turned away to hide her embarrassment. He didn't know whether to offer her his hankie, kept especially for moments like this, or pretend not to notice. Snatching a piece of paper towel, she dabbed at her eyes and turned to face him, trying for a smile.

'I'm sorry. It's just when I think how it has ruined his life. I don't think he'll ever be the same again. I worry about him all the time.'

'At least he has you.'

Giving another wipe to her eyes, she added, 'That's the problem. I don't know how long he can stay here. Ian, my husband, wants him to go. We're trying for a baby you see.'

As she stopped to pour the coffee, Matt waited before asking, 'That would be a problem?'

'Not for me, but then, I don't think Dave is dangerous.'

'Ian does?'

'Yes.' Again, the pause, and he remained quiet while she gathered her thoughts.

'Yes. It's not just the original incident you see. He has nightmares and…and…gets these thoughts that he could harm someone else. I'm sure he wouldn't, it's just in his head, but Ian doesn't want to risk it, and well, part of me can't blame him.'

'Does Dave see any of the old gang?'

'No. He hardly goes out, except to the hospital group.'

'Did you know that Jonathan James is dead?'

'No, but don't expect me to be sorry. He was always a bad one, used to get our Dave into all sorts of trouble, right from schooldays. And yes, I know Dave has a mind of his own, but I can't believe he would have kicked that man to death on his own.'

Matt was inclined to agree but he needed to find out more about Dave's thoughts of harming people. There was just the faint possibility that Dave had decided to finish off the cause of all his problems, although he thought it unlikely. Taking a sip of coffee, he thought of the best way to bring up the subject, aware also that Mrs Pritchard made no enquiry as to how Jonathan died. It was as if she read his thoughts.

'How did he die, the James lad?'

'It is uncertain at the moment but we think it was a drug overdose. Did the lads get into drugs when Dave was with them?'

She shook her head. 'Nothing heavy, mostly grass and alcohol. The psychiatrist thought the grass might have affected Dave. Some people have long-term effects apparently. I wonder sometimes if he goes out at night to get some, although he's not supposed to mix it with his tablets. I daren't tell Ian though. You won't tell him, will you?'

'If Dave has nothing to do with Jonathan's death, then no, certainly not.'

'I don't understand – you said that he died of an overdose?'

'It looks that way. These thoughts Dave has about harming people, how do they manifest?'

'Oh no. I shouldn't have said anything. Now you'll try to blame it on him.'

'I'm just intent on finding out what happened, Mrs Pritchard, and, if Dave has nothing to do with it, in ruling him out.'

She gave him a long assessing look before continuing. 'I only know about them because I go to him when he has nightmares. In them, he sees what happened over and over again…wakes up shouting. Then, while I'm calming him down, he rambles on about how he might harm someone. It could be anyone, someone he sees at the hospital, or in the street. It's as if he doesn't trust himself not to do it again. There's nothing much I can do, except reassure him.'

'Does his psychiatrist know of these thoughts?'

'I've tried to get Dave to talk about them, but I don't think he has. He's scared they'll say he's dangerous and lock him up.'

'It might be a good idea to have a word.'

'It's not that easy,' she sighed. 'Dave has to give his permission for me to talk to them.' She thought for a moment. 'But you are right. I'll sit him down on a good day and ask him.'

Matt nodded in agreement. Finishing his coffee, he peered into the living room. Dave was talking in a low voice. He couldn't hear, but Dave seemed at ease with Jane. Mrs Pritchard came to stand beside him.

'It's a pity she's not his psychiatrist. He's usually only with her for a minute. Probably gets no chance to talk.'

'DC Meadows is the best.'

Just then, Jane looked up. She nodded before reaching out to thank Dave, who stood to shake her hand.

'You can both definitely come again,' Mrs Pritchard said.

'I hope that won't be necessary, but thanks for your help.' Matt joined Jane in the hallway.

Outside, they waited until they were in the car before talking. Jane broke the silence. 'I didn't expect to feel sorry for him, but I do.'

'Yes,' Matt agreed. 'Sorry for the whole family. Sister's in a bind, as the husband wants him out. Can't really blame him. Don't think I'd want Dave around my new baby.'

'Got something to tell me, guv?' she teased.

'God no. Still settling in together. And don't you go putting the idea in Eppie's head.'

'Wouldn't dream of it.'

74

Matt hadn't really thought about it before. He and Eppie met and married within six weeks, but now he felt a sudden excitement. He could, no, probably would be, a father within the next few years. What would it be like to have a son?

She brought him out of his musings. 'I don't think Dave is capable of planning the killing of Jonathan. For one thing, he's frightened of his own shadow and rarely goes out. His ideas of harming anyone are all in his mind. Besides, I can't see how he would get the drugs.'

'I agree. But he and his family have suffered a lot through his involvement with Jonathan, so I don't think we can rule him out completely.'

They completed the rest of the journey in silence and Matt returned to thinking of his role as a father. It would be fun teaching him things, to get him playing rugby. But what about the sleepless nights? How would he or Eppie cope? And where would he sleep? The flat was just about big enough – according to him, not Eppie – for the two of them, but they would need more room for a baby. Resolving to talk to Eppie about waiting for a few years, he tried to push it to the back of his mind.

Back at the office, Matt gathered the troops together for a briefing, conscious of the need to get away early for the dinner party. He'd only just started when his phone rang. As it was Sam, he decided to take the call, indicating for Jane to take over.

'Matt. No need to worry, but we've had a minor accident.'

# Chapter 22

Matt cursed as he entered the hospital grounds. The evening stream of visitors all having to pass one at a time through the car park barrier made his progress towards the emergency department agonisingly slow. Finally, through the crowd, he pulled in behind two squad cars, put the official note on his car and headed inside.

The emergency department was busy. Patients with makeshift bandages leaking blood, others with black eyes sat resigned for a long wait. At the reception desk, he slipped in behind a family with a small girl held in her daddy's arms, her arm covered in a tea towel and her dark eyes wet with tears. Matt guessed a scald or burn. He knew he could show his badge and get priority, but made himself hold back, reasoning that if Sam could talk to him, he couldn't be that bad.

At last, he received directions and hurried down a corridor to a curtained cubicle. Drawing the curtains aside, he breathed a sigh of relief to find Sam smiling up at the pretty nurse who was attending to the wound on his head. Matt could see the head wound was minor and there didn't seem to be any other damage.

Sam turned and saw him. 'Matt.'

'Talk about scaring me to death.'

'Sorry.'

'What happened?'

'Tell you later.' Sam gave a nod towards the nurse. 'When Clare has finished.'

Clare glanced at Matt and he noticed that beside her long lashes, she had a dimple in her chin.

'Just about done. The doctor should be along to discharge you soon.' Clare gathered her tools and with a nod to Matt, threw a special smile to Sam, before wheeling the small trolley out of the cubicle.

Sam gave a sigh as he watched her go.

'So this is all about pulling the girls, is it?'

'Merely a welcome side effect.'

'Clare seemed quite taken.'

'I've given her my number, so it's up to her now.'

Matt thought that Clare probably received a fair amount of offers, but didn't say anything.

'So what happened? The truth.' Matt watched as Sam struggled with how to explain. It was always tricky to tell tales about a colleague, but he needed to know.

'He's always difficult to work with, so I suppose I try harder with him, give him the benefit. Today, he wasn't talking at all, just the odd grunt. He seemed kind of sluggish, like he was coming down with a cold or—'

'Had been drinking?'

'Yes, I guess so. His reactions were slow. Even my mum could have missed that bollard. Grant was lucky it was old Duffer who came out. He just wanted to get back to his warm office.'

Matt nodded. Uniform Superintendent Derek Duffin was months away from retirement and wouldn't have been happy to be called out, as required, to a minor traffic accident involving a police inspector. Grant had been lucky he hadn't been breathalysed. If left to Traffic, he certainly would have been.

'Sorry, Matt.'

'Don't be. I've been worried about him lately. Meant to have a word before anyone got hurt. I should be saying sorry.'

Thinking about what he should do next, he knew confronting Grant was not going to be easy. It sounded as if he should have been charged with drink driving. But it was now two hours since the accident so blood alcohol levels would be diminishing, and Grant knew the score. If he had any sense, he'd be drinking gallons of water. Then there was the effect on the team and the force as a whole, especially if the papers got hold of the story. He'd have to tackle Grant and talk to McRay. Although he wasn't looking forward to doing either.

Sam interrupted. 'Can't say he smelt of drink, or I wouldn't have got into the car. Probably a hangover from last night.'

'That sounds likely. I'd better go and find out.'

'Good luck with that one.'

'I'll hang on and drop you home.'

Before Sam could reply, the curtain swished aside and a harassed young man in a white coat entered.

'Detective Sergeant Withers?'

'I'll wait outside.' Matt went outside into the hectic ward. He saw Clare entering another cubicle and an older male in a suit, with several nervous-looking young people gathered at the end of the ward. Matt thought they looked like a new intake of doctors. His job was bad enough, but he didn't know how anyone could cope thrown into this high-pressure environment.

Glancing at his watch, he was shocked to see how late it was. Eppie would be expecting him home as he'd promised to help her set up the folding table. Yet he felt duty bound to get Sam home safely and catch up with Grant. He needed to see for himself the state of the man. Not wanting to get into a conversation, he decided to call Eppie after he had dropped Sam home and seen Grant. By then he would have a better idea how late he would be.

# Chapter 23

By the time he left college, it was already dark. Harry didn't mind; it always felt warmer at night. He tugged his scarf around his neck and began to cross the car park, heading into town.

Usually on a Thursday he went to see his gran. She would have supper ready and then he'd catch up with Nick, have a couple of pints, before coming back to his room at the college. Gran still treated him as human, unlike his visits home. Mum and Dad were wary, never knew what to say to him. It was worse when his brothers were there as they acted as if Harry might contaminate them. He couldn't blame them, not after what he'd done.

Tonight, though, he was due at rehearsal with the Gilbert and Sullivan society. As it was Gran's friend, Ida, who had invited him, he was sure she was instrumental in it.

Harry stopped as a car pulled up alongside. The driver's window was down and a nondescript man nodded to him. He didn't know the man so gave a brief nod and went to walk on.

'Harry Winters?'

'Yes?'

'Someone would like to have a word.'

Harry couldn't see anyone else in the car and shook his head.

'It's about Jonathan.'

As the man dropped his voice to a whisper, Harry had trouble hearing. He stepped closer to the car.

'Who?'

'Jonathan James.'

'Well, I'm not the right person. I haven't seen him since…in years.'

'You've heard what happened to him though, haven't you?'

'Yes.'

'This person just wants to talk to one of Jonathan's old friends.'

Harry hesitated. Most of his memories regarding Jon were

unpleasant, but there had been some good times in the past. Maybe it was Jon's mother. She must be devastated. When they were young, Harry remembered her welcoming them to play in the garden, even providing biscuits and pop, as long as Jon's dad wasn't home. He guessed it wouldn't hurt to have a word. 'Okay, I've got a few minutes to spare.'

As he got in the car, Harry wondered if he was doing the right thing. He had no idea where he was going. The man spoke as if guessing his thoughts.

'We thought it best to meet in town. Big crowds tonight with the Christmas market. I'll drop you at the top of Henley Street. He'll be waiting.'

Harry noticed the *he'll be waiting* and was suddenly afraid. Why had he agreed to do this? What if it was Jon's dad? He was a bully and he didn't want to talk to him.

It was a short drive complicated by the mass of cars making their way into town tempted by the offer of free parking, the Christmas lights and market. It would have been faster to walk.

The man dropped him at the top of Henley Street, right next to the statue of *The Jester* by James Butler, reminding Harry of the project they had done on the statues in Stratford. Out of all of them, this one with its sense of movement and fun remained his favourite. The statue held two poles, small heads on sticks, one representing comedy, the other tragedy.

Wandering down the street, Harry passed the Creaky Cauldron, a magic shop that sold butterbeer and chocolate frogs, before stopping to listen to the University of the Third Age's steel band playing in front of Shakespeare's Birthplace. The rhythm was infectious and he felt himself tempted to join in with several toddlers dancing in front while their parents smiled at their antics.

The mingled smells of food enticed him on towards the bright, canopied stalls further down the street. Although it was cold, the light from the overhead lights gave out a warm magical glow. Forgetting for the moment why he was there, Harry decided to get something to eat and headed towards the hot pasties stall. Before he could decide what to have, someone tapped him on the shoulder and he turned to see a short man with a domed shiny forehead. Behind the thick glasses, his pale grey eyes seemed huge, giving him the appearance of a professor.

'Hello, Harry. How very kind of you to meet me.'

'That's okay. Don't think I'll be much help though. Haven't seen Jon in a long time.'

'I'm sure whatever you can tell me will be a great comfort to, er, shall we say, my friend. Maybe if you can tell him, for instance, what has happened to Jonathan's other friends? The ones arrested with him for, shall we say, that most regrettable incident.'

'I haven't seen any of them since.'

'Come, come now, you live in the same area, and can surely provide me with some information. Take your time and think now, very carefully.'

'Well, Beanie, Dave, went to live with his sister. He hasn't been well, since...' Harry stopped. He didn't know this man, shouldn't be telling him anything. The man's voice had a soft, soothing quality, yet Harry sensed the threat beneath it and he could feel the sweat beginning to bead around his neck. There was no way he wanted to talk to this man, or tell him that he and Nick met up for the occasional drink. Beside Beanie, he had no idea what the others were up to, anyway, except Nick's girlfriend, Tilly, who was pregnant. She used to be Jon's girlfriend. Harry wondered if he should just walk away and lose himself in the crowd, refuse to answer any more questions.

The man reached out and grasped Harry's arm as if he could read his mind. 'Where are my manners? You are probably hungry. Let me take care of that while you think. How about one of these delicious-looking pasties?' The man led Harry to the stall, still holding onto his arm. 'Come now, what's it to be, my boy?'

Passersby would not see any threat, just a mild-mannered man buying his companion, most likely his son, a treat. It would be useless to ask for help. The stallholder was smiling and waiting. People began queuing behind them, so Harry nodded towards the steak and onion and took the warm offering, even though he had lost his appetite. Still tightly holding onto his arm, the man manoeuvred them both away from the crowd into a shop doorway.

'My friend is particularly interested in the young lady known as Tilly. He feels this dear girl might like to know what has happened to Jonathan, and could possibly be somewhat of a comfort to his dear mother.'

Harry did not intend to talk about Tilly. He wouldn't betray his friends. 'You know how Jonathan died?'

'Sadly, it was a drug overdose.'

'Yes, I'd heard that. But he'd never touch anything.'

'Now there you are, young man. Already such a great help. You confirm my friend's suspicions that Jon was murdered. As you can understand, he is desperate to find out who would wish him such harm.'

Harry thought there must be quite a few people who would be glad that Jon was dead, but he stayed quiet.

'You can understand that my friend is anxious that justice be done. He is worried that the police will simply write Jonathan's death off as accidental. These days you can't rely on the police to figure it out, can you? He will be most grateful that you have confirmed his suspicions. Most grateful. Now I am going to leave you, give you time to think about all you know. You have until tomorrow to give me the information I require. Should you not be forthcoming, then my friend will be very disappointed. Do you understand?'

Harry nodded and the man smiled, a condescending sickly smile, one that belied the menace in his words.

# Chapter 24

The Black Hound pub, though a bit grubby and rundown, was convenient to the police station. To cops coming off a long and difficult shift, it provided warmth and comfort, a favourite place for all ranks. Many stopped off there to relax before heading home. Matt used to do the same, before Eppie.

Now, he had the unpleasant task of seeking out Grant, of giving the man a chance. Grant had struck lucky having Duffer attend the incident, but Matt needed to see for himself if he should take it further. He spotted him at the back of the pub, pint in hand, propping up the bar, and headed towards him. Grant showed no surprise.

'How can this help, Grant?'

'What the hell would you know?'

'You're right – nothing at all.'

'Then sod off and let me get on with it.'

'I can't do that.'

'Yes you can. It's easy – turn round and walk out that door. I'm nothing to you.'

'Not true.'

'Why – because I turn out and do my job?'

'You're a valuable member of the team.'

'Rubbish.'

'You certainly keep me on my toes.' Grant laughed at this and Matt felt as if he had gained some ground.

'Someone has to.'

'True. I would become unbearable if you weren't there.'

'Even when I am there.'

Matt grinned. He decided to relax. It might be the best way to get Grant on side. Catching the eye of the barman, he ordered two coffees. 'Join me?'

'Why not?'

As they waited for the coffee to arrive, Grant continued to take swigs of his pint. He made no effort at conversation and Matt racked his brains as to what to say, conscious that he didn't know anything about the man, except that he had risked his life to save Eppie. Maybe this was a mistake. Would it have been better to confront Grant in the office? But he wanted to avoid making judgements, at least until he had the facts. He waited until the coffees arrived and, after taking a sip, tried again.

'Used to come in here all the time, before—'

'The wife. Tie you up in knots, if you let 'em.'

'You married?' Matt was ashamed that he didn't know.

Grant took a long drag of his drink, ignoring the coffee. 'No. Not now. The job, usual story.'

'I'm sorry.'

'Don't be. You won't be any different.'

Matt thought of Eppie and hoped not, but, given the strain the job brought with it, marriage breakups in the police were common. And, if McRay and Grant were anything to go by, the odds were against him. Mind you, Grant and McRay were hardly the easiest of characters. How could any woman enjoy living with either of them? He and Eppie must have more of a chance. 'I can try.'

'Good luck with that then.'

Matt wondered how to bring up the subject of the car crash.

'It was an accident.'

'Yes?' At least the drink hadn't dulled Grant's perception.

'Nothing more.'

'Not like you though.'

'Happens.'

'But shouldn't.'

'Then do what you have to.'

'I will. Just wanted to talk to you first.'

'Don't do me any favours.'

'I won't. Maybe we should go through it tomorrow, in the office.' Matt watched as Grant shrugged his shoulders as if he didn't care. He'd given the man a chance, damn him. Now, from what Sam had said, there was no other way but to make it his business. Matt doubted he would get any more sense out of the man tomorrow and he didn't want to put Sam on the spot. The way Grant was knocking back that pint, which was probably his second or third and still early evening, was bearing out Sam's thoughts that he'd been hung over from the night before.

Matt pushed away his half-finished coffee. 'This is already official. I need you in the office early so we can talk. Right?' He got no acknowledgement from Grant as he turned and walked out, nodding to the officers he knew.

# Chapter 25

Kathy hurried past the crowds browsing the food stalls towards the joyful music of the steel pans. It floated out over the shoppers, creating a carnival atmosphere. Kathy could see her friend Maureen concentrating on a huge steel pan, only looking up as the piece finished. Kathy waved and received a nod and a smile as she aimed her camera. She stayed to enjoy a couple more seasonal tunes before turning away. The cold was biting and she couldn't wait to get to rehearsal.

It was then she saw Harry with an older man at one of the food stalls. But something wasn't right. The man was holding Harry's arm tightly and the look on Harry's face said he wished he were somewhere else. Kathy hesitated, decided to walk past, but as she got closer, she could see that Harry was terrified. She stepped forward.

'Hello. Harry, isn't it?'

The man turned to her and his eyes raked over her like an X-ray, taking in everything. He smiled and nodded to her and turned to Harry.

'Aren't you going to introduce me, dear boy?'

Kathy stepped forward to introduce herself, as Harry seemed at a loss. She was now sure something was wrong. Harry visibly relaxed as the man walked away. Although she had given him her first name, he hadn't obliged with his.

'Who was that man, Harry?'

'I've never seen him before.'

'So what did he want?'

'Oh, some information about an old friend who died recently. I couldn't tell him anything as I haven't seen him for years.'

Was this to do with Jonathan? If they hadn't been in touch recently that was a good sign. Maybe it was true that he'd left his old ways behind. She decided to watch him tonight and perhaps consider putting him to the end of her list.

'Are you on the way to rehearsal? Ida said you'd be joining us.'

'Yes.'

'Would you like a lift?'

'Yes. Thanks. I'm not sure where it is.'

As they began to walk down crowded Bridge Street to the car park, neither of them noticed the man following closely behind.

# Chapter 26

Eppie was getting anxious. Matt should have been home by now and the dinner was past ready. She'd taken the shepherd's pie out of the oven and put it in the warming drawer. The starter was cold – Parma ham and feta cheese – so there were no worries about that. Even though Matt wasn't looking forward to this dinner, she didn't think he would resort to deliberate sabotage. Was he alright? After what happened two months ago, when serial killer Clive Draper had injured them both, she'd gained an insight into what Matt's job entailed. In some ways, she wished she had remained ignorant.

However, she couldn't allow her worries to spoil the evening. This was the first time she'd cooked for Matt's parents, Sue and Paul, and she wanted it to be a success. Matt had said that his dad would be her slave for life once he'd tasted her shepherd's pie. Eppie had been thinking of having a roast or steak and although she'd taken his advice, it still didn't seem the right thing to have at a dinner party.

She offered Sue and Paul more wine, thinking they would all be tipsy before dinner at this rate. 'Sorry about this. I'm sure Matt won't be long.'

In reply, Paul gave a resigned humph, while Sue smiled. 'Don't worry. We're enjoying having you to ourselves for a change. Aren't we, love?'

'Yes, yes, of course. Can only apologise for that lad of mine. The job will always come first. Besides, something smells delicious and well worth waiting for.'

Eppie had the feeling that she ought to stick up for Matt, but as the hostess, she didn't want to upset her guests. Matt had told her how disappointed his father had been at his choice of career. Now she could see first-hand that what he said was true; his dad had never forgiven him. Feeling awkward, she decided she'd rise above it all and ignore Paul's comments.

'It's shepherd's pie. Matt said it was one of your favourites.'

'It certainly is.'

'We could start without him, if you like.'

'No, let's give him a little longer. Paul can wait, can't you?'

Before Paul could reply, the phone rang and Eppie moved to answer it.

'Hi.' She was relieved to hear Matt's voice.

'Sorry, Epp. Just sorting out a bit of a mess. Sam and Grant had an accident. Sam ended up in A&E.'

'Is he alright?' Eppie saw the disgusted look on Paul's face and turned away, moving into the kitchen.

'Yes. Just a bump on the head. I've dropped him home and caught up with Grant so shouldn't be long.'

'I hope you gave Sam my love.'

'Not likely.'

'Well, you know what I mean.'

'Yes. Sorry. Tell the folks I'll be there soon. Don't wait for me.'

'Okay, we'll carry on.'

As Eppie put the phone down and returned to the lounge, Matt's dad burst out.

'He's not coming, is he? I knew it.'

Sue laid a warning hand on his arm. 'Come on, Paul. It's not Eppie's fault.'

'No, it's that damn job.'

'One of his colleagues has been injured. Matt went to hospital to see how he is. He won't be long, said to start without him. Hope that's okay?'

'Of course. Can I help at all?'

'Thanks, but I think everything is ready. I won't be a minute.'

As she returned to the kitchen to collect the starters, she could hear Sue quietly telling Paul to behave himself. Hopefully he would listen to her, as she didn't want Matt coming home to his father's snide comments. Wondering how Sam was, she carried the plates through to the table.

Throughout dinner, Eppie heard all about Paul's position as a history professor at the University of Warwick. His specialist subject was the Tudors. Despite his interest in history, Eppie couldn't see Matt enjoying the academic life and thought he had been right to follow his grandfather into the police, although she was careful not to say so.

Hearing Matt's key turn in the door, Eppie stood to greet him. 'Are you sure Sam will be alright?'

'He'll be okay. Back to work tomorrow, knowing him. Sorry, folks.'

'Nothing more than we expect, Matt,' Paul snapped.

'It couldn't be helped, Paul. Matt would hardly be missing a dinner like this on purpose,' Sue reproached him.

'I'm sure he has lots more important things to do than sitting down with his parents.'

'As a matter of fact I did.'

Eppie heard the angry edge in Matt's tone and tried to intervene. 'I'll just get your dinner, Matt. You must be starving.' She turned towards the kitchen, before realising that he was ignoring her.

'It was essential to check on my sergeant, and friend, given that he was involved in an accident while on duty.'

'This is how it's going to be, Eppie. Work will always come first.'

Eppie turned back from the kitchen wondering how she could calm this down. Sue looked at her in despair. She'd obviously seen it all before.

'When people's lives are in danger, yes, work will come first. But then you wouldn't know anything about having a job with real responsibilities, would you, living up there in your ivory tower?'

Eppie put her hand on Matt's arm. 'Matt.'

Matt shook her off. She knew he wasn't sleeping well on the sofa bed and that he must be worried about Sam, and now this wasn't helping matters. Paul stood up.

Sue followed, placing herself between her son and husband. 'I think we should be going, Paul. So sorry, Eppie.'

Eppie saw Matt turn away in despair and went to him.

'Ask them to stay for coffee, Matt, please.'

At first, she thought he was going to pull away from her. As he looked down at her she realised she'd never seen him look so tired. He turned back to his parents. 'Look, I'm sorry. Please stay and have a coffee. Eppie's bought a special blend and it would be a shame not to try it.'

'We'd love to. Wouldn't we, Paul?'

Some of the tension dissipated as Paul sank back down on his chair and nodded. 'That would be nice.'

Eppie smiled up at Matt and went into the kitchen to get the coffee going. She hoped that the night could end on a peaceful note. There was no sound of conversation as she measured out the coffee and when she took Matt's dinner through, everyone was sitting as if engrossed in their own thoughts.

'Coffee won't be a minute.' Eppie sat down at the table and tried to think of something to say that wouldn't cause a row between Matt and his dad. Sue spoke first.

'We've had a lovely time with Eppie spoiling us, Matt.'

'She does that, Mum.'

'You need to make sure you look after her.' As Paul spoke, Sue and Eppie held their breath.

Matt finished a mouthful of food before he spoke. 'I don't think she has any complaints – have you, Eppie?'

'None at all.' Eppie leaned across to Matt and put her arm around his shoulder, feeling the tension beneath his muscles. Maybe she had been wrong to force this dinner on him. In fairness, when she had planned it, he wasn't busy at work. Now he had a case, she knew he would be aiming to have 'thinking time' in his old comfy chair. He was unlikely to get that tonight, as by the time his parents had left, Angela would arrive home, no doubt full of herself and wanting to regale them about her evening. He wouldn't be able to get an early night either.

# Chapter 27

Vinny was beginning to feel at home. Dan proved a willing servant, restocking the fridge with beer and fetching whatever takeaway Vinny fancied. The boat was warm and apart from banging his head every time he stood, he reckoned he could put up with it for a while, especially if it was a means to an end.

Listening to Dan washing the dishes, he'd almost dozed off. Footsteps on the deck outside woke him and he jumped up, catching his head on the overhead locker. Cursing, he was relieved to hear Ops' familiar voice.

'Good evening, gentlemen.'

'Bloody hell, couldn't you have given us some warning?'

'Now, now, Vinny, you know I dislike bad language. I can go away again – call back tomorrow with an appointment if you wish. Yet, I thought you might be interested in my meeting with young Harry.'

'What did he say?'

'A coffee would be much appreciated.'

'Dan,' Vinny snapped.

Ops composed himself on the small bench opposite Vinny and waited while Dan prepared an instant coffee. Vinny wanted to strangle Ops. It would be so easy to grasp that plump pink neck, watch those grey eyes pop. But this infuriating man held information that could lead him to Jon's killer and he forced himself to wait, turning his anger instead on Dan.

'How bloody long does it take to make a coffee?'

Ops sighed, shook his head and waited until Dan slopped a mug of coffee in front of him. Only then did he speak. 'I met up with young Harry earlier this evening. He turned out to be a most pleasant and helpful young man.'

'Well?'

'He tells me that he has had nothing to do with Jonathan since the start of the trial.'

'Bugger.'

'However, he did confirm your suspicion that Jonathan would not take drugs.'

'I told you that.'

'Yes, but it is nice to have it verified, so to speak.'

'Is that all?'

'No. He mentioned someone called Dave. Beanie, I recall is his nickname.'

'I know him. Used to live down the road. Useless little sod. His sister was the brightest in that family.'

'That is who the young man is living with at the moment. I've checked and her married name is Pritchard. Apparently, Dave has mental health problems and rarely goes out.'

'He was always into the funny stuff. Probably done his head in, although he was dopey to begin with. Now, he could have got hold of the gear to kill my lad.'

'I think it is unlikely, but I will follow it up. Also, I intend to see Harry again soon. In the meantime, I'm having him followed. So you can rest assured that I have all bases covered. Oh, I almost forgot, a lady of about fifty came by, said hello to Harry. She gave her name as Kathy. Would you know who she might be?'

'No idea.'

'Oh well, I'm having her followed as well, just in case she proves useful.' Ops stood. 'Thank you for the coffee, Dan. Vinny, have patience. I am working hard on your behalf.'

'I'd rather be out there sorting it myself.'

'And getting caught before your task is completed?'

'Don't automatically follow.' Vinny stood so that he towered over Ops.

Ops merely smiled at this obvious display of muscle. 'We shall see. Good evening.'

As Ops made his way up the steps, Vinny cursed, gave his usual one-finger salute to Ops's plump backside and turned to kick the stove in frustration. He wanted to be out there, to find out for himself who had killed his boy. Still, it should be easy to sneak out while Dan was asleep.

# Chapter 28

Every time he'd drifted off to sleep, his cold feet had woken him and Matt hoped he hadn't kept Eppie awake. She appeared to be sleeping peacefully so he eased himself off the edge of the sofa bed, forgetting that he would land on Eppie's favourite plant; a small Yucca that she nourished with great care. He couldn't help crying out as his toe met the heavy pot. 'Damn.'

Eppie stirred.

'Sorry, go back to sleep. I was trying not to wake you.' He leaned over to kiss her and she turned to him.

'Are you okay?'

'I'm fine.'

'And my plant,' she murmured sleepily.

'No damage.'

'Good,' she said, snuggling back down.

At least she had put him first, Matt thought, grinning to himself. After a quick shower and an instant coffee, he crept out. Eppie's alarm clock would go off at seven fifteen, so at least she could have another half hour. Matt wanted to be in the office early to prepare himself for Grant and he wasn't looking forward to what must be done.

There were already a number of cars on the road and a frail sun tried to break through. It just caught the highest of the ruined towers of Kenilworth Castle. Matt often thought, if he could time travel, he would go back to the time of John O'Gaunt to be there to watch him arrive with his knights and chargers. It would be all bustle and noise as the stable lads received the sweating horses while John strode into the castle impatient to see his mistress, Katherine Swynford. Now, with the ruins left to the blackbirds and rabbits, all was silent and still. Matt pulled away from one of his favourite imaginings to concentrate on the icy road.

At work, it looked as if it had been a slow night given the lingering smell of curry and the empty cartons littering a desk. Matt didn't appreciate the stench first thing in the morning, but by the time he'd made himself a coffee and attacked the biscuit tin, he had become accustomed to it. Feeling better prepared, he sat down to sort through what needed doing today. It was a pity that Phil Nodding hadn't been seen due to the accident, as he could be a vital witness. He'd put him down for a visit today.

Half an hour later Grant ambled in. Matt, relieved that he had shown up, went to the door of his office and beckoned Grant to join him. Without even looking at Matt, he sauntered in. Indicating a seat by the coffee table, Matt thought he looked rougher than yesterday. Sitting down opposite, he waited to see if Grant would look up, but was disappointed. 'You know what this is about?'

'Yes.'

'Tell me what happened yesterday.'

'Moment's lack of concentration. That's all.'

'Which could have killed you both?'

'But didn't.'

Determined not to lose his patience, Matt fought to stay calm. He wondered if Grant realised the trouble he was in. 'One of my officers ended up in casualty. That's more than sufficient. You were damn lucky it was old Duffin or you could be on a charge right now.'

Grant didn't reply. His tolerance beginning to slip, Matt decided to tackle him head-on. 'Grant, had you been drinking the previous night?'

Shrugging his shoulders, Grant looked up for the first time. 'Nothing else to do.'

'How much?'

'The usual.'

'So you might have been over the limit? Just like you are at this minute.'

'Unlikely.'

'Shall we take a test?' Matt was pleased to see the smirk leave Grant's face. 'No? I didn't think you would like that. You do realise how I should deal with this?'

'You'll do what you want.'

'No. What I have to, damn you.' Matt wanted to thump the coffee table for emphasis, but resisted. How could he get through to the man? He tried to rein in his anger, took a breath and started again. 'When you drove yesterday, were you aware that you might be over the limit?'

'Didn't think about it.'

Matt wanted to snap back, *Well maybe you should have,* but stopped himself in time. 'Or, that if you have been drinking heavily each evening, you could be over the limit every day?'

Grant declined to answer. So Matt continued. 'Do you want to lose your job?'

Grant shook his head.

'Because, unless we get to grips with this, that's exactly what will happen. I need to understand what is going on for you.'

Grant remained silent.

'Bloody hell, Grant, you're not making this easy. If you're not willing to help, I can't do a damn thing. Don't you understand, this might be your last chance?' Matt waited, and as the silence lengthened, wondered how long he should give the man.

Grant finally spoke. 'It's a long story.'

'I've got time.' Matt sat back, making sure his posture was open and relaxed. He didn't think Grant was going to reply as he watched the man fight with the demons in his head.

'It's the job.'

'It's tough at times.' Matt couldn't help thinking of the danger Eppie had been placed in because of his position.

Grant looked up. 'You think facing up to the villains makes us men? That's the easy bit. It's the way it takes over, creeps into your head, leaves no room for anything, or anyone. You're a policeman twenty-four seven, no turning it off. You hear the neighbour shouting at his kids and think you should interfere, a pal fiddling his tax and wonder whether to report him.'

Matt watched as Grant became lost in his thoughts. He decided to wait, let him continue in his own time.

'I was in the middle of my Inspector's exams, living and breathing the bloody job.'

In the stillness, Matt became aware of the ticking of the wall clock.

'I didn't want to know. I knew what he was going to say and I couldn't face it. She'd asked me to have a word with him and I kept finding excuses.' Grant lowered his head into his hands.

Aware that whatever was bothering Grant had been torturing him for a long time, Matt knew he didn't have the skills to deal with the man's pain, yet, if this was the first time he had opened up, there was nothing else he could do but listen and wait.

'I didn't know what to say to him.'

'What happened, Grant?'

'I left it too late.'

'Too late?'

Grant took a deep breath and the words shot out. 'He killed himself because I couldn't face the fact that he, my son, was gay.'

Matt sat back, stunned. Whatever he had been expecting, it wasn't this. He had been thinking of the usual marriage break-up due to stresses of the job. Grant's persecution of homosexuals made sense now. It was as if he had turned all his grief and anger onto them. No wonder Jane's relationship with Jenny had riled him.

'I'm sorry.' It tumbled out as he searched in vain for something adequate to say. Grant's shoulders relaxed. Maybe it was a relief that it was finally out. 'Thanks for telling me, Grant.'

Grant gave a grunt.

Matt thought of the implications of Grant's position. He'd need the man's cooperation if his job was to be saved. Realising this might be difficult to get, he laid it on the line. 'Grant, do you want to keep your job?'

'Of course. I've nothing else.'

'Then we'll need to work out what we do next. For a start, we'll have to get McRay on side.'

Grant looked up at that.

'No other way, sorry. Then, there will be no driving.' Matt waited to see if there would be a reaction from Grant, but he merely gave a shrug, so he continued, knowing that the crux of the matter was to come. 'You'll cut down on the drinking and, if that means getting help, then you will accept it.'

'See the counsellor?'

'Yes.'

'Fat lot of good that will do.'

'It's part of the deal. If this goes through the system, as it should, you won't stand a chance.' He paused before adding, 'I certainly don't want to lose you.'

Grant stayed silent as if assessing the truth. 'For how long?'

'As long as it takes.'

After a long silence, Grant nodded consent.

'Good. I'll talk to McRay.'

Grant shuffled to his feet.

'And we'll keep this to ourselves until then. Okay?'

Receiving a brief nod from Grant, Matt took this as a yes. Now all he had to do was talk to McRay.

Grant left the office and Matt couldn't help sighing. He didn't need this. Before approaching McRay, he'd have to get his argument clear so he could persuade him that Grant was worth the risk. Matt cheered up at the sight of Sam walking into the office, stopping to give his usual grin as he received the well wishes of colleagues.

# Chapter 29

Last night she'd watched him at the rehearsal. Harry seemed shy at first but relaxed once they started singing. Kathy could hear his clear tenor adding strength to the row behind her. This alone would ensure his welcome as there was always a shortage of tenors.

During the break, she saw him chatting to some of the others and caught glimpses of that wide smile. Would they still welcome him if they knew what he had done? She still couldn't believe he'd ever been vicious enough to take part in Jack's horrific death. Could anyone really change that much? She wanted to hate him, was prepared to kill him, rid the world of a wicked character, but now everything was turned on its head, leaving her confused and uncertain.

Besides Harry, there was another newcomer, Angela, and Ida had asked Kathy to help her. Kathy personally thought that no one, Angela or Harry, ought to join at this late stage, but it wasn't up to her to decide. As for helping her, Angela was convinced she knew it all and tried to tell Kathy what to do. No matter what the passage called for, Angela was intent on singing louder than anyone else and Kathy was relieved when, at the break, she made a beeline for the men.

This morning she'd woken from a fretful dream about Harry. Trying to push him from her mind, she prepared for a busy day at college. She enjoyed working on reception and sometimes felt like a mother hen to the students. Although Ida had told her when Harry started his course in the drama department, she'd resisted seeking him out, her need for revenge only nebulous then, a hot angry lesion slowly turning itself into a solid cold ball of hate.

After a busy day, she arrived home, annoyed to find herself still thinking about Harry. Tired of the dilemma, she mentally put Harry to the bottom of the list, and decided she'd check out David Beeson. Relieved at making a decision, she made a cup of tea and sat down to relax with the local paper.

'Heartbroken mother' the caption read underneath a picture of Jonathan's mother. That pathetic little woman who had hovered, lost, as the court officials ignored her. She had felt empathy for her then. The article told her little she didn't know already – Mary James couldn't understand what had turned her son into a killer, but she thought having a violent father hadn't helped.

What would the newspapers make of her? Would heartbroken mother be the headlines, or cruel and heartless killer? She always imagined herself on the side of good, but Mary James would think differently. Kathy hoped she would never have to face her.

# Chapter 30

Phil Nodding lived in a high rise flat on the outskirts of Leamington Spa. Seeing at least one vehicle propped up on bricks, Matt was uneasy leaving *his* car, but there was nowhere else. He pushed down his fears of coming back to find all four wheels gone and followed Jane to the entrance. The flats had the pretence of security, and needed a code to enter. Trying the caretaker's bell brought no response and Matt was starting to get impatient when two young mothers, complete with pushchairs and numerous toddlers, came out. Matt held the door open for them and ushered Jane inside.

Declining to take the lift after only one sniff, they began the long climb to the eighth floor.

'I'll go up on my own if you like?' Her reply was a raised finger and he gave up. He would have been glad if she had stayed in the car to keep it safe. By the time they reached the eighth floor, Matt was slightly out of breath as he laboured up the last few steps, while she stood at the top waiting. 'Okay, I get it.'

She nodded at his resignation and turned to walk along the corridor. Phil's flat was two doors along and she banged on the door. By the time Matt reached her, she had resorted to banging again, this time louder, before bending to peer through the letterbox. 'Someone's home.'

After another attack on the door, they heard shuffling inside, followed by bolts being drawn back. The door opened an inch secured by a chain. 'What?'

Matt stepped forward. 'Phil Nodding? We just need a quick word. We are investigating the death of Jonathan James and I understand that you were friends with Jonathan? I'm DI Turrell and this is DC Meadows. May we come in please?' Both of them held up their warrant cards.

Cursing came from inside, followed by fumbling before the chain was released and the door opened. A skinny young man stood shivering in his boxer shorts. He stood back to let them in, before ushering them into the tiny room that served as a bedroom, living room and kitchen. The sofa obviously doubled as a bed, with a dingy pillow and duvet laying half on the floor. Matt guessed they had woken him up.

Phil picked up the duvet to wrap around him. 'Jon dead?'

'Yes. Sorry.'

'When?'

Jane checked her notebook. 'He was found early in the morning on the sixteenth of December. Were you with him that night?'

'Suppose so.'

'Where did you meet?' Matt asked.

'By the shops.'

'Which shops?'

Phil waved his right hand vaguely. 'By the off-licence.'

'The one on Alderton Road?'

'Yep.'

'Why there, Phil?'

'Sometimes one of the punters will get us cider.'

'Did you get lucky that night?'

'Nope. Least *we* didn't.' Phil stopped as if recalling something. 'Nope.'

'Who got lucky, Phil? Was it Jonathan?'

'Dunno.'

Matt sighed. It was obvious Phil had remembered something and had just as quickly shut it away again. He tried a different tack.

'What time did you last see Jonathan?'

'Dunno.'

'Please think. It could be important.'

Phil plonked himself down on the sofa and pulled the duvet tighter around him. 'It was cold. No hope of getting anything. The off-licence had shut. Some of the lads went into town. I came back here.'

'What were they going in search of, Phil?' Matt hoped the answer wasn't going to be, *Dunno*.

'Booze I suppose.'

'Not drugs?'

'Jon didn't do 'em.'

'And the others?'

'Maybe. I dunno.'

Matt thought it might be best to wind it up for now before they lost what little cooperation they had. He decided to risk one more question but he could guess the answer. 'You have been very helpful, Phil. I'd like to ask you just one more question and then we'll leave you in peace. Do you know the names of any of the lads who were with you that night? Just a partial would help.'

Phil looked as if he were scanning his memory, but eventually shook his head. 'Nope.'

'Well, if you remember anything, anything at all, it might be a great help to us. Here's my card, just call me. Thanks for your help.' He would have liked to add *such as it was* but refrained.

Going down the stairs was much easier than coming up, and reaching the car park, Matt was relieved to find the car intact. He guessed that at night time it would be different. All the layabouts, like Phil, would be out roaming, looking for any opportunity.

Safely in the car, he turned to Jane. 'Impressions?'

'He remembered something, but didn't want to tell us.'

'Yes, that was my feeling too. Maybe a trip down the station would encourage him.'

'Could do, or shut him up completely.'

'Let's check out the off-licence.'

Although Mrs Johnson at the off-licence was helpful, they drew a blank. The CCTV worked on a loop and the footage from the night of Jonathan's death had already been taped over. Mrs Johnson never worked the evening shift, but looked up the rota and gave them the name and number of a Reg Storey, who had been on duty from four to ten pm on the evening before Jonathan's death.

# Chapter 31

After finding out that Dave Beeson lived with his married sister, Kathy found the Pritchards' house with the aid of the sat nav. Parked opposite the house, she questioned what she was doing, sitting here in a strange street on one of the coldest nights of the year. She'd promised herself she'd just stay for ten minutes, to get the lie of the land. The lights were on in the front room and Kathy could see the flicker of a television set. At just gone ten, a man entered the front bedroom and drew the curtains while downstairs the lights remained on.

Eight minutes later, freezing and feeling a bit of a fool, she was about to head home when the front door opened and a lanky youth came out. He wore dark colours and blended silently into the shadows. Arguing with herself as to whether she should follow, she reasoned that this was her chance to find out more about him. Despite the bitter cold, she forced herself out of the car and pulling up her scarf to cover her mouth, began walking after him, stepping gingerly to avoid patches of ice.

The youth turned towards town and she realised a man, about ten yards in front of her, also seemed to be trailing him. Each time David turned a corner, the man turned too. He only became visible when a streetlight illuminated his face and from those brief glimpses, Kathy didn't recognise him. At a guess, she'd say he was about 5'11", thick-set and muscular.

Worried by his presence, Kathy slowed her pace and increased the distance between them. Now certain the man was following Dave, she made up her mind and returned to the car, glad to get inside out of the biting cold.

# Chapter 32

Vinny spotted him shambling forward, keeping in the shadows close to the buildings, as if afraid the rays of the streetlights would annihilate him. He decided to follow for a while, see what he was up to, but guessed he was out to score.

Why hadn't Jon dumped this idiot? He had warned him, but Jon always liked to surround himself with the weak and easily led. The sort who jumped at his bidding, making him appear the big man. The stupid little sod hadn't realised a unit was only as strong as its weakest link. This was the useless specimen who yelped to the pigs before they'd even laid a hand on his shoulder and got them all nicked.

It should be easy to get the information he needed, but Vinny decided to follow him anyway, just to check. If he had contacts in the drug world, then he could be the one who killed his son.

The dealer was some low-life Vinny didn't know but he didn't seem much of a player. He watched from the shadows as the deal took place.

The idiot turned for home. Vinny waited until he came to a patch of waste ground before pouncing. 'Arsehole, I want a word with you.' He pulled the unresisting bundle into the dark side of a skip and raised his fist. 'You're going to tell me what I need to know. Understand.'

Taking the creature's nod as agreement, he dropped his hand. The sight of its terrified eyes and the slack, dribbling mouth disgusted Vinny. Clenching his teeth in an effort to control the anger, he reached into the lad's pocket to retrieve a packet of white powder. 'You know where to get this filthy stuff.' Vinny tore open the packet and threw the powder all over him. 'This is what killed my Jon. Did you do it?'

'No. No.'

'Then who was it?'

'I don't know.'

'You're supposed to be his mate.'

'He put bad thoughts in my head.'

'And I'll knock 'em out if you don't tell me.' Vinny raised his fist to emphasize.

It flailed its thin arms in a useless effort to protect itself.

But it was easy to push them aside. The first punch was like hitting a leaking balloon. The coward made no attempt to defend himself, or hit back, just collapsed on the ground, whimpering like a lost kitten. Vinny stood over him. It didn't seem right for this pathetic coward to be alive while Jon was dead. He reached down and drew him to his feet, ramming his body so hard against the skip that bones cracked. The mewling increased and he brought his face closer. 'Who was he with?'

'Don't know.'

'Don't know, don't know. Pretty useless, aren't you?'

'Yes.'

'Where's the old gang?'

'Don't know.'

This was a waste of time. In frustration, he aimed a blow to the side of its head. The creature whined and sank to the floor, covering his head with his hands. Kicking out, Vinny discharged his anger into the unresisting softness.

# Chapter 33

There was something sad about Dave in life, but in death he was pathetic. He lay there like a baby, curled up into himself, with one arm over his head as if to ward off blows. Livid bruises showed on his pale skin, while blood matted his lank hair and streaks ran down his face. Someone had done a right job on him. Who would want to pick on such a defenceless young man? His vulnerability reminded Matt of Gracie and the familiar feelings of inadequacy arose of letting them both down. The only difference between them was that Dave hadn't fought back. Matt guessed he must have slid out into the night, probably in search of drugs.

Matt had seen enough and he moved back to let the forensic team erect the tent over the body. Slim would feed him the gruesome details later.

His next job was one he didn't relish. Dave's sister would have to be told. Matt was just wondering if Jane was on her way when she drew up at the outer perimeter. Matt moved towards her as she got out of her car, noticing the dark circles under her eyes. There wasn't going to be much of a chance to ease her in now they had a second suspicious death on their patch. He could send her back to the warm office, but knew it would be best if she came with him to inform Julie Pritchard.

'Sorry about the early start.'

'I'm not sleeping anyway. Is it Dave?'

'Unfortunately, yes. Looks like someone gave him a right beating.'

'Poor sod.'

'Yes. Just retribution, some would say.'

'Think he was suffering enough already.'

'A blessing then? I doubt his sister will think so, although her husband might. We'd better let them know.'

Before he could get into his car, a man, so well wrapped up against the cold that only his eyes showed, came forward. Matt assumed he was a reporter.

'Can you give me a statement, sir?'

'Not at this point. I'm going back to base now and we'll have a press release later.' Matt pushed past the man and got into his car. Jane followed in her car.

Dawn had lightened the sky and a watery sun was rising behind the icy bare branches of the trees. It was only a short distance to the Pritchards' house.

As they walked up the path, Jane spoke. 'Good work dumping the reporter.'

'The Pritchards don't need that lot door-stepping.' No lights showed and as Matt rang the bell, it echoed shrilly through the silence. They waited, hearing movement inside.

Soon, a tall man answered the door, still tying his robe. His blond hair was tousled and he didn't look pleased. 'Yes?'

'Detective Inspector Turrell and Detective Constable Meadows. Mr Pritchard?'

'Oh no, don't tell me. This is to do with that barmy brother of hers.'

'Yes, I'm afraid it is. May we come in?'

He ushered them in while calling up the stairs. 'It's about Dave.'

Mrs Pritchard appeared at the top of the stairs. 'Dave? What… Inspector?'

She hurried down the stairs, alarm showing on her face. 'Come in, take a seat, please.' She led the way into the living room, before turning to face them. 'Do you want to see Dave?'

Both Matt and Jane remained standing. 'Maybe you should sit, Mrs Pritchard.'

At the seriousness of his tone, Mr Pritchard came forwards to his wife as she sank into a chair. Matt sought for the best way to break the news. 'I'm sorry to say there has been an incident.'

Mrs Pritchard broke in before he could continue. 'Involving Dave?'

'Yes. It seems he was attacked last night.'

'That can't be. He's asleep upstairs. I told you he rarely goes out.'

Mr Pritchard seemed to have grasped the seriousness of the situation and took hold of his wife's hand. 'Let them finish, love.'

Matt thought it best to say the awful words he had to say quickly, put them out of their misery. 'I'm afraid he didn't survive his injuries, Mrs Pritchard.'

For a moment, he wondered if she had heard. She shook her head and jumped up. 'Don't be stupid. He's asleep upstairs.'

She made a dash for the stairs and they could hear her footsteps above their head, followed by a scream. Mr Pritchard made to follow his wife, but Matt put out a hand to stop him and indicated for Jane to go instead. As she left the room, Mr Pritchard sank into the armchair vacated by his wife.

'It is probably best if I talk to you, Mr Pritchard. Would you be able to answer a few questions for me?' He waited until Pritchard nodded and chose a seat opposite him. 'When did you last see Dave?'

Pritchard shook his head as if to clear it. 'It would be about ten last night. He was down here watching some rubbish so I went up early, as I wanted to catch the news. What happened to him?'

'At first glance, it looks as if he was beaten.'

'Oh my God.'

'What was your relationship with Dave, Mr Pritchard?'

'I'll tell you straight. I never wanted him here.'

'Why was that?'

'After what he'd done, would you?'

'This isn't about me.'

'No. So it's easy for you to sit there and judge.'

'I'm not doing that. But I am trying to find out what happened.'

'Of course. I'm sorry. It's just that it's been a bone of contention between us. We're hoping to start a family soon, and, well I wouldn't feel safe having a baby in the house. Not with him here.'

'Why is that?'

'I know he couldn't help it, but he was strange at times.'

'In what way?'

Pritchard sat for a moment, recalling. 'He would sit and mumble to himself. And, although Julie thinks I don't know, he was having nightmares. You could hear him shouting from our room. Julie always got up to him. She said he was worried that he might hurt someone else. That it was all in his head, but I wouldn't like to take a chance. He'd done it once already hadn't he?'

'I doubt he would have initiated an attack.'

'I'm sorry he's dead, Inspector. Despite everything, I wouldn't wish that on Julie.' As he said his wife's name, he rose. 'I should go to her.'

'Before you go, will Mrs Pritchard verify that you were here all night, sir?'

'What! You think I would do that to Julie? You seriously…?'

'You have openly admitted that you didn't want Dave living with you, so I have to ask.'

'I didn't want him here, that's true. But listen to my wife sobbing. I want that even less. Julie came to bed about 10.20 pm. She made Dave a drink of cocoa as he seemed restless, more than usual, last night.'

'Thank you, Mr Pritchard.' Matt couldn't see the sense of detaining him. Relieved, Mr Pritchard thundered up the stairs. Matt listened as he reached the top. He could hear Julie Pritchard's voice as she broke down and her husband trying to comfort her. Given how the man felt, he wondered how easy that would be.

Jane made her way downstairs and gave him a rueful grin. 'Wouldn't like to be in his shoes. Are we leaving them to it?'

'Arrange for a Family Liaison Officer. She can take them to identify Dave tomorrow, if they're up to it.' Raising his voice, he called upstairs, 'We'll be off for now, but I'll leave my card here on the hall-stand. Ring if you need anything.' Above the renewed sobbing, they heard Mr Pritchard acknowledge them.

'He has his hands full,' Jane said as they let themselves out.

'I don't think they had anything to do with Dave's death, do you?'

'Mrs Pritchard, definitely not.'

'Right, let's get to the office. I'm dying for a cup of coffee.'

# Chapter 34

By the time they arrived at CID, Sam had posted a picture of the death scene on the board. Matt tried not to dwell on it. Instead, he took his place at the front and turned to face the team.

Nodding his thanks to Sam, he took a breath. 'We interviewed this young man, Dave Beeson, a couple of days ago. He was one of the original gang involved in the death of Wylde. His death would seem to confirm that this is indeed someone seeking vengeance for that crime.'

'Such a different method of killing though, sir,' Grant called out.

'Yes, that is a puzzle. It could mean that we have more than one killer. But are they working together?'

Sam scratched his head. 'Could the first murder have prompted the second?'

'So someone is intent on avenging Jonathan? Yes. Good call, Sam. However, it doesn't seem possible that Dave killed Jonathan James. He was frightened by his own shadow and still terrified of him.'

'And who would avenge Jonathan? There's only his mother,' Jane added.

'What about the father? We have no idea where he is.' He turned as Grant, never one to say much, spoke up. 'Vincent James. I arrested him for armed robbery, over four years ago. First court appearance, he legs it. Jumps right out of the dock. The bastard should be locked up; instead he's probably out there in Spain, spending his loot.'

Matt had never seen Grant so involved. Could this be a glimpse of how he used to be? 'Would he risk coming back to avenge his son?'

'He always liked to think of himself as the big man, hence his name change to Vinny. So it's likely he'd take someone killing his son as a personal insult.'

'Grant, as you have first-hand knowledge of this man, could you check him out from all angles? Known associates, old haunts, prison records, cellmates and the like. And let's have a picture for the board.'

'Glad to.'

Matt was relieved that he could engage Grant while keeping him tied to base. He continued. 'There is also the possibility that the murder was drug related. Dave is known to be a user and it's the only reason he would venture out alone. However, as dealers don't usually kill off their customers, this seems unlikely. Unless he was killed for the drugs. When found, he had no money or drugs on him. We'll need to arrange a door-to-door and check CCTV. Could you liaise with uniform on that, Sam?'

'Will do.'

'We have Dave's mobile and it's being analysed. That might give us some indication who he was meeting. It certainly looks as if he was beaten to death, but no doubt Slim will fill us in. There's nothing back from SOCO yet.'

'Do we need to warn the remaining members of the gang that they may be in danger?' Sam asked.

'If one of them is the killer, they'll know we're onto them,' Jane suggested.

'True, but there is no way we can leave it as they could be at risk. We do need more information about Dave's death, as there is a chance it's unrelated. And we have no evidence yet that Vincent James is involved or is even in the country.'

Matt was about to continue when McRay came out of his lair and made his way to the front. Matt stepped to one side in case he wanted to address the team.

McRay looked at the board before addressing him. 'This is a nasty one, Matt.'

'Yes, sir.'

'Any leads?'

'We're working on one or two angles, but nothing definite. The thinking is that this murder may be linked to that of Jonathan James.'

'Makes sense as they were in the same gang. Let me know what you need and I'll do my best.'

'Thank you, sir. We're starting a door-to-door. Sam is coordinating with uniform on that.'

'Good.' McRay turned and spoke to the team. 'I've got a feeling if we don't get on top of this one fast we'll be faced with more victims. Also, it could mean missing Christmas with your families. So let's have a hundred per cent dedication. I'll try and get authorization for overtime as needed.'

The team were silent, unused to McRay in this reasonable mood. He had been like a snarling bear until a couple of months ago. Matt guessed the near destruction of the team during the Clive Draper case had snapped him out of his self-pitying bout that began after his wife left him. The old McRay was back and very welcome, Matt thought.

# Chapter 35

Grant was relieved that he had a legitimate excuse to remain in the office. It meant the rest of the team wouldn't comment. He was aware that there were already rumours circulating about the accident. Today he had to see McRay and he wasn't looking forward to facing him, even though Matt had smoothed the way. McRay would tell him what plans had been put in place to help him retain his job. Grant knew he should consider himself lucky in having this second chance. Had the decision been his, he wasn't sure he would have put his neck out for a colleague, especially one who could bring down the whole team.

Since he had been shifted out of division and no longer in charge of his own team, Grant felt a compulsion to undermine every decision Matt made. Now Matt stood by him, giving him a second chance and Grant couldn't understand why. Even in his own eyes, he wasn't worth it. The only way to repay him was to get all the details about Vinny James and, with his knowledge of the man, he was the one to do it. The bastard had cheated him once and he relished the chance to get him behind bars where he belonged.

Grant began jotting down all he knew about Vinny. The computer added details of Vinny's past prison sentences and the inmates who were incarcerated at the same time. Some of these individuals formed the gang Grant had arrested for the armed robbery. He checked on them, cheered to find them all still in prison. It could be worth having a word with them. No doubt they would be feeling fed up with Vinny living the high life, while they were still inside.

As he worked through the records of those who had shared a cell with Vinny, he came across one who didn't fit the usual pattern of robbers, muggers and burglars. Harold Harper-Jones was a solicitor who'd been caught fiddling the books. He wouldn't have survived the prison regime, unless Vinny had seen his usefulness and offered him protection. Grant spent the rest of the morning searching out more details about him and some of the others, becoming so engrossed that he was surprised to realise it was time to see McRay.

McRay didn't look friendly and left Grant standing. Fuck him, thought Grant. Just get it over. Finally, McRay looked up.

'Are you aware of the seriousness of your situation, DI Grant?'

'Yes, sir.'

'If it had been left to me, you would be disciplined and out of the force.'

Grant dropped his head in mock shame.

'However, it seems that DI Turrell would prefer to give you another chance. I hope you are suitably grateful.'

'I am, sir.'

McRay gave him a long assessing stare before shaking his head. 'I've made you an appointment with the counsellor at three pm this afternoon. You will follow, to the letter, whatever type of treatment he recommends. This may involve following a specialised programme for your alcohol problem. Do you understand?'

'Yes, sir.' Grant felt that he should salute and all of sudden wanted to laugh. McRay noticed.

'What on earth can you find funny about injuring a colleague, putting the public at risk and bringing shame to the police force?'

Grant tried to recover ground. 'I think it must be nerves. Sorry, sir.'

McRay shook his head in disgust. 'There will be no driving on duty and I would advise you not to drive in your own time either, at least until the programme is having some effect.'

'Yes, sir.'

'Get out of here.'

Relieved that his interview with McRay was over, Grant left the office. He would have loved to bang the door, but thought he'd tried the patience of the old bugger enough for today.

Would he be required to give up alcohol completely? He'd normally have lunch in the Black Hound and fit in a pint or two, but today it wasn't an option, so Grant settled for a quick sandwich. Maybe he could sneak in a pint on the way home, just to relax. If he stuck to the pubs in Warwick, near to his flat, he could count it as research as these establishments were the ones frequented by Vinny. If Grant knew anything about villains, he'd bet Vinny, despite living the life of luxury somewhere, wouldn't have changed his habits. Back on home turf, he would soon resort to his favourite pubs and old running mates, providing Grant with the perfect opportunity to redeem himself.

# Chapter 36

Harry didn't intend to meet up with the man with glasses again. Last night he debated whether to stay in his room or ask his gran if he could stay over. Despite chiding himself for being too imaginative, he'd ruled out going to gran's, not wanting to bring any more trouble to his family. The softly spoken man with glasses seemed threatening, but maybe he was just anxious to help his friend. Instead, he'd decided to stay in his room all night, pleading an upset stomach when mates tried to get him to go into town.

Tonight, he decided to avoid town again, just in case the man was watching. Instead, he placed himself in the middle of a crowd of students heading to the sports hall where Ben, his friend, was playing basketball. Ben was keen to get Harry playing and suggested he come and watch.

From the centre of the crowd heading to the hall, he tried to scan the dark parking lot for signs of the man who'd accosted him the other night. It was impossible to see if the same car was there, but he felt sure the man wouldn't approach him unless he was on his own and Harry relaxed.

Enjoying the basketball match, Harry forgot all about the man. As he moved to congratulate Ben, whose team had won, he was aware that someone was at his side. Without turning, he knew who it was.

'Hello, Harry. Great game wasn't it?'

'I don't want to talk to you.'

'Now I can understand that, Harry. What young man would want to talk to his uncle while surrounded by so many friends? But it is most important that you allow me five minutes of your time.'

Harry felt most of this speech was for the benefit of those around them. He could already feel people moving away and giving them space.

'You see, I would be really upset if you succumbed to the same fate as your friend.'

Harry stopped. 'What friend?'

'The boy you mentioned to me the other day.'

'Dave?'

'Yes, I believe that was his name.'

'Was?'

'Oh, my dear boy. I'm so very sorry to be the bearer of bad news. It seems young David was brutally attacked and has died.'

'You killed him?'

'Harry, Harry, look at me. Can you honestly see me attacking a poor defenceless young man?'

Sick with horror, all Harry could do was shake his head.

'Of course not. I like you, Harry. In fact, the only reason I am here is because I do not want the same fate to befall you.' He paused to allow his threat to hit home. 'You see, Harry, my friend is so distraught, he is lashing out in his despair. Now, if he knew who killed Jonathan, only that person would feel the brunt of his anger and no one else needs to get hurt.'

'I've told you, I don't know. Why don't you listen to me and leave me in peace?' Harry turned and started to walk away, not wanting the man to see how distressed he was, but the man caught his arm.

'I am inclined to believe you, Harry. However, I do need to return to my friend with some snippet that will help us solve this puzzle, otherwise there will be no telling what he may be driven to. You do understand, don't you, Harry?'

'I know nothing. Leave me alone.'

'That is a shame as I would hate to see you...or your family, hurt. For instance, who was the lady who introduced herself as Kathy?'

'Just some woman from the hotel.'

'Yet you accompanied her down Bridge Street and got into her car. I wonder why that was.'

'She's in the same choir, that's all.'

'There, you do have more information. Does this lady have a surname?'

Harry hesitated. Dave had been killed because he gave this man his name. There was no way he wanted to be responsible for someone else's death. Anyway, he didn't know her name.

'I don't know her name. Honest.'

The man studied him before patting him on the arm. 'I think you can do better than that.'

Harry, welling up with anger, turned to face the man. 'Even if

I knew her name, I wouldn't tell you. Now go away before I call my friends to help throw you out.'

'Harry, Harry, there is no need to be like this. No need at all. I expected you to be upset, after all, David was your friend. As, I assume, is this lady. You can safely tell me her name, unless, of course, she is responsible for the death of Jonathan James. And I wouldn't think this is likely. Would you?'

'No.'

'Then what is the harm, especially when a tiny snippet of information could protect those closest to you, like say, your dear grandmother?'

Harry froze. This man could do what he liked and he caused Dave's death. He thought of his gran; she had always stood by him. He couldn't let anything happen to her.

'Now, when you see this lady again, I want you to find out her surname. You will do this one thing for me, won't you, Harry?'

Harry nodded. All he wanted was for the man to go away, leave him alone. He was relieved when he seemed satisfied and with a final pat to Harry's arm, was gone. Sick with worry, Harry lost interest in joining Ben's celebrations and returned to his room. Should he try to warn Kathy, or would it be better to call that detective who had come to see him? Getting out Sergeant Withers' card, he laid it on the bed and wondered if it was too late to call. What would he say? Would he get into trouble for not calling him before, especially after Dave's death? Deciding he didn't want another death on his conscience, he dialled the number, heard it ringing, then cut it off, scared.

# Chapter 37

Matt drove through the avenue of trees towards the crematorium, thinking how tastefully it was set out. It added a dignity to the final ceremony for the dead. Not that he expected many would attend Jonathan James's last appearance or would turn up to mourn his passing.

Both he and Grant were dressed in sombre clothes, aiming to fade into the background as much as possible, although this could be difficult if the turnout was small. It was a well-known fact that murderers would sometimes turn up to see the fruits of their labours, enjoying one last thrill in the power of their handiwork. In addition, Vinny James may turn up to say farewell to his son.

Surprised by the amount of cars in the tree-surrounded car park, Matt drove on to the overspill area. Surely all these people weren't here to honour Jonathan. He had expected that some press might turn up but nothing like this. Then, as they made their way to the entrance, everything became clear. People began to spill out as they approached. There was no one he recognised. Two strapping young men were supporting an older woman, dressed all in black, and Matt guessed this was the funeral before Jonathan's.

He and Grant stepped back out of respect as the large crowd of mourners stopped to give their condolences to the widow. It seemed an age until they dispersed and the wind, carrying a hint of snow, was beginning to bite.

Finally, the black limousines glided forward and the rest of the party began to make their way back to their cars. It was then he saw Mrs James sheltering on the other side of the thinning crowd, shivering in the cold. The man accompanying her showed a likeness, although he was much taller. Matt moved forward to repeat his condolences and she introduced the man as Richard, her brother who had come down from Sheffield. He was obviously a man of few words as he nodded to her introduction of Matt and Grant and turned to lead his sister inside.

Inside it was blessedly warm with the air overlaid with the scent of flowers. The soft background of organ music made Matt want to talk in whispers. The sense of light and peaceful colours gave out an ambience of calm as if to persuade those entering that it was going to be a pleasant experience. Overall, it reminded Matt of the dentist's with their decoys of fish tanks and mood music.

They followed Mrs James and her brother into the main auditorium, choosing to sit in the middle row. Mrs James went down to the front of the raked seats, looking lost in the large space. Just as Matt was wondering if they were to be the only mourners, two elderly women came in and moved to sit behind Mrs James. She turned to acknowledge them. Matt guessed they were probably neighbours.

Then a young man entered and, from Sam's description, and his own memory of arresting him two years ago, Matt was sure he must be Harry. He seated himself across the aisle from Matt and Grant.

'Hope you've got a loud voice, sir,' Grant hissed in a loud whisper as he flipped through the hymnbook to find the first hymn.

'Might have to rely on you for that.'

'You'll regret it.'

'I'll take my chance.'

Eventually, the music swelled and the small group stood as the coffin entered. Mrs James began to sob quietly and her brother looked embarrassed, feeling in his pockets for a crumpled hankie to hand to her. Matt felt uncomfortable and glancing at Grant, he guessed he was feeling the same.

Once the coffin was placed on the central plinth, the organist began the chords of the first hymn. Mrs James and her brother couldn't manage to sing at all, but the elderly women were giving it their best, so Matt and Grant joined in to support. Surprised that Grant had a strong voice, which seemed to be on key, Matt followed him as best he could. With the young vicar adding his rich baritone and Harry's tenor, between them they managed a fair sound. Matt was pleased for Mary James's sake. This was the final send-off for her son and although he had been nothing but trouble, he meant the world to her.

They sat down and the vicar began a reading. Matt, aware that someone else had entered, risked a quick glance round. A man wearing a fur hunting hat, the kind with flaps that come down either side of the head, had slipped into the last row. He had a reporter's notepad on his knee. Matt wasn't surprised to see a reporter but couldn't place him to any of the local papers.

Harry too turned around before slumping down in his seat, as if he didn't want the man to notice him. It could be he didn't want to appear in any newspaper report connected to Jonathan James, but Matt wondered if it was anything else. From his quick glance, he couldn't tell if the man was Vincent James, but he would have tried to disguise himself in some way.

The vicar's recap of the deceased's life seemed to go on a long time and Matt wondered how he found so many kind things to say about Jonathan James and thought it must be a skill they developed. He barely touched on the trouble he had been in, dismissing it as 'losing his way'.

They rose to sing the last hymn, the one where the coffin slides gracefully from view. Mary's sobs became louder, prompting the singers to raise the volume. Hearing a movement behind, Matt turned to see the reporter leaving. He gave Grant a nudge and put down his hymnbook, sliding out as quietly as he could.

They arrived at the entrance as the man was walking away. Matt raised his voice.

'Could we have a word, sir?'

The man turned around briefly and then began to run. Matt and Grant sped after him, now certain he was no reporter. Although he had the advantage of a head start, Matt was closing the gap with Grant panting at his heels.

The roar of an engine caused the man to slow. Looking towards the sound, Matt saw a nondescript car racing down on them. It shot between Matt, Grant and the man they were chasing, slowing for the man to jump in, before speeding off down the drive.

'Bugger.' Matt stopped, allowing Grant to catch up with him.

Grant managed to get out between pants, 'Vinny.'

'Shit.'

Grant bent over recovering his breath while Matt phoned it in. 'Vincent James, wanted for armed robbery. Just leaving Oakley Wood crematorium in a dirty, dull green car. I think it was an old Escort. Number plate concealed in mud. Yes, thanks.'

Grant straightened. 'So he was involved.'

'Looks like it. Come on, I want a word with young Harry. He recognised Vinny too.'

'Yes, he didn't want to be noticed, did he?'

By the time they got back to the crematorium, the small group had gone through to look at the floral tributes. Matt and Grant joined them at the pitiful display. Just four wreaths and one small bouquet with a handwritten note occupied the grass under the sign, Jonathan Bernard James.

Matt bent to view the note. The handwriting was hard to read and he crouched down. 'Bye Son', it said, but the line beneath made Matt catch his breath: '*I'll sort out the bastard who did this to you, don't you worry. Dad.*' Matt stood, wanting to swear, but stopped himself out of respect.

'What's up?' Grant asked.

'Take a look.' He nodded to the bouquet and as Mary was approaching, he stepped forward to offer her his condolences. She spoke before he could begin.

'Thank you for coming, Inspector.'

'Glad to be here, Mrs James, and it was a very moving service.'

'Thank you. He did his best, didn't he? Brought out all the good points of Jonathan. There were some, you know, Inspector.'

'I'm sure of that. Can I ask you if that young man is Harry Winters?' Matt indicated Harry, who was standing on the edge of the group. Mary turned to look.

'Yes. It was kind of him to come, wasn't it?'

'Very.' Matt was aware that Grant had straightened and that he needed to speak to Harry before he left. The vicar approached so he relinquished his place, pausing only to pat Mary on the arm. With Grant beside him, he moved towards Harry.

Harry glanced up, obviously aware they were police. It showed how much the young man had changed in that he made no attempt to move away.

'Is it Harry?' Matt asked, wanting to keep it as low key as possible for his sake.

'Yes.'

'You were Jonathan's mate?'

'A long time ago. Before...before, well you know what.'

Matt nodded. 'We aren't here to talk about that, Harry. Just wanted to ask you if you recognised the man who sat at the back during the service?'

Harry glanced away as if he didn't want to answer.

'He's gone, Harry, so there's no need to worry.'

Harry looked around as if to make sure.

'Has he threatened you?'

'I know what he's like.'

'Who?' Matt and Grant asked simultaneously.

'Him. Jon's dad.'

'Vincent James?'

Harry nodded, ill at ease even talking about the man. 'He'd tried to make himself look different, but it was him.'

Matt decided to let Harry off the hook as he had given them everything they needed and besides the vicar was walking Mary towards them.

'Thanks, Harry.'

Harry nodded and went to move away, then turned back. 'He's the one who killed Dave, isn't he?'

Matt moved swiftly to his side. This wasn't the place to discuss this, not with Mary a few yards away. 'Look, Harry, best not talk of this here. Maybe we can drop you somewhere?'

Harry was quiet for a moment, then nodded. Matt watched as he stopped to speak briefly to Mary. Sam had described him as a good lad and Matt thought he had that spot on.

Grant echoed his thoughts. 'Seems like he's learnt his lesson.'

'Yes.' He moved Grant away from the others. 'Did you notice if Mrs James looked at that bouquet?'

'I'm sure she didn't have the time before we caught up.'

'Good. I want that card, but think it is best if we wait until Mrs James has left. Don't want to upset her.'

'So she had no idea he was here?'

'Looks like it.'

'Poor cow.'

Matt nodded, wondering if Vincent James had tried to contact his wife and if she would tell them if he had. He would have to make another visit to see her.

Once Mary had left with her brother, Matt turned back to the flowers. He was glad the vicar had disappeared inside as it felt wrong to take the note, but Matt assured himself that he would keep it safe and return it. Putting on his gloves, he crouched and detached it, sliding it into an evidence bag before making his way to the car park amidst those arriving for the next funeral. Grant and Harry were waiting for him in the car.

'They certainly do a roaring trade, don't they?'

'Roaring being the operative word,' Matt retorted.

'Very funny.'

'Well, you said it first.'

Conscious that Harry had just attended the funeral for an old mate, Matt thought it was not quite the thing to be making light of and tried to change the subject.

'Where can we drop you, Harry?'

'Anywhere. Thanks.'

Harry seemed uncomfortable. Even though this was an unmarked car, Matt guessed it was bringing back memories he would rather forget.

'Why did you think it might be Vincent James who killed Dave Beeson, Harry?'

'When I saw him there today, it seemed like something he would do.'

'And you haven't seen him around recently?'

'No.'

Matt glanced in the rear-view mirror and saw Harry's lips firmly shut. He was sure Harry knew more than he was letting on but decided to leave it for the moment. Maybe Sam would be able to get more out of him. It was obvious the lad was afraid of Vinny and probably with good cause.

'Harry, I can't comment on any specific case, but I'm thinking that Vincent James is bad news. We need to talk to him urgently. If you see him again, will you give DS Withers or myself a call?'

After a moment's hesitation, Harry gave a nod. Matt had to be content with that and passed over his card as they dropped Harry at a bus stop.

Grant broke the silence as they pulled away. 'Want me to call and see if uniform have had any luck with Vinny and his mate?'

'You can try. Depends which way he went.' Matt thought of the winding road that led to the crematorium. If he had gone north towards Warwick and Leamington, he'd have a choice of roads to take, including the M40. The other way would take him into Wellesbourne and again numerous ways to turn off. It would all depend on if a patrol car had been in the right area.

# Chapter 38

Matt was glad to arrive back at the warm office and wrap his hands around a hot mug of coffee. Dipping into the biscuit tin, he was delighted to see it full of his favourite jammy dodgers. Still munching, he called the team together.

'First of all, congratulations, Sam, you were spot on. We can now confirm that Vincent, or should I say Vinny James is back on the scene. Not only that but he appears intent on avenging his son. This note, left with flowers at the funeral, substantiates it.' Matt held up the evidence bag containing the note. 'If we can find out where those flowers were bought, we may be able to pinpoint the area he is holed up in. Wendy, can you contact local florists, see if they recognise Vinny? I'd go as far as Warwick, just in case. The note can then go to forensics. We'll need to circulate his picture too and put uniform on alert.'

Wendy nodded and Matt thought how invaluable she was – always ready to help and usually came up trumps.

'Grant, care to share what you know about Vincent James?'

Grant stood and moved to the front. 'Glad to, sir. He's a known bullyboy, a local big man, who'd been in and out of prison for robbery and assault. He is a violent man who likes to imagine himself in the top league. I arrested him for armed robbery over four years ago, but he escaped custody so never went to trial. Some of the others involved in that attack are still in prison, so it might be worth having a word with them, especially as we never recovered the considerable proceeds of that robbery.'

'They must be seething that Vinny is out and has access to their share of the takings. Yes, we'll see them and use that angle. See if there really is honour amongst thieves. Thanks, Grant. Anything else?'

'Before his arrest, he was known to frequent both the Leamington and Warwick areas, especially some of the pubs in Warwick. I've made a list. I'm still working on his known associates, old cellmates and the like. There is a rather unusual one from several years back, a Harold Harper-Jones. He was a solicitor who was in for fraud. Thought he might be worth looking up.'

'Yes. Someone like that would know his way around concealing money. And he would have been very glad of some protection. Address?'

'Still working on that.'

'Do you need any help, Grant?'

'Not at the moment. Be good if someone else can talk to the rest of the gang.'

'We'll take care of that. Good work. Sam, do you fancy a trip to Long Lartin prison?'

'Okay.'

'Get the details from Grant.' Sam nodded and Matt turned to the next problem. 'We need to let those who might be in Vinny's firing line know that he is back on the scene. Jane, would you talk to uniform and have them find and warn Nick and Tilly that they may be in danger? Sam, on the way back from the prison, would you call in and see Harry? We spoke to him briefly after the funeral and I have the feeling he knows more than he is telling.'

'Will do, guv. Had a call from him last night, but he rang off before I could answer so I was thinking of catching up with him today.'

'I'm interested to see how Kathy Wylde takes the news. Fluff, sorry, Jane – could do with your input there. Then I can warn Mary on the way home.'

Matt dismissed the team and walked towards McRay's office, intending to get some protection for Mary. McRay saw him coming and called him in.

'How is it going, Matt?'

'We now know for sure that Vinny James is back on the scene, sir. Grant spotted him at Jonathan's funeral. We suspect that he might be responsible for the death of Dave Beeson. I would like to offer some protection to Mary James, Vinny's wife. It seems logical that he might show up there and it could facilitate an arrest.'

'Why her and not the rest of Jonathan's gang members?'

'Ideally, I would like to extend protection to them all, but I know we'd have a hard time justifying the funding. Uniform are informing the ex-gang members while we are visiting Mrs James and Mrs Wylde. We think Harry may be holding something back, so DS Withers will try and talk to him later, sir.'

'What level of protection are you advocating, Matt?'

'Ideally, full protection, but I know we can't run to that. Maybe a patrol car in the road after dark?'

Matt waited, knowing how McRay's mind worked. He had suggested one of the cheapest options and hoped he would agree. McRay sat back in his chair and scratched his left ear, something he always did when he was weighing things up.

'We could probably get a patrol car to pass by each hour. Sorry, Matt, think that's the best I can do.'

Knowing it was no use arguing, Matt accepted the offer with good grace. 'Thank you, sir.'

Leaving McRay's office, he rang Mary James to ask if he could visit on the way home.

# Chapter 39

'I'm paying you. That means you don't fucking tell me what to do. Understand?'

Ops gave a sigh and took his time moving past Vinny to sit at the small table. 'Now, now, Vinny, just remind me, if you would, why you hired me?'

'Not to get stuck in this shit hole.'

'This hole, as you described it, is perfectly adequate for the purpose. You have shelter, food, warmth and companionship. You are also in the heart of the community, exactly where you need to be. No one will find you here.'

'No bugger else would think to live on a boat in the middle of bloody winter.'

'If you are unhappy with my services…'

'It's not that. I had to see my lad off. Even you can understand that, surely?'

'If it was that important to you, you should have consulted me. I did not realise attending your son's funeral was more important than avenging his death.'

'Well it was. It was worth it too. That bloody copper, the one that arrested me, was there.'

'This simply gets worse. If you recognised him, then it follows that he also recognised you, or Dan. I take it you coerced him into taking you? This makes my job even harder. Surely, you can see that. I should pull out completely. Yet, this is something I am reluctant to do.'

'Don't want to lose out on all that cash, more like.'

'Believe me, Vinny, that is the least of my worries. I have obtained a reputation for an excellent service and I do not intend to allow your indiscretions to sully what I have worked hard to achieve.'

'You need to remember what I did for you inside, you pompous shit.'

'Indeed, I do remember your kindness and protection. Now, sit down and let's work out the best way forward.'

Vinny hesitated, not used to taking orders from anyone. Ops waited as if it was inevitable that Vinny would obey, tapping his fingers lightly on the plastic table until Vinny slumped onto the bench opposite.

'Now, my orders were that you stay safely hidden here, while I undertook investigations on your behalf. I am keeping my part of that bargain and have already fed information back to you. I am extremely disappointed that you have gone against my direct orders and acted irresponsibly. You have exposed yourself unnecessarily to the police for a start.'

'Could pay off, though.'

'In what way?'

'I know that copper, much better than he knows me. He's a drinker. Couple of pints and he's anyone's. And, I know some of the pubs he goes to.'

'This information is certainly useful. However, I cannot comprehend that you fail to recognise the danger this puts you in. Do you imagine this police officer is going to forget that he has seen you? We've had you hidden away abroad for some years now and he certainly won't want to lose you again.'

'He's got to find me first.'

'And you intend to make that easy for him.'

'No.'

'Let us come to the other little matter you have forgotten to tell me about.'

'Like what?'

'Need I elucidate? I passed on information regarding a certain David Beeson.'

'That little toad.'

'Yes, as you put it, that little toad. Here again you took matters into your own hands and now the young man is dead. Was he the one who killed Jonathan?'

'He wouldn't have the guts.'

'So, a completely unnecessary killing?'

'No. The bloody little sod pissed me off.'

'And that was worth putting your whole venture in jeopardy, bringing you to the attention of the police, and causing danger to those trying to help you?'

Vinny half rose to reach into the tiny fridge, extracting two cans of beer. He offered one to Ops.

'No, thank you.'

Vinny swigged back his beer, refusing to look at Ops. The silence in the small cabin grew tense. Finally, Ops broke it. 'We need to clarify our contract, don't you think?'

'I need to be involved. Can't just sit here playing cards with that dickhead.'

'So you are unwilling to follow my orders, even those that move you closer to your stated goal of finding and dealing with your son's killer?'

'Yes...no. I don't know.'

'Then I suggest you take time to think it over. You may let me know if you wish me to continue.'

Ops stood, turning his back on Vinny, and moved to the steps leading to the deck.

'Wait.'

'Yes?'

'Yes. I do...do need your help.'

Ops turned to study Vinny. 'Very well. Then this is how it will work. You stay put here until I identify the person who killed your son. And—'

'But...'

'No buts, none at all. I will tell you what you need to do, and when you need to act. Harry told me about David. Now you have acted on this information, he is, of course, reluctant to trust me. He has, however, given me another name. I will investigate this and let you know if I find anything relevant.'

'Tell me who it is, you bastard. I'll find out if it's relevant or not.'

'If you imagine for one minute that I would entrust such information to you, after what happened last time, then you are a fool. What I need you to do is write down everything you remember about the detective who arrested you. What is his name?'

'DI Grant.'

'Good. He could give us much inside information.'

'He's not likely to do that.'

'I have my methods and you did say he likes a beverage or two.'

'A kitten wouldn't be frightened of you.'

'Then rest assured I shall address him in a language he will understand.' Ops moved towards the steps again. 'When you have written down everything you can remember, call me using a new sim card.'

Behind Ops's back, Vinny stood, stooping to avoid the roof, and gave his usual salute. He did not intend to sit waiting on Ops to get the information he needed. He had his own methods.

# Chapter 40

Kathy greeted them cheerfully, without a twitch of guilt or worry. This time there was no smell of baking coming from the kitchen and she led them into a tidy, if a little overcrowded, living room. 'Can I get you a cup of tea or coffee, officers?'

They both declined and she sank, somewhat reluctantly Matt thought, into the leather chair by the fire. 'I thought I would bring you up to date on the case of Jonathan James.'

Matt watched as she shifted her glance away. It was as if she didn't want to hear. 'You may have heard that another member of Jonathan James's gang has been murdered.'

'Yes, I saw it on the television, Inspector.'

'We thought at first that the same person had committed both murders, but have decided against that.' He had her attention now.

'What changed your mind?'

'The method of killing. One was almost, if any unlawful death can be, merciful, while the other was brutal in the extreme. The first could have been carried out by a woman, while the second was more obviously a man.'

Her eyes didn't leave his face. She sat still, almost as if she didn't want to draw attention to any movement that might signify guilt. He carried on. 'We now believe that the second murder was mistakenly carried out to avenge the first.'

Now she diverted her eyes, gave a gulp and covered it with a cough before asking, 'And do you know who carried out these murders, Inspector?'

'The second, yes.'

'So you've arrested someone?'

'Not yet. We're trying to find him before he kills again.'

'Oh.'

'We think he is trying to find out who killed Jonathan.'

'I see. But what is this to do with me?'

'We're simply warning anyone connected with Jack's murder, Mrs Wylde.'

'Should I be taking any precautions?'

'I think you'll be the last person he will think of. But we felt we should let you know.'

She stood up. 'Thank you, Inspector. I'm most grateful. Oh and whom should I be watching for?'

'Jonathan James's father, Vincent, a dangerous and vicious career criminal. He is stocky, light brown hair, goatee beard, about five ten or eleven, early forties. You already have my card, Mrs Wylde. Ring me if you are at all concerned.'

'I will. Thank you.'

Kathy almost shooed them from the house. Matt waited until they were on their way before speaking. 'What do you think, Jane?'

'She's definitely hiding something. It's like she either knows who did it or did it herself.'

'I agree. We'd better keep an eye on her. I don't want Vinny James to get to her first. If she did kill Jonathan, she might have designs on the others too. Find out a bit more about her. See where she goes, who she sees.'

'Will do, guv.'

Matt glanced at her. She seemed a little better today. He wondered whether it was the right time to mention Jenny and decided to risk it. 'You're looking better.'

'Thanks.'

'How's Jenny?' He knew immediately from the silence that he had stepped on a sore spot and inwardly cursed.

'I don't know. We're not together anymore.'

'Oh. Sorry.'

'No need. I'm with someone else. A fellow patient undergoing physio. We helped each other through it.'

'Good.' Matt thought it best not to pry anymore and they continued back to the station in silence.

# Chapter 41

It was one thing to plan and carry out a murder herself, but it was another matter that she had caused Vinny James to batter that young man Dave to death. What had she done? The inspector's description of Jonathan's dad fitted the man who had been following Dave Beeson last night. She set him on that path and Dave wouldn't have stood a chance against him. Now she had two deaths on her conscience, three if you counted Ken. What on earth had she become? Should she give herself up, tell Inspector Turrell everything? It would be the way to stop anyone else being hurt. Shaken, she set about making a cup of tea.

While the kettle was boiling, Kathy shut the kitchen window and checked that the back door was locked, resolving to go through the whole house once she had had her tea. After two cups of tea, she began to calm down.

Thinking about the inspector's visit, she wondered why both he and his constable had come. The woman hadn't said anything but she had the sense she was watching, waiting for a reaction. Did they suspect her? Kathy couldn't imagine how they could. She'd strived to keep her responses to a minimum. Did they really think she was on the murderer's hit list? Maybe they were just trying to scare her and in that case, they had succeeded.

Kathy put her cup in the sink and, satisfied that downstairs was secure, went upstairs, even closing the bedroom window she usually left open.

It was only as she got ready for rehearsal that it struck her. This murderer could be doing her a favour. He was doing what she had set out to do in the first place. Yet, this way, she wouldn't be able to form a decision about them. Look at Harry; he'd thrown all her theories straight up in the air. She liked him, could see he'd changed and deserved another chance. Vinny James wouldn't give that a thought. She realised she sounded like both judge and jury. After starting out certain, now she was puzzled. Maybe she was no better or worse than Vinny James, who was also seeking revenge for his son. The man must be very determined to risk his freedom and he'd thought nothing of beating that poor young man to death.

Thinking about Dave from the trial, Kathy remembered him as a pitiful creature who never looked up and who snivelled throughout. Would she have been able to kill him? Kathy doubted it. His sister had spoken up for him. She must be devastated. A new thought struck her: what if Vinny James targeted Harry? She didn't want him harmed. Maybe she should tell DI Turrell about the man following Dave. Yet how could she do that without giving herself away? Her head in a daze, she filled the kettle again.

# Chapter 42

Sam hated these places; the smell reminded him of school dinners with loads of cabbage and sweaty feet. He hated even more being frisked. It should be taken for granted that a police officer would not be bringing forbidden items into a prison. Finally, the officer gave a nod to his companion.

'Follow me, sir.'

'Thank you.'

The officer led Sam through several barred gates and corridors before finally stopping at a small room.

'The first one's here. Don't think you'll get much joy out of Doggy Smith. As soon as you've finished with him, we'll bring you the next one.'

He opened the door and ushered Sam into a small room with minimum furniture, just a table and two chairs. Inside another prison officer stood with arms folded guarding an older man with greying longish hair. Sam wondered if his nickname came from his long face that had a sad hound dog look. 'Thank you for agreeing to talk to me, Mr Smith.'

'Can't do that with him there, can I.' He nodded towards the guard.

Sam turned. 'Do you mind?'

The guard grunted and went out.

'What's this about then? You gonna get me out of here?'

'Sorry, I'm not here for that reason.'

'Bugger it then. Call him back.'

'You know that Vinny James isn't serving the same sentence as the rest of you, don't you?'

'So?'

'And that he's out there enjoying all that freedom plus the money. Your money.'

'He'll be keeping it safe.'

'Will he, though? Just think of all the expenses he'll have keeping his head down. Who's to know if he takes a little dip into funds now and again?'

'He wouldn't be so stupid. We're not going to be in here forever. He'd have the four of us to answer to.'

'You'd have to find him first.'

Doggy was silent for a moment and Sam could see he was thinking it over in his mind.

'I know what you're doing. You buggers are all alike.'

'What am I doing, Mr Smith?'

'You're doing that splitting us up routine. I saw it on *Lewis* the other day. It ain't gonna work. I can tell you that.'

Sam silently cursed all TV cop shows and changed track. 'We're not after the money, only Vinny.'

'A likely story. Why chase him now?'

'Because he's back in the country and we believe he murdered a young lad.'

'Why'd he do that?'

'You might have heard that his son died. We think he's out to avenge his death.'

'Bloody hell. He'd do that. Never did let anyone cross him.'

'So you see, he's not really thinking straight and is hardly a careful guardian for your money.'

'I ain't worried about the money. Vinny's got it all safely tied up.'

'Someone to make it look clean?'

Before he could stop himself, Doggy nodded, then realised what he had done and tried to pull back. 'Here, I didn't mean that.'

'It makes no difference to me. We only want to stop Vinny killing again. Of course, when we catch him, as we will, we'll probably lock him up for a long time. You'd better be sure you know the particulars of who is handling the money. Vinny might be tempted to keep them to himself. If that happens you could be waiting thirty years or so.'

Sam was pleased to see Doggy's face drop even further, but disappointed when he pushed himself away from the table and folded his arms.

'You're wasting your time with me. I ain't talking.'

There was little left for Sam to do but signal for the guard to return and take Doggy away. While he waited for the other member of Vinny's crew to arrive, he tried to think of a better approach. He had the feeling that this track wouldn't be successful.

While waiting, Sam gulped a cup of the weak tea provided by the guard. It was at least hot and to some extent revived him. This and the knowledge that he would soon be out of there gave him renewed hope that was heightened when Pete Scunthorpe arrived. He was much younger than Doggy Smith and seemed nervous, twisting his fingers and refusing to look at Sam.

'Good morning, Mr Scunthorpe.'

Pete nodded without looking up. Sam sought for a way to reach him. From reading about the robbery, he understood that Pete was the getaway driver and unlikely to have much inside knowledge about the job. He was also serving a shorter sentence than the others and due for release in two months.

'I'm guessing you're looking forward to getting out soon?'

'Yes.' Pete looked up.

'Got any plans?'

'Going home to me mum.'

'Home-cooked meals. Lucky lad.'

'Mmm.'

'You've got a nice little stash tucked away. What are you going to spend it on?'

'Don't know.'

'Do you think Vinny has kept it safe?'

'Said he would.'

'And you trust him?'

Fed with doubt, Pete looked hard and long at Sam. 'Had to.'

'No choice then?'

Pete nodded again.

'Pete, we're looking for Vinny at the moment. We think he may have murdered a young man – about your age. Can you tell me anything about him, anything that would help us find him?'

'No.'

'If he wanted to keep all the money for himself, do you think he could do it?'

'Don't know.'

'We're not interested in the money, just Vinny. If you help us catch him, then your money would be safe for you to enjoy. I guess your mum could use a bit extra, couldn't she? If you could give us any tips on where we might find him, it would look really good on your record.'

Pete was silent for a long time.

Sam prompted. 'Do you know where your money is, Pete?'

'Doggy said I weren't to say anything.'

'Do you always listen to Doggy?'

'He's my uncle.'

Sam sat back and sighed. This was a losing game, but at least they'd tried. The only information gained was that they'd used an intermediary to wash the money clean. Not much joy for nearly a day's work. He was glad the rest of the gang were incarcerated further north. Maybe he wouldn't have to visit them.

# Chapter 43

By the time Matt left the office, it was later than he hoped and Mary was waiting for him with a tray set out with mugs and biscuits.

'I've just got to boil the water. You will have a cup of tea, won't you, Inspector?'

Matt wanted to refuse as he was longing for home and his dinner, but he hadn't the heart to say no. 'That would be lovely. Thank you.' He waited while she boiled the kettle, thinking of how to break the news that her husband may be back. The last thing he wanted was to scare her. Once Mary returned with the teapot, he cleared his throat.

'Is it bad news, Inspector?'

'You may find it distressing, Mrs James.'

'Then best to get it over with. And please call me Mary.'

'When did you last see your husband?'

'It must be over four years ago now.'

'And you haven't heard from him?'

'No. I knew he'd escaped from the court, but didn't think he would hang around here. Why are you asking?'

'We think he may have heard about Jonathan's death.'

'Oh.'

Matt watched the colour drain from her face.

'I hadn't thought of that. Do you think he will come here?'

'That's why I'm here, Mary.'

'Then you think it is a possibility?'

'We're just erring on the side of caution in wanting to protect you. Plus, we would like to pick up Mr James.'

'He killed that lad, the one in the news, didn't he? The one involved in the murder?'

'David Beeson. What makes you say that?'

'It's just like him. Lashes out with his fists, thinks afterwards. He'll be trying to find out who killed Jon. He'll take it as a personal slight against himself.'

'Have you any idea where he might be staying or who might be hiding him, Mary?'

'No. He never confided in me and I never asked. Sorry.'

'If Mr James does show up, or you do think of anything that might help us, please give me a call, day or night.' Matt passed over his card. 'My home number is there too. You won't hesitate to call?'

Mary nodded in agreement and took the card, rising to place it behind the clock on the mantelpiece. Matt took the opportunity to rise.

'It might be best if you stay somewhere else until Mr James is in custody. Is there anywhere you could go?'

'No. I'm best here, it's handy for work. And...and I can't let him bully me anymore.'

'Try not to worry, Mary. We have arranged to have a patrol car pass by every hour to keep an eye on you. If you'd like, I can assess your security?'

'I think I'm pretty safe, but come and see for yourself.'

Mary led the way into the kitchen. The windows and doors had been upgraded to double glazing within the last few years. The windows had good locks, as did the kitchen door. As long as Mary kept them locked, she should be alright. Yet Matt knew nowhere was completely safe if someone was determined to get in.

'Please make sure you keep everything locked, Mary.'

'Yes, of course.'

'It's just a precaution but it's better to be on the safe side.'

She nodded, but didn't seem reassured. Matt tried to imagine what it must be like knowing your violent husband was on the run and likely to drop in on you. He wished there was more he could do. When he left her at the doorstep, she peered out into the gloom as if worried that Vinny might be out there. Matt was only a few steps up the path when he heard the door shut with a bang. He resolved to ask McRay tomorrow if they could stretch to giving her more protection.

Driving home with Mary James still on his mind, he didn't even take in the grandeur of Kenilworth Castle, not that there was much to see in the dark. At home, a delicious aroma greeted him and he wondered what delight Eppie was preparing. Trying to decide what treat lay in wait, he drew her to him and ignoring the rigid figure of Angela on the sofa, kissed her soundly.

'About time. It's not good for me to be kept waiting for my meal,' Angela snapped.

Matt and Eppie grinned at each other and kissed again, this time lingering deliberately.

# Chapter 44

Determined to prove his worth, Grant worked late. He felt like a bloodhound following a trail. Putting aside his search for Harold Harper-Jones, he turned instead to the list of pubs he was compiling. Some of the Warwick pubs were close to his flat, but not the ones he'd chosen to drink in, although maybe it was time to try a few. Having always felt cheated by Vinny's escape from court, he wanted to be the one to bring him in. It would be a double triumph. No one could blame him for stopping for a drink on the way home, especially in the name of research. Knowing his job was on the line, he'd have to be careful not to be hung over in the morning. Besides, if he wanted to nail Vinny, he needed to keep a clear head.

The first port of call was the Railway Arms, a small establishment near to Warwick railway station. Although small and old, it had a welcoming atmosphere and the outside gleamed with new paint. The barman was hospitable and the clientele, intent on their conversations, barely looked up as he stood at the bar and enjoyed his pint. Grant decided that this was an unlikely place for Vinny to patronise and, finishing his beer, headed for home and his microwave dinner. Maybe he'd try another pub later.

While he waited for the microwave to heat his beef and mashed potato dinner, Grant crossed the Railway Arms off his list and decided the Golden Acorn might be worth a try, especially as it was close by.

The Acorn was at the end of a dingy street. This was more like it; Grant could visualise Vinny here. Before he pushed open the grimy door, he paused to consider what he would do if Vinny was inside. No doubt he would have a few henchmen with him. Considering it worth the risk, he went in. Something about the place immediately felt right, but a quick scan showed no sign of Vinny.

Grant decided he'd stay for a pint, try to relax and suss out the other customers. Placing himself at the end of the bar so as not to attract attention, he ordered a pint. The barman tried to be the chatty, all friendly type, but Grant felt he was only digging for information. The young, dark-haired barmaid stayed at the other end of the bar.

Grant felt under observation.

Before his glass was half-empty, the barman came towards him. 'Another, mate?'

Despite knowing that he should refuse, Grant nodded. If the barman was trying to keep him there, he wanted to see why and he'd need to keep a drink in front of him otherwise it would look suspicious. Half an hour later, after downing three pints, the desperate need to keep drinking was fighting with his common sense.

The pub was filling up with the regular evening crowd and other men joined him at the bar. Grant had just convinced himself that another couple of pints wouldn't hurt when a red-headed woman pushed in next to him. Although the red came straight from the bottle, Grant thought she wasn't unattractive and moved over to accommodate her.

'See if you can catch the barman's eye for me, will you, love? Bloody impossible for me to.'

Grant thought this woman would be able to capture anyone's attention, but nodded and raised his arm.

'Another pint, mate? And whatever the lady's having.'

'Thanks. Gin and tonic, Ben.'

'Coming up.'

Although his head was starting to get hazy, Grant gathered she was a regular. Maybe she could fill him in on one or two things. He returned her smile.

'You didn't have to do that,' she said.

'I know.'

'You from round here?'

'Not far away.'

'Me too. I've never seen you in here before.'

'Felt like a change.'

'I know that feeling.'

Silence descended between them while Grant sought to bring up the subject of Vinny.

'Used to meet up with a guy here. Few years back now. Wondered if he was still around?'

'What's his name?'

'Vincent – well, he calls himself Vinny now.'

'What's he look like?'

'Five ten, eleven, brown hair, thick-set, a goatee beard.'

She laughed. 'You sound like a copper.' She touched his nose playfully. 'And in that case, I shouldn't be talking to you.'

Grant kicked himself. The last pint had dulled his senses. He forced himself to concentrate, laughing in return and leaning towards her.

'Now, now, young lady, haven't anything to hide have you? If so, I don't know where you would put it.'

She giggled. 'Oh, officer.'

'Let's find a seat, shall we?' Grant knew he must move away from the bar and temptation.

'Let's take another drink with us, shall we?'

Grant paid for another gin and tonic and a pint for himself. She led the way to a seat next to the stairs and they squeezed onto a table already occupied by two burly men who moved along to accommodate them.

'So, are you a copper?'

Grant wished she would keep her voice down. He was sure one of the men shot a glance at him.

'Would it make a difference?'

'Depends.'

'On what?'

She put a hand on his arm. Her nails were a strange yellow, the colour of sputum, and they looked like claws ready for the kill. He was beginning to regret encouraging her.

'Well, if for instance you're working on a case. It wouldn't do my reputation any good to be seen as a grass, now would it?'

'I'm looking for a friend, that's all.'

'I might have seen him.'

'Where?'

'Around. Look, why don't I make a few enquiries and get back to you?'

'When?'

'Impatient, aren't you? How about tomorrow, around seven?'

'You're on.'

Excited that he might be getting somewhere, Grant was tempted to leave his half-finished pint, but deciding it would be a waste, downed it in one, said goodbye to the woman and left.

Outside the cold made his head fuzzy. The lamplights had a nebulous halo around them and the pavements were shiny with ice. As he made his way home, he slipped and landed flat on his back. Glad that no one was around to witness his undignified position, he scrambled up and headed for the warmth of his flat.

# Chapter 45

Kathy thought how smart Harry looked tonight. He was overdressed for rehearsal and she wondered if he had been somewhere special. At the break, she decided to find out. 'Been for a job interview, Harry? You do look smart.'

'No. My friend's funeral.'

'Oh, sorry.'

'Don't be. I hadn't seen him in a long time. He wasn't very nice.'

With a shock, Kathy realised he must be talking about Jonathan. He seemed glad of the chance to talk.

'We did something really bad together. I can hardly believe it was me...involved in... I'd give anything to go back and change...change what we did.'

Kathy wanted Harry to spell it out, say exactly what he had done. 'Surely it couldn't be that bad?'

Harry looked up and hesitated before looking down at the floor and answering. 'We, there were five of us, we...we attacked a man. He died.'

'Why?'

'To be honest, I don't know.'

'You don't know why you attacked someone?' Kathy tried hard to keep the anger out of her voice, aware it was bursting out, raising her tone and turning the words into an accusation.

Harry flushed and kept looking at the floor, one hand twisting the other. For a moment, Kathy felt a tiny shoot of compassion until another surge of anger swept it away. Jack's death had been for nothing, a mere whim. She stayed silent.

Rescued by the musical director calling an end to the break, Kathy moved back to her place amongst the sopranos. Unable to concentrate on the music, she couldn't wait for the rehearsal to end.

Finally came the moment when everyone began to stack the chairs. Ida came up to Kathy as she was putting on her coat.

'I've said you wouldn't mind dropping Harry off in Leamington, Kathy. He's visiting his grandma. Hope that's alright with you, dear. I'm sure he'll be happy to walk from where you drop me.'

All Kathy could do was smile and say, 'Of course, no problem.'

The journey along the Warwick Road began in silence that continued almost until the Longbridge Island. Ida made a futile attempt to break it.

'I saw you two chatting earlier and it is so lovely to see you both putting everything behind you.'

Kathy decided to ignore this and instead asked if they could add some colour to their costumes as the black seemed rather dull. Ida thought it would be fine to add ribbons or flowers.

This topic safely filled the rest of the journey until it was time to drop Ida off at Miranda Court. Harry went to get out too until Kathy stopped him.

'I'll take you onto your gran's, Harry.'

'Here, come into the front.' Ida held open the door to the front passenger seat and Harry had no chance to refuse. He sat and fastened his seat belt without looking at Kathy. There was an uncomfortable silence in the car after Ida said a cheery goodnight.

Kathy drove back into Kenilworth past the castle and down towards the Parade.

Harry broke the silence. 'You knew?'

'Yes.'

'You must hate me.'

Kathy stayed silent, a welter of emotions colliding. She pulled into a lay-by. 'Did you know the man?'

'No.'

'Then why?'

'He shouted at us 'cause we were sitting on his car.'

'Drinking.'

'Yes.'

Her stomach churned but she made herself carry on, needing to hear, needing to feel the pain.

'So you killed a man simply because he told you to get off his property. Something he had every right to do.'

'Yes. It was…terrible.'

'For you?'

'Yes.'

'Yet you did it. Put the boot in – felt it connect with living flesh.'

147

Kathy was compelled to keep verbally striking out at him, to feel each comment hit home, just as he had done when he kicked out at Jack. She couldn't stop. Is this what it had been like for him?

'Please stop.'

'You didn't stop, even when a man was dying.'

'I did. Jon carried on.'

'So this is blame someone else, is it?'

'No. I didn't mean that. I…I stopped when I saw the blood.'

'Stopped and watched your mate.'

'I tried to stop him, we all did. We knew it had gone too far. Dave had already run off. Tilly was crying. The woman was screaming.'

'And the rest of you did nothing.'

'I grabbed his arm, told him to leave it. It was like he was possessed.'

'Were you scared of him?'

Harry was silent for a moment. 'Yes.'

Kathy stopped. Harry was shaking and in tears and she was bullying him. It had helped get something out of her system, but it was an unforgiveable way of doing it. She rummaged in her pocket for a tissue.

'Here.'

Harry wiped his eyes and blew his nose before he spoke. 'Did Mrs Davis tell you?'

Kathy wasn't sure she wanted to share this information and didn't answer.

'Why would she do that?'

The words burst out. 'He was my son.'

'Your son?'

'Yes.'

'Oh my God.'

Kathy was aware that Harry was staring at her. 'Then…then you came to the hotel especially to find me?'

'Yes.'

'Why?'

'I wanted…no, *had* to see what kind of person you are.'

'And?'

'I like you.'

Both deep in thought, it went quiet. Harry broke it as he undid his seat belt, one hand on the door handle. 'Did you find Jon?'

'I…I—'

'It was you. You killed Jon.'

Kathy remained silent, unable to face him.

'And me? Do you plan to kill me too?'

'No…yes. 'Til I met you.'

'Dave?'

'No. Of course not.'

'Wasn't that the plan?'

'Yes.'

'Nick, Tilly? She's pregnant, in case you didn't know.'

'That was the plan.'

'So you're no better than me? Worse – 'cause you planned it all.'

Kathy couldn't answer. It was what she had been telling herself, but to hear someone else spell it out felt like a physical attack.

Harry opened the door and got out, banging the door fiercely behind him, and strode away.

Kathy burst into tears.

# Chapter 46

Vinny woke early and after manoeuvring and cursing around the tiny bathroom, headed for the delights of the main cabin. Dan was fast asleep on the narrow cushioned bench that served as a sofa. He looked cosy curled up in his sleeping bag, giving Vinny the intense desire to shake him. Why should he be sleeping when the day had started and the little rat could be making his breakfast? Struggling against his instinct, he managed to hold back, knowing he needed Dan on his side.

Vinny had already hinted that there might be room for Dan in Spain where he could lead a charmed life loafing in the sun. He'd watched Dan's eyes light up at this suggestion. It was time to up the stakes and secure the little git's full cooperation.

He squeezed past Dan, found the kettle, and filled it before facing the small stove. How hard could this be? He turned a knob, surprised and delighted to hear a hiss of gas, followed by a flame that set the ring alight. Soon, the kettle was boiling and he woke Dan with a mug of instant coffee. Sipping from his own mug, he watched Dan struggle out of his sleeping bag, surprise etched on his face at this unexpected service.

'Morning, Dan. We have things to discuss.'

Despite being half asleep, Dan was suspicious. 'I gotta do what Ops tells me.'

'I know that, Dan. But you must remember who is paying Ops. That's my money. That makes me the boss. Understand?'

'Suppose so.'

'And, it's not as if I want you to disobey him. Just do one or two things for me on the side. For extra money of course.'

'Can I tell Ops about these things?'

'No. You see, he's doing his best, but we both know that some things can only be done in a certain way – with a bit more force. While

Ops is more of a gentleman, you and me are hard men. I'm not asking you to go against him, just not tell him everything. See?'

'Like what?'

'There's someone I need to see.'

'I ain't allowed to take you anywhere.'

'I'm not asking you to. But you could bring them here.'

'Who are they?'

'Just someone who knew and cared for my Jon.'

# Chapter 47

Last night Matt had brushed down his dark suit and made sure his shoes were polished, ready for the press conference. He never found these events easy. When the grieving relatives broke down under the strain, it was hard not to feel their pain.

He drove the long way round so he could see Warwick Castle from the bridge. Somehow, the magnificent building, which had survived for hundreds of years, through wars, battles and intrigues always nourished him.

Arriving at CID, he found both Sam and Jane already there. There was now a picture of Vinny James on the board, taken at the time of his arrest four years ago. Matt looked at the face. It could have been pleasant, except for the curl at the corner of the mouth and his hard, bright eyes. It was easy to imagine this man beating someone to death. When they'd encountered him the other day, it was obvious he had tried to alter his appearance and Matt was pleased to see that Grant had noted the differences alongside the photo.

Also on the board was an unknown face. 'Someone new?' Matt asked Sam.

'Dave's drug contact, Jackson Groves. Picked up from his mobile. Minor local dealer. Drug squad have info on him. They're hoping to reach the big boys through him and would be glad if we didn't lift him for now.'

'They are aware this is a murder enquiry?'

'Yes. They're willing to send in one of their undercover guys to ask any relevant questions as long as we don't disturb the nest.'

'Suppose we'll have to make do with that. There's little likelihood that he was involved in the murder, but he may have seen something and will know what drugs Dave bought. Will you liaise with them, Sam?'

'Will do, guv.'

'Did you catch up with Harry yesterday?'

'Tried, but couldn't get hold of him. I'll have another go today.'

'Okay.'

Matt stood looking at the board. 'We're clutching at straws, aren't we?'

'Maybe the press conference will bring something in.'

'I doubt it. But suppose it's worth a try.'

'Can't do any harm.'

'No. No, you're right.' Matt loosened his tie and turned towards his office, aware that there would be a pile of reports to read from overnight. Settling at his desk, he noticed Grant arriving with two cardboard cups of coffee that he set down in a deliberate, careful way. Matt knew it wouldn't be easy for Grant to stay on the wagon, but this was just a few days in and he looked hung over. He made a mental note to have a word with him later. Sighing, he settled at his desk. Jane joined him, bearing coffee.

'All set, boss?'

'As I'll ever be.' Looking up, he thought she looked better. There was a sense of lightness about her, colour in her cheeks and the dark circles were disappearing. Matt wondered again about her love life. He resolved not to be nosey and leave her to tell him when she was ready. After all, their brief fling, long past, did not give him the right to question her.

On top of the pile of reports was one from SOCO on the Dave Beeson murder scene. They'd found a small amount of white powder scattered over and around the body and after the body was removed, a plastic packet. This contained remnants of the same powder, now known to be cocaine. As he read on, Matt became excited. They'd lifted a finger mark from the packet that matched Vinny James. Now they could place him at the scene. All they had to do was catch him.

By the time he had ploughed through several files, making decisions and notes of the actions to take, it was time to leave for the press conference. After updating Sam, who would run the team meeting, he stopped by Grant's desk.

'How's the Vinny enquiry coming on, Grant?'

Grant didn't look up but merely nodded and grunted.

'Let's have a catch up later.'

'Fine.'

Matt had to be content with that and made his way downstairs to the purpose-built suite. He wasn't looking forward to seeing Julie

Pritchard and her husband, as despite their best efforts, Dave's killer was still at large.

The Pritchards were with the press officer. Julie stood white-faced, staring straight ahead, except for a brief glance in his direction. Matt sensed the accusation in her glance. Mr Pritchard stayed by her side but nodded to Matt.

While the press officer ran through the format of the press interview, Matt pulled PC Foster aside, the FLO, to ask how the Pritchards were coping.

'She's still in shock. I think she feels guilty for not protecting him. Ian's doing all the right things to support her. Pretty typical I would say, sir.'

'Thanks. OK, let me know if anything changes.'

'Yes, sir.'

Walking through to face the press, Matt recognised several faces in the front row. They would all be hoping for tears and recriminations and Julie would certainly satisfy them on that score. He could almost see the headlines now. 'Grieving sister begs for help to catch brother's killer'. Sometimes these press conferences did awaken something in the memory of an unsuspecting witness. Yet usually they yielded nothing worth putting the likes of Julie through the distress of it all. When asked if he thought the appeal might help, Matt mentioned Dave's murky past and suggested the reporters might bring this up and so defeat the object. How many people would choose to put themselves out when they heard he'd helped kick a man to death? Many, like McRay, would be thinking his death was no loss.

As the press conference began, Matt concentrated on his role. The superintendent gave the opening speech and Matt gave a brief outline of the case, before handing over to Julie and Ian Pritchard.

Ian held his wife's hand tightly, encouraging her to begin. Matt could see Julie steeling herself and she began speaking in a quiet, wavering voice. One of the reporters called for her to speak up so Matt bent to adjust the microphone. Julie stumbled on, forgetting the prepared statement in her hand. By the time she was finished, the tears were running down her cheeks and Ian's arm was around her.

The press started to ask questions, most of which the super or Matt fielded. Just as Matt was thinking it was about time to wind it all up, someone asked the question he was dreading.

'Mrs Pritchard, do you think your brother got what he deserved? He did commit murder, did he not?'

Matt recognised the man at the back. Rob Peters, a reporter from one of the London papers. The same one who stirred up the dirt after Gracie died. Julie simply stared in horror at the man and buried her head in Ian's shoulder. Matt jumped in.

'Take her out, Ian. Perhaps I can answer that. Dave Beeson was indeed involved in a killing two years ago, when he was only sixteen. He was arrested, tried for that offence and has served his time. Not only that, but, haunted by what he had done, he suffered a breakdown and had been ill ever since. Are you really proposing that we only investigate those cases where the victim is snow white and forget about the others?'

Greeted by silence, Matt added. 'I didn't think so.'

Matt was relieved when the super thanked the press for coming and closed the meeting. Hoping that the reporters had enough to make a story and feature the appeal, Matt left, pausing only to thank the Pritchards for their help. Shaken by the presence of Rob Peters, he couldn't get away fast enough. Seeing his mistake amplified in print had only served to exaggerate his sense of guilt over Gracie. What if Rob Peters decided to drag it all up again, use him to make headlines? The memory of her was always with him, reminding him not to let anyone down. Yet a small persistent voice reminded him that he had failed both Gracie and Dave.

Sam was just finishing the team meeting when Matt returned.

'Anything new, Sam?'

'The PM is on your desk.'

'Thanks. Anything unexpected?'

'Not really. Not much luck with the door-to-door, except one sighting of a woman sitting in a car outside the Pritchard house. I've put the report on your desk.'

'Thanks, Sam. Nothing on the CCTV?'

'Sorry.'

The post mortem confirmed that David Beeson was beaten and kicked to death. There were no defensive wounds. Matt turned to the door-to-door reports and found little of interest, except a statement made by a neighbour who had seen a woman parked opposite the Pritchards' house at about ten twenty. Thank God for the nosey, Matt thought. The woman, described as middle-aged, was driving a red Peugeot. Matt immediately thought of Kathy Wylde. He was sure there had been a red Peugeot in her drive. Matt strode from his office to ask Wendy if she would get the registration details for him, citing that she was a suspect in a murder case. If CCTV could place her car in Leamington on that night, it would be a start.

Leaving Wendy, he decided this was a good time to talk to Grant. Although he wasn't looking forward to berating the man again, it had to be done.

'Shall we go over the Vinny details, Grant?' Grant jumped up straight away, gathering documents ready to follow Matt back to his office. He seemed alert and a different man from first thing this morning. Matt wondered if he was mistaken in thinking him hung over, until he saw numerous empty coffee cups in the bin.

Impressed by the amount of detail in Grant's report, Matt thanked him while wondering how to bring up the subject of drink. His eyes lighted on the list of pubs Grant had compiled and he picked it up. 'Hope you haven't been tempted to investigate any of these on your own, Grant?'

'I did pop in to a couple yesterday, just for a look around.'

Although Grant aimed for casual, he didn't meet Matt's gaze. 'I asked you to compile a list, not check them out yourself, Grant. Surely you can see that it puts temptation in your way. That's why you were hungover this morning.'

Grant raised his head and Matt thought he was going to argue the point. Instead, he shrugged his shoulders. 'I can understand you wanting to follow through on your research, Grant, but in this case, it can't be done. We both know the dangers. How about I share out this list between Sam and some of the others?'

Grant looked up at last. 'You don't trust me?'

'After this morning, no.' Matt was determined not to make it easy. Grant had to stay away from the booze or lose his job. It was that simple. 'How's it going with the counsellor?'

'Only had one meeting. Another this afternoon.'

'Stick with it.'

'Mmm.'

Matt wondered what he could say or do to help. He needed to engage Grant and keep his mind off the drink. Flipping through the papers Grant had placed before him, he noticed a list of other places associated with Vinny. He passed this across to Grant. 'How about you and I see a couple of these tonight? I could spare a couple of hours. Knock a few off the list.'

'I suppose so.'

'Good. Say six o'clock? Let's start with Mike's Gym.'

'Okay. You're the boss.'

As Grant left, Matt made a quick call to Eppie to say he would be late, before picking up the next report.

# Chapter 48

Just before six o'clock Grant was ready and waiting. Glancing towards Matt's office, he was relieved to see him standing, getting ready to leave, and then dismayed to see McRay approaching. He went into the office and both men sat down.

Moving closer to Matt's office, Grant tried to catch his eye, without any luck. He couldn't hang about forever, had to get to the Golden Acorn by seven to meet the red-headed woman.

By six twenty, his impatience rising, Grant was ready to walk. It had been a slim chance anyway, but he still might just have made it if they'd left on time. Frustration building he paced up and down, an eye on the clock. Finally, McRay left and Matt strode towards him.

'Sorry about that. Couldn't ignore the boss.'

'I know that feeling.' The words shot out before he could stop them.

Matt shot him a glance but didn't say anything and Grant realised he would have to calm down or Matt would get suspicious. It was almost as if this was some kind of test and, if it had been anyone else, he would tell them where to go, but Matt had stuck up for him, saved his job, so he had a right.

Leamington was their first port of call. Mike's Gym had been in business for over thirty years and, according to a tattered notice, seemed to offer more in the defensive arts than the usual workout. Situated above a shop at the bottom of the Parade, the entrance was through a grubby side door. The stairs were narrow and uncarpeted, designed to discourage the customary gym trade. Reaching the top, they were faced with a wide expanse that encompassed a boxing ring on one side, while the rest of the space was filled with several pairs of white-suited men, all engaged in attacking each other.

None of the men took any notice of their arrival. Although Grant was certain they were aware, no one came forward to greet them.

Unable to stand any delay, he stepped forward to grasp the arm of one of the young men. 'The boss?'

With a glare, the man shook his arm free and nodded to a door in the far corner, before returning to attack his partner with renewed energy. Grant followed Matt around the other combatants to the small room with a fading sign of office painted on its glass door.

Not bothering to knock, Matt opened the door. Inside a well-built young man was on the phone. He stood as they entered and stopped talking. Grant guessed he was expecting them and that the place must be fitted with an early warning system.

'I'm Detective Inspector Turrell and this is Detective Inspector Grant. We need to have a word with the manager.'

Following Matt's lead, Grant held up his warrant card while watching the man. He put the telephone down and folded his arms.

'Well, you can't. He's not here.'

'Then who's in charge?' Grant asked.

'Tony.'

'And where is he?'

'Gone for his break.'

'Who were you phoning?'

'None of your business.'

Grant experienced a sudden rage towards this bastard who was messing them around. Before Matt could stop him, he shot forward and pinned the man against the wall, rejoicing to know his strength and weight had the man at bay.

'Stop messing us about, you arsehole. Let's have some straight answers, or else.' With the blood rushing to his head it was a moment before he heard Matt's quiet command.

'Let the man go, DI Grant.'

With an effort, he obeyed, taking a step back.

'I'm sorry about that. We are anxious to find this man.' Matt offered a picture of Vinny James. 'You may know him as Vincent or Vinny. Have you seen him recently?'

Keeping a wary eye on Grant, the man peered at the photo. 'No. Never.'

'Thanks. We may need to come back. Come on, Grant.'

There was silence between them until they reached the car.

'Was that really necessary?'

'He was messing us around.'

'What we would expect, surely?'

159

'But shouldn't put up with.'

'What would be the point of beating the man up?'

'It would show him we mean business.'

'And lose us any possible co-operation.'

They continued in silence along the Myton Road towards Warwick, their next stop a small cafe. Grant, aware that Matt was unusually quiet, sought to lighten the mood. 'Should get a better reception here.'

'And if we don't, will you be tempted to threaten another member of the public?'

'Hey, he was asking for it.'

'I didn't see that.'

'You see what you want to see.'

'Meaning?'

'Seeing the good in everyone, treating them right. It's not a language these bastards understand.'

'So I was wrong to give you another chance?'

'No. I won't let you down.'

'If you do, it will be the last time.'

'Is that what you're hoping for?'

'Bloody hell, Grant. I could do without this hassle. I need you working at full capacity, just like the rest of us. Right now I want to get home, so let's get this over with.'

Matt got out of the car and headed to the cafe. For a moment, Grant was tempted to walk in the opposite direction, but clamping down on his temper, followed behind.

It was a brief visit as the place was full with late-night shoppers. Matt questioned the busy waitress, showing her the picture of Vinny, while Grant stood sullenly behind him. Afterwards Matt drove in silence to Grant's flat. Before Grant could leave, Matt spoke. 'I'm wondering if this is working for you, Grant?'

'Early days.'

'You might be better taking some leave.'

'No bloody way.'

'Let's talk about it in the morning.'

Too angry to speak, Grant left, slamming the door behind him. Watching the tail lights of Matt's car disappear, Grant glanced at his watch. He was already half an hour late for his meeting with the woman, yet he daren't go straight to the pub in case Matt drove round the block just to check on him. Something Grant wouldn't put past him. He went into his flat, pausing only to abandon his suit and slip into casual gear.

Five minutes later, he was ready to leave and after a brief check for Matt's car, he rushed to the Golden Acorn, hoping against hope that the woman was still there. He'd show Matt he wasn't ready to be put out to pasture. Bringing Vinny in would make everyone realise what a valuable member of the team he was.

Inside the Acorn, the same crowd were busy enjoying their drinks. Grant could smell the alcohol as soon as he entered, but as he made his way to the bar, he couldn't see the woman anywhere. Disappointment almost put him off buying a drink, but he needed an excuse to be there, so he waited his turn at the bar. No one appeared interested in him; even the barman gave him only a brief nod and before Grant could mention the redhead, he'd turned away.

Frustrated, Grant tackled his pint, forcing himself to take it slowly instead of gulping it down, as he wanted, while he waited for the rush to calm down. When a brief respite came, Grant jumped in to order another pint. This time the barman was less hassled. 'The young lady, the one with the red hair, has she been in tonight?'

'Yes. Couldn't stay. Said to meet her here at six tomorrow.'

'Thanks.'

The barman just nodded and Grant downed his pint. He fought against having another, knowing he had to have a clear head in the morning and excited by the prospect of getting closer to Vinny.

# Chapter 49

When it was announced that they were to have a rehearsal in the Royal Shakespeare Company's Clore Centre, everyone in the choir had been thrilled. Not only that, but they were to have tuition from an RSC movement coach. Tonight was the night, but for Kathy, the excitement was washed away by the events of the previous evening.

Last night, it had taken a long time for Kathy to calm down enough to drive home. Bent over the steering wheel, waiting for the tears to stop, she realised this was the first time she had really cried since Jack died. In those early days, she'd tried to stay strong for Pam and the girls by telling herself that is what Jack would have wanted, until it was too late and the pain became like a splinter, buried deep and healed over on the surface.

A couple walking by had peered in on her, looking concerned, and dreading any offers of help, she wiped her eyes, blew her nose and started the car. Waves of tears washed over her as she drove home, making it hard to concentrate on the road. When she noticed a police car approaching with its blue light flashing, Kathy thought they must be looking for her, but the car sped past intent on someone else's crisis.

This morning her head ached and her eyes were swollen and red. She was glad she had the day off, although she wondered if she would have been better working. All night she'd been on edge listening for that knock on the door, certain that Harry, knowing she had killed Jonathan, would have gone to the police. If he showed up tonight, she didn't know how she would face him.

In case the police arrived to arrest her, she decided to get the house straight and by the evening, it was spic and span. It had been a long day. Just after lunch Kathy thought the moment had come, but it was only a neighbour returning a cake pan.

The door to the Clore Centre would have been easy to miss if she hadn't been told it was next to Carluccio's Italian restaurant. A small group from the choir stood shivering outside and as she joined them, Kathy learned they had pressed the bell and were waiting admittance. Somehow, this formality added to the excitement and led to light-hearted laughter and comments that Kathy attempted to join in with, all the time wondering if Harry had arrived.

When the door opened, they signed in and followed their guide upstairs to a long corridor before being shepherded into a room on the right. It looked like a classroom. Eager for the experience of working with an RSC movement expert, most of the choir had already arrived. Kathy scanned the room but couldn't see Ida or Harry. Maybe he couldn't face her. She tried to join in the conversation as they waited.

Directed to a large rehearsal room, they spread out, as told, across the floor. It was marked out with tape for different productions. The centre was mostly used for educational purposes, but at times the RSC actors rehearsed here. This gave it an air of magic and Kathy wondered what famous actors had stood on this very spot. Being here felt like a validation that they were doing something worthwhile.

Just as they were about to begin, Ida and Harry arrived. Kathy guessed they had come together. She risked a whisper as Ida came to stand by her.

'Thought you weren't going to make it.'

'Wouldn't miss this for the world. John had trouble finding Harry's gran's. He's very quiet tonight. What have you done to him?'

Kathy was saved from answering when Greg Doran, Chief Associate Director, welcomed them to the centre. A warm, charismatic man, he spoke of how the RSC looked forward to opening the new theatre and went on to say that their performance, along with the other amateur groups, was essential to test out the new stage in all its aspects.

Buoyed up by his speech, Kathy threw herself into the loosening up exercises, feeling silly at first, but then as everyone joined in, relaxing enough to enjoy it.

After several exercises, they began working on the final floor plans for their performance and received suggestions and pointers for improvement. As the hour ended, everyone joined in a hearty round of applause for the help received and began to filter out. Kathy looked around for Harry and seeing him at the end of the file, forced herself to go over to him. As the queue moved forward, she tried to speak to him. 'I'm sorry.'

He wouldn't look at her. 'For what?'

'For bullying you.'

'And Jon?'

Kathy remained silent, unsure if she was repentant about killing him.

'Dave?'

'Sorry isn't enough.'

'I've found that.'

Kathy was quiet, thinking how right he was. She hadn't been prepared to give him a second chance, or even consider anyone in the gang could be remorseful about killing Jack. Much had changed in these last few days. Harry was moving away from her. She hurried to catch up with him. 'Harry, I was wrong.'

'Tell that to Vinny James.'

'Wait.' Kathy caught at Harry's sleeve as he moved away. He shook his arm free. 'Why?'

''Cause he's got his own list. And we're all on it, including you.'

'How would he know about me?' She stood still, shocked.

'The man in Henley Street. You introduced yourself.'

'I only gave him my first name.'

'Well, now he wants more.'

'You...you haven't told him it was me?'

'No.'

'Will you?'

'He's threatening my gran.'

'Oh my God. Harry, you have to protect her.'

Seeing that he'd scared her, Harry seemed to relent. 'The police are looking for Vinny; maybe they'll catch him soon.'

'I'll go to the police.'

'How will that help? Besides, she's going to Auntie June's for Christmas; she'll be safe there.'

'But the rest of you?'

'We're taking care. You should too.'

'Harry...' Kathy watched as Harry turned his back on her. No wonder he wanted nothing to do with her.

# Chapter 50

Trying to keep his attention on the road, Matt thought about Grant. He'd tried hard not to lose his temper with the man, knowing it wouldn't help. But he was testing his patience and Matt couldn't afford to keep giving him second chances. Tomorrow, he'd need to deal with the situation, but how depended on Grant.

By the time Matt reached home, he was tired and longing for his dinner. Putting the key in the lock, he heard raised voices. Guessing the cause was Angela, he sighed and pushed open the door to find Eppie facing her mum. Angela hastily pulled her dressing gown around her as Matt entered.

'If you want to behave like this, then you will have to do it else-where.'

Matt tried to get Eppie's attention. 'What's going...?' He stopped as a middle-aged, rather bemused man, still fastening his shirt and carrying his shoes, tiptoed gingerly from the bedroom and the cause of the row dawned on him. Bloody Angela had brought a man into their bedroom. Anger rising, he stepped to Eppie's side.

'If this is what it looks like, then I agree with Eppie.'

Angela waved her arm. 'Oh really, you young people think you are the only ones who are allowed to have any fun. This is Derek.'

Derek smiled and nodded. 'Maybe I'll be on my way.' He put on his jacket and still carrying his shoes and tie, slid cautiously by Matt to the door.

The closing of the door seemed to restart the anger. Eppie shook off Matt's restraining arm and moved towards her mother.

'You really are disgusting. How dare you bring a man in here – to our bed!'

'My bed at the moment, surely?'

'Not any longer. It's time you found somewhere else. You can start packing.'

'You're going to throw your own mother out on the street?'

Matt thought it time to step in. 'No. We are simply going to find you alternative accommodation.'

'I won't be forced to stay in some cheap hotel.' Angela disappeared into the bedroom, banging the door.

Matt guessed that was her way of telling them it wasn't going to be easy reclaiming their bed as they could hardly drag her kicking and screaming out of the flat. Maybe if they managed to find her somewhere nice. Although it would be expensive, it would be worth it to have some peace and a decent night's sleep.

'It might not be easy, Matt. Everywhere is full for Christmas and the toy conference.'

'We can try. You get the laptop, I'll try the phone book.' Matt bent over the phone book, thinking how thin and anaemic it was nowadays, a former shadow of itself, mostly full of adverts.

Over half an hour and several phone calls later, Matt was desperate for his dinner. He sighed and leant towards Eppie. 'Any luck?'

'No. What are we going to do? I can't put up with her anymore, Matt. God, that sounds awful.'

'But for you, I wouldn't have stood her for a minute.' Matt paused, noticing the tears in Eppie's eyes. 'Hey, come here.' He pulled her to him and felt the tears release. This was much worse for her. For him, it would be like having his dad here and that would drive him crazy. He held her until the tears subsided and as she pulled away, pushed a box of tissues over to her. 'You have a shower and relax while I rustle up something for supper.'

'I can't let you do that.'

'Yes, you can.'

'If you're sure?'

'Yes.'

'There's some leftover lasagne. You could warm that up – have it with salad.'

'What about...?' Matt nodded towards the bedroom.

'Guess we'd better feed her. Thanks.'

As Matt began preparing supper, he thought about the situation and wondered if he could pull in a favour from anyone. They couldn't go on living like this indefinitely.

Matt was just about ready to dish up when a knock came on the door. He went to answer it while Eppie, fresh from her shower, took over. It was Ida.

'Sorry to bother you, Matt, but it's John's card game tonight and we need the table back.'

'I'm so sorry, Ida, we should have returned it sooner. I'll bring it right now.' Lifting the table from its place against the bookcase, he called out to Eppie. 'Won't be a minute, love.' This could be his chance to ask Ida about Kathy and as he followed her, he thought of ways to bring it up.

'How are rehearsals going?'

'Oh, very well. We're working really hard.'

'Did you have a rehearsal last Monday?'

'Yes, but why do you want to know?'

Matt wondered how much to tell her. 'Spoke to Kathy Wylde the other day. She mentioned it, that's all.'

'Yes, she enjoys it. I think it's helped her get over Jack's death, although she was feeling under the weather and left early on Monday. I do hope she will be alright for the concert.'

'We're looking forward to it.'

'Well, I'm sure you will enjoy it.'

Carrying the table through, he nodded to John and turned to leave. 'Must get back, Eppie's dishing up.'

On the way back to his flat, Matt thought about the consequences of what he had just learnt. He couldn't rule Kathy Wylde out of the enquiry. She had both motive and opportunity. The only thing that puzzled him was where she could have obtained that amount of morphine.

# Chapter 51

Next morning, working through the usual load of information, Matt couldn't keep his mind off Grant and the tough decisions he may have to make. Grant was a loose cannon who couldn't be allowed to continue. He would have to stick with the programme or face the consequences, although losing an officer now was the last thing Matt needed. It would have been good to discuss it with McRay, but he'd already pushed him to give Grant a chance, and this time he might insist on suspension. Matt wondered if that would be the best thing for Grant, but decided if that happened, he'd go downhill fast. No, he'd see how he was this morning.

By the time Sam arrived, he was ready for a break and joined him in the small staff room to refill his coffee cup. From his grin, Matt guessed he might have some news that would move the case forward.

'Morning. You look pleased with yourself.'

'Managed to catch up with Harry yesterday. He's been approached by a man who said he was acting for someone close to Jonathan. At first, Harry thought it might be Jonathan's mother, so he was happy to help. But on talking to this man, he became scared and thought Jon's father could be behind it.'

'Description?'

'Yes, fairly comprehensive. And he's coming in later to look at mug shots.'

'Great. Good work, Sam.'

'There's something else – not sure what. I agree he's holding something back. Thought I'd try and get him to tell me today, unless you'd...?'

'No, you have the rapport, go for it.'

Matt returned to his office and feeling somewhat guilty, pushed aside the reports to spend the next ten minutes attempting to sort out the problem of Angela. Having no luck, he gave up and sighed as

Grant appeared at the door. He didn't appear hung over this morning and stood straight.

Before Matt could say anything, he took a step into the room. 'I have to apologise. My behaviour yesterday was unforgiveable.'

Shocked by this straightforward admission, and prepared for battle, Matt didn't know what to say. 'I'm glad you realise that, Grant.'

'I wasn't thinking and could have brought the team into disrepute.'

Thinking Grant's speech sounded rehearsed, Matt wondered what was behind it. He'd never taken much notice of anything Matt had said before. 'You could have jeopardised the enquiry.'

'That's the last thing I want to do.'

'Good. Think it's best if we keep you away from the public for a while though.'

'Fair enough. There's a lot to do.'

Now Matt was sure Grant was up to something. It was as if someone had taken his place and left the growling, awkward Grant at home. However, he may as well take advantage of the new version while waiting to see what was behind it all. Standing, he ushered Grant towards the door. 'Unless there is anything else…?'

'No, I don't think so.' Reaching the door, Grant turned back. 'Just one thing.'

Here it comes, Matt thought. 'Yes?'

'I'd like to get away at five, if possible.'

'Can't see a problem with that.' Matt had a sense this was what he wanted, but couldn't see why Grant needed to go through the charade. Still, if it brought a more co-operative man for a while he would go along with it and there were plenty of other things to think about.

After Grant had left, Matt picked up Jane's interim report on Kathy. Reading it made her sound like a model citizen, with not even a parking ticket. She worked as a part-time receptionist at Stratford College. Matt realised that is where she must have met Ida, who used to work there before she retired. Another thing they had in common besides the G&S society. The thought crossed his mind again that he could simply ask Ida about Kathy, but he dismissed it as unprofessional, at least for now, as he had nothing to go on but the sense she was hiding something. In addition, Wendy had obtained Kathy's car registration number and there had been no reported sightings in Leamington on the night of Dave's death.

# Chapter 52

Sam decided not to use an interview room, thinking they would hold too many memories for Harry. Instead, he begged use of the press office while the staff attended a meeting. He'd brought up the computer database of local mug shots and checked where Harold Harper-Jones was located, a quarter of the way in. This would give Harry time to settle down before having to face him.

Harry looked nervous when Sam met him in reception, and he could understand. Coming into this building would remind him of the worst time in his life.

'Thanks for coming, Harry. It can't be easy.' Sam led him to the press office and indicated a seat in front of the computer, before sitting down opposite. 'Can I get you a drink, Harry?'

'No, thanks. I'll get started, shall I?'

'Please.'

Sam sat quietly, watching Harry's face. Over the years, he'd learnt to read the signs that were significant: a hesitation, a slight frown, moving the body just a fraction away or forward. There was no reaction for a while and Sam guessed Harry should be approaching Harper-Jones. His response was immediate and he stood as if the man was in front of him.

'That's him.'

'Great work, Harry.' Sam walked around the desk to verify and make sure it was Harper-Jones.

'He's creepy. Speaks quietly but with a threat in his voice. Acts like he's your best friend and pretends he's doing you a favour.'

'What did he want from you, Harry?'

'He wanted to know who killed Jon. Said he was working for a friend.'

'And he didn't say who this friend was?'

'No, but I'm pretty sure it's Jon's dad.'

'Why did you think that?'

'It was the second time. After Dave…'

'Yes?'

Harry sank down into his seat again, trying to find the words. 'I think I caused Dave's death.'

'How?'

'I mentioned his name to this man. Then he was dead. There has to be a connection, doesn't there?'

Sam thought it was probably likely, but he didn't want to add to Harry's feeling of guilt. 'Is it possible Dave could have killed Jon?'

'No, of course not.'

'You sound pretty sure.'

'He wouldn't hurt anyone.'

'Yet he'd been involved in a murder before.'

'Not really. He ran away.'

Harry was now avoiding direct eye contact and Sam was sure he was hiding something. Maybe it was time to take a chance.

'Do you know who killed Jon, Harry?'

'No.'

The answer came too quickly and Sam was sure this was the question Harry had been dreading. He did know and was obviously shielding someone. Was he scared of them? Was it the same person who had killed Dave?

'Did this person also kill Dave?'

'No.'

'How do you know?'

'They told me.'

'You realise having this information is putting you at risk?'

Harry sat silent, looking like he wanted to be somewhere else. Sam wondered how far to push him.

'Are you scared of this person?'

'No way.'

'So they are a friend and you're trying to protect them? We're the only ones who can do that, Harry. You can't help yourself or them by keeping quiet. You could also be laying yourself open to a charge.'

'Can I go now?' Harry stood up.

Cursing inwardly, Sam realised he wasn't going to get any further. Harry had a sense of misplaced loyalty to this person. Maybe if they could pick up Harold Harper-Jones then he would feel safer and be willing to trust them.

'Thanks for coming in, Harry. You've been a big help.'

171

'Glad to.'

'I want you to remember that the person who killed Dave is violent and extremely dangerous. You, and the person you are protecting, wouldn't stand a chance against him. It would be much better to tell us who this person is, or persuade them to give themselves up. Believe me, they would be safer in prison.'

Harry looked pale, but simply nodded, eager to leave.

'I want to help you, Harry. Do you still have my card?'

'I think so.'

'Here, have another and ring me anytime, okay?'

'Yes. Thanks.'

# Chapter 53

Eppie calculated the time in Hawaii – 9 pm – and decided it would be a good time to catch her dad, unless he was out drinking with Howie.

'Dad.'

'Thought you'd be calling. Don't tell me – that woman is playing up already.'

'How did you guess?'

'I did warn you not to give in to her.'

'Wasn't that easy.'

'No, I suppose not. Epp, you need to put you and Matt first. Your marriage hasn't had an easy start. Don't let your mum mess it up.'

'How do I get her out of here? She says she has no money.'

'Book her into a hotel. I'll transfer the money. She'll soon find some other mug to look after her.'

'I couldn't let you do that, Dad.'

'Then I'll come over and sort her out. About time I saw my girl too. It's fairly quiet here and I'm sure Howie wouldn't mind.'

'Thanks, Dad, but let me and Matt work on it first. I'm thinking of asking Aunt Sandra if she could put her up. Plus we're both looking around for a reasonable hotel.'

'Your Aunt Sandra didn't do you any good. I still feel bad about leaving you there, Epp.'

Eppie thought back to that time. Mum had just left and Dad, as a round-the-world yachtsman, had no other option than to leave her and Mike with Mum's sister, Aunt Sandra. Hating it there, Eppie had run away and straight into danger from the gangs that prey on such youngsters. She shook off the memories, not wanting to burden her dad. 'It was good for Mike and his exams though. And surely she'll help her own sister.'

'I wouldn't bank on it. They're not alike.'

'Chalk and cheese.'

'Do you want me to ring her?'

'No, thanks, Dad. My escapade in London was a long time ago now and Aunt Sandra can't tell me what to do anymore.'

'That's my girl. However, I'm here if you need me. Understand?'

'Thanks, Dad. I'll let you know how I get on. How's the business going?'

'Good. More customers every day. You and Matt must come over. Catch up with Mike.'

'How is he?'

'Fine. Getting pretty serious about an American girl. We could have another wedding on the cards soon.'

'About time. Give him my love. How's the *Mary Lee*?'

'If I'm honest, missing the deep sea challenges, just like me. Still, she is a perfect lady with the punters. You'll have to come and see for yourself.'

'One day soon. I promise, Dad.'

After she put the phone down, Eppie sat and thought about the time she'd worked with her dad and of the extraordinary countries they had visited in his yacht, the *Mary Lee*.

Smiling at the memories, she got ready for work, deciding she would ask her boss, Chris, for help to find her mother a hotel room. If that didn't work, it would have to be Aunt Sandra.

At work, they were busy preparing for a large medical conference early in the New Year and Eppie had no chance to speak to Chris until they snatched a break for lunch. She laughed as Eppie explained the problem.

'Newly wed and your mum turning up. Sounds like a sitcom. Sorry, I shouldn't laugh. I'll have a ring around later, but I wouldn't get your hopes up, not at this time of year. Why don't you pop over to the Chalice and ask. They were very pleased with the Bellemy conference.'

Abandoning her sandwich, Eppie decided to use the rest of her lunchtime to walk the two minutes to the Stratford Chalice hotel. She could smile now at the memories of Natasha Bellemy. With Harry's help, she'd pulled it off.

Entering the elegant lobby, she was surprised to find Harry at the reception desk looking smart in the staff waistcoat and shirt. He seemed slightly ill at ease, but still managed a big grin as she approached.

'How can I help you, madam?'

Eppie sensed he'd been rehearsing the words. 'Nice to see you again, Harry. Are you enjoying your time on reception?'

Glancing at his colleague, who was busy with another guest, Harry lowered his voice. 'This is my first day.'

Although Eppie guessed as much, she didn't want to mention it. 'I'm sure you will do really well. Just keep smiling.' Her query was one Harry couldn't answer, but, after seeking help from his co-worker, it was confirmed that the hotel was fully booked until early in the New Year.

Walking back to work, she began wondering again about Harry's past.

# Chapter 54

Vinny was stretched out enjoying a football match when Dan warned him of Ops's approach. Pleased that the lure of Spain appeared to be putting Dan under his control, he sat up.

'Glad to see you are taking it easy, my friend.' Ops came cautiously down the narrow steps.

'Thought about it and realised you were right. Why keep a dog if you're going to bark yourself?'

'How true. Although I wouldn't automatically liken myself to a dog.'

'Just a figure of speech.'

'Of course. I have some news for you that I think you will like. I expect to have your police inspector in my hands by tonight.'

Vinny sat up. 'And what do you intend to do with him?'

'We will sit down together for a little chat. I expect him to tell me about the case and if they have any suspects for Jonathan's murder. This information may confirm my suspicions so that we can move forward with your quest.'

He wanted to ask *how the hell are you going to do that?* but managed to stop himself, modifying it to a simple, 'How? He's a tough man.'

'Please rest assured I have all the angles covered. If loosening his tongue with the drink doesn't work, other methods are in place to prompt him.'

'Let me be there.'

'I do not think this will help our cause.'

*His* cause, damn him. Had he forgotten this was *his* job, *his* son who had been murdered, and *his* responsibility to avenge his death? 'I have a right.'

Ops gave a sigh. 'Why did you hire me, Vinny? Don't answer as I can tell you. You had the common sense to realise you couldn't be seen on the streets asking questions. I believe there is a reward on your head that many of your so-called friends or acquaintances would be eager to claim. It would be such a shame to fall at this last hurdle. Let me do what you are paying me for and I promise that you will know immediately when I have the information you require.'

Vinny sat back, recognising the wisdom of Ops, but the fury inside wanted to burst out, grab him by the throat and demand to be there facing the copper who'd ruined his life. If the bastard hadn't arrested him, he could have been here to stop Jon getting killed.

Ops watched him, bemused. 'I am aware how difficult this is for you, Vinny. However, I do feel that I am offering the best service I can, both as an old friend and as your adviser. Shall I proceed?'

All Vinny could do was nod. He daren't speak, as he knew his rage would explode.

Ops gave a gracious nod and rose to leave. 'I need a quick word with Dan.'

'Wait. You said something about confirming your suspicions.'

'Maybe I shouldn't have mentioned that. It may be nothing.'

'Tell me,' he demanded, taking a step towards Ops.

'Very well. The lady called Kathy. I don't have the connection yet. It may be nothing, but I am working on it. I will let you know.'

Vinny watched as Dan walked with Ops to his car, wishing he could hear what they were saying. If Dan told Ops about his plans, it would be the last thing he did. The little sod wasn't a good liar and he would soon know. But, more importantly, who was Kathy?

# Chapter 55

Harry arranged to meet Nick at a different pub in Leamington, in case anyone was following, and chose to travel by train instead of the usual bus. He didn't want to put Nick and Tilly at risk, but felt desperate to talk to someone about the turmoil in his mind over Kathy. Since seeing Sam he'd been over and over the pros and cons of telling him everything, even though he knew this would lead to her arrest.

Nick looked around at the unfamiliar pub. 'Why the change, Harry? I like the Lion, feels like home.'

Harry wondered how much to tell his friend. With the arrival of his baby in a couple of months, the last thing he wanted was to frighten him. Nick talked about nothing else and was already upset at the thought of Vinny James on the loose. Yet, Harry reasoned he had a right to know so he could protect Tilly.

'Thought it best. Given what's going on.'

'You mean Vinny?'

'Yep. He killed Dave. So I thought—'

'Hang on. How do you know that?'

Evading the direct question, Harry answered, 'Makes sense, doesn't it?'

'You're saying we might be next?'

'Could be.'

Nick glared at Harry. 'Think you'd better tell me the truth?'

Harry gave a sigh and decided to tell Nick everything. Deep down, it was what he wanted. 'I've been approached by a man who is working for Vinny. He threatened me, wanted to know about us...you know, Jon's gang.'

'And?'

'I refused to tell him. Except...except I let slip that Dave lived with his sister. I didn't know then who this man was working for, or I wouldn't have done it. Honest, Nick. Then Dave was dead and it's like I killed him.' For the first time since the trial, Harry felt like crying.

'Tilly, me, did you tell him where we lived?'

'No. No, of course not. That's why I made sure I wasn't followed tonight and suggested we meet here...'

'Fucking hell. If you've put Tilly in danger...!'

'...once I realised.'

'You better be right.' Nick looked around him, sizing up the others in the pub.

Harry couldn't help doing the same. They all looked innocent and engaged in their own conversations. No one was on their own, although that didn't mean anything. Harry shifted uneasily in his seat. 'Nick. I know who killed Jon.'

'Good, so shop the bastard and get us all off the hook.'

'It's not that easy.'

'So tell me and I'll do it.'

'It's Kathy Wylde. His mum.'

'Fuck.'

'I don't want to turn her in.'

'Tough. She did it. I can understand why, but what the hell, we had to pay for what we did. Why shouldn't she?'

'She's only doing it because of us.'

'Look. If it comes to a choice between her and Tilly... Anyway, how do you know so much?'

Harry hesitated. 'Jon was only the first on her list.'

'Shit, then...'

'I was next.'

'So...'

'She said she couldn't do it.'

'Why?'

'I dunno. Guess she's not a natural.'

'So we're off one list and on another, more dangerous one, thanks to her.'

'She didn't know that.'

'Bloody hell.'

'Can't you get Tilly out of town for a bit?'

'She's got a scan in two days. She won't miss that. It's late 'cause she had the flu. Then maybe she could go to her sister's in Barford.'

'Good. Make sure no one follows you.'

'I'd better go, make sure she's safe.'

'Will you tell her?'

179

'We don't have secrets. The police told us about Vinny James already.'

'Best we don't meet up 'til...'til this is all over.'

'Yep. You take care, Harry.'

'And you.'

After Nick left, Harry lingered over his pint, reluctant to go back to Stratford where the man could find him. Still, he had nowhere else to go, so he drained his glass and headed off to the train station, making sure no one was tailing him.

# Chapter 56

Tilly went into the nursery, paused to run a finger over the crib rails. She loved this room, the soft primrose walls; well, that's what it said on the tin, chosen before they knew the baby was a boy.

Once they knew she was pregnant, they'd thrown themselves into preparing the nursery. The border and stencils showed frolicking animals, from puppy dogs to piglets. One night, Nick surprised her by bringing home an old rocking chair. She wasn't thrilled, wanting everything new and shiny in the nursery, but now he'd renovated it, it had become her favourite. She sank into it and tried to imagine holding her son, feeding and singing to him.

By the time Nick came in, she had almost rocked herself to sleep. She stood as he enfolded her in a bear hug and wondered at the intensity of it. Pushing him away, she looked at him, trying to read what was wrong, while not wanting anything to spoil the moment. 'What is it?'

'Come and sit down.'

'No. Tell me what's wrong. Is it Harry?'

'He's fine.'

Tilly allowed him to lead her into the tiny living room. Seated on the sofa, she demanded, 'Tell me.'

'Harry knows who killed Jon.'

'Good. Is he going to the police?'

'No.'

'Why not?'

'It's not that easy.'

'Why?'

'Because of what we did.'

'The man...that died?'

'Yes. It was his mother, Kathy Wylde. She's got a list and we're all on it.'

'Oh my God.' Of course, it was how she would feel if anyone harmed

181

her son. She held her abdomen as if to protect him. 'So why did the police warn us about Mr James?'

'I guess it made sense to them, after…after Dave.'

'Did she kill Dave?'

'No. Harry was next on the list. But then she decided she liked him.'

'That would be easy.'

'The trouble is Mr James. He's still out there and he probably killed Dave. I don't want you, or him,' he paused to rub her tummy, 'in danger. Can you go to Lynn's after your scan?'

'Yes, she's always asking me to stay. But what about you?'

'Do you think I'm going to miss out on seeing our son? I'll take great care and I want you to do the same. You're taking a taxi everywhere from now on. No argument.'

Tilly nodded, feeling like crying, the wonderful dreamy mood of before completely lost.

# Chapter 57

At last, they had an idea who was working with Vinny. If they could trace Harold Harper-Jones, he might lead them to Vinny before he killed again. Grant had started the process and they should have some leads soon.

Matt was still musing on how to deal with Kathy Wylde as he drove home. While she could possibly be guilty of the murder of Jonathan James, he was certain she hadn't physically beaten Dave Beeson to death. Yet, if she had been on the scene, she could be working with someone else. Deciding that he would have her brought in for questioning tomorrow, he turned to the problem of Angela. He was disappointed that he hadn't had time to find a solution and hoped Eppie had had more luck.

He entered to find the flat quiet, although Eppie should be home by now. Trying to recall if she had mentioned working late, he removed his jacket and hung it in the hall closet. Moving into the living room, he found her, curled up like a child, fast asleep on the sofa, still in her working suit. Having Angela around was really taking it out of her. He wondered where Angela was now. Any sort of mother would be preparing dinner and helping out.

Thinking of dinner, he moved into the kitchen to investigate the fridge and freezer, looking for ideas. Deciding on a frozen chicken pie – Eppie always made double and froze one – he wondered what heat to set the oven before choosing the middle range to be safe.

Twenty minutes later, he was pleased with himself: the pie was in the oven and the delicious aroma was starting to spread through the kitchen, making his stomach rumble. The broccoli was sitting in a pan of cold water and while he stood debating whether to have rice or salad, he felt her arms reach around his waist.

'Sorry.'

Turning to hug her, he bent to kiss her. 'Hey, no need. You're allowed to be tired. Besides, it is good for me to remember my way around the kitchen.'

'Something smells good.'

'Chicken pie. Not sure of the temperature though.'

Eppie turned to check the oven, moving the dial to a higher range. 'You take it easy, I'll take over now.'

'Yep, now it's all done,' Matt teased.

'Go on, get out of here.'

'Where's…?' Matt nodded towards the bedroom.

'Out to dinner. Don't ask me where or with whom.'

'Wouldn't this be a good time to…?'

'I've thought about it, but not like this, Matt.'

'Just a thought.'

Matt turned to answer his mobile, hoping it wasn't work. The caller sounded like Grant, but it was hard to hear and he sounded like he was in the middle of a fight. He moved out of the kitchen to try to hear better.

'Matt – trouble. Golden Acorn, Wa—'

'Grant, where are you? Grant?' Matt listened, hearing only a background of scuffles and thumps. Various scenarios ran through his head – was Grant drunk, had he dropped his phone, or had it been taken from him by force? Why would Grant call him? Matt couldn't recall him ever doing so outside of work for the entire time they'd worked together.

The rest was impossible to hear, just more scuffling before the phone went dead. He recognised the Golden Acorn pub from Grant's list of the places where Vinny used to hang out. What the hell had Grant got himself into? He'd warned him to stay well away from the pubs on the list.

There was no time to worry about that now. Grabbing his jacket, he dashed back to Eppie.

'Sounds like Grant's in trouble. Let Sam know I'm going to the Golden Acorn pub in Warwick. I have him on speed dial – I'll only ring if in trouble and need backup.'

'Got it – but, Matt—'

Matt kissed her and left.

The Golden Acorn was tucked away in a side street, next to a scruffy bookies shop. It looked anything but golden, more grey and in need of a coat of paint. The minute Matt walked in he sensed something was wrong. The volume of chattering voices dimmed so he could hear the sound of his feet across the sticky floor. There was a feeling that everyone knew who he was and expected him. He was the main floorshow. Matt made a mental note of the areas of the room to avoid if he needed to make a quick exit. On his left, three elderly men sat next to a passage-way marked by a faded toilets sign. Matt guessed the passageway led to a rear entrance with an enclosed yard.

To his right, next to the door, a party of six lads, the oldest in his mid-twenties, sat watching him with wary eyes. They might be a problem if he had to get out of here fast.

There was no sign of Grant. Matt wondered if he had come to the wrong place, but his instincts told him not. He hadn't picked up much from Grant's phone call, but the Acorn bit had been clear and there were no other pubs around here of that name.

Matt moved to the bar where a young dark-haired girl stepped nervously forward. He gave her a smile and ordered a half and she scurried to serve him. After he had taken a sip, he leant on the bar as if completely relaxed before venturing, 'I'm meeting a friend. Thought he'd be here by now. You might have seen him – brown hair, five ten, stocky?'

The scared shake of her head told him that Grant was here some-where. He watched her eyes dart to a small alcove near a staircase where two burly men sat. Matt guessed this was where the power lay. Picking up his glass, he smiled at the girl and went to join them.

'This space free?'

The men glared at him.

'Waiting for a friend. I think you know him.'

The men seemed fazed at this head-on approach. Eventually, the larger of the men, arms and neck heavily tattooed, spoke.

'Nope, nothing to do with us.'

His mate, a smaller carbon copy, nodded in agreement.

Matt wondered if he should leave and call for backup. Yet what would he tell them? He thought his colleague was in trouble, trouble of his own making, that he might be lying drunk somewhere or had fallen in with the wrong crowd. If he was right, then it would be the end of Grant's career. If he was wrong, he would look a fool. He made up his mind: he was on his own, just like Grant had been when he tried to save Eppie.

'Then you won't mind if I take a look around,' he said, rising in one swift movement and striding towards the stairs.

Both men leapt to their feet, but they weren't fast enough and Matt made the stairs first, taking them two at a time, aware the men were scrambling after him. Ahead, he could hear shuffling and a thump followed by a groan coming from behind a door to his right. He kicked open the door and burst in.

The first thing he saw was Grant, barely on his feet, sprawled against the wall, with a bruiser preparing to land a right-hander. From the look of Grant's bloody face, he'd already suffered many blows. Matt banged the door shut and shot forward to deliver a swift uppercut to the bruiser's jaw. It hardly fazed the man, who shook his head as if a fly had landed. Matt, realising this wasn't going to be easy, positioned himself as if for a rugby tackle.

The bruiser looked across the room to the man seated at a small table. Matt recognised Harold Harper-Jones. He posed no physical threat and appeared completely at ease, oozing a quiet sense of power and control. The light caught his bald forehead and intelligent but cold bespectacled eyes.

Harper-Jones gave a nod and the bruiser turned to Matt. As the door began to open, Matt kicked out, hearing a yelp as it caught one of the men from downstairs.

Bruiser threw a punch at Matt's head that he dodged without difficulty. Grant seemed to recover a little. Matt nodded towards the door and was relieved when Grant got the message and staggered to lean his weight against it.

Matt wondered if it would be any use declaring that he was a police officer and telling Bruiser he was under arrest. He should cover himself, but didn't think it would work. They probably knew Grant was a police officer. He'd get Bruiser into an arresting hold and then tell him. Although his punches might be deadly, he was slow and he wasn't keeping up a good guard. If Matt could dodge the next punch, he figured he could seize his arm and turn it into a subduing hold.

The man's heavy fist shot forward, Matt stepped backwards and ducked, then moved forward to seize his free arm, bringing it up behind his back. The man cursed and tried to pull away, but Matt held him firm.

'I am arresting you for assaulting a police officer. You do not have to say anything, but it may harm your defence—'

'Really, Inspector Turrell, there is no need for such formality. This was just a little falling out amongst friends. No harm done, none at all.'

Harper-Jones spoke in almost a whisper. His voice had a singsong quality that would have been pleasant in another situation. To Matt's ears, it sounded sinister. 'Call off your dogs then.' Matt glanced towards the door. He could see Grant wouldn't be able to hold it shut much longer, not with the renewed attack from the men outside.

'Of course. Of course. When you have released my friend.'

It was a stalemate, as Matt did not intend to give up his advantage. Grant was tottering, either drunk or damaged by his attacker. The men would soon burst in. Matt doubted that he would be able to get Bruiser past them. He must ring Sam. If Grant could reach his mobile. Twisting himself around, he prayed that Grant would understand. 'Grant. Mobile, top pocket, speed dial one. Backup.'

It seemed an age before Grant acted and Matt was conscious that Harper-Jones had stood and taken a step forward.

'That really won't be necessary.'

'Grant.'

Finally, Grant had the phone in his hand. Matt saw him hit the number. After a renewed battering, the two men burst in, knocking Grant forward towards Harper-Jones. Bruiser gave a twist, trying hard to break free. Matt maintained the hold but found himself attacked by Tattoo.

Grant was on the floor and Harper-Jones reached forward to take the phone from his hand. Carbon Copy kicked Grant hard in the ribs. Matt had no idea if he had managed to get the call through. A stinging blow from Tattoo caught his eye. He turned Bruiser around to shield himself and had the satisfaction of Tattoo's next blow landing on Bruiser's nose.

He couldn't hold out for long against all of them. Grant was out of the picture, lying still on the floor.

The door was ajar. If Matt could get his back to it, he might be able to reach the stairs. There was a chance for him to escape, but what of Grant? There would be no way he could carry or drag him down the stairs, not while fighting all three. However, if he could get away, he could raise the alarm.

With a heave, he shifted Bruiser around so Tattoo was directly in front, and gave a violent push so that the two men collided. Feeling backwards for the door, he raced through it while the men fought to become free of each other. Carbon Copy turned from Grant and lashed out. Matt thought he caught the glint of metal.

Over his shoulder, he shouted to Grant.

'Hang on, Grant. I'll be back.'

Clattering down the stairs, Matt recalled the layout and people in the pub. As long as the group of older men didn't join in, he thought he might have a chance to reach the street. The group of young men were a problem, but years on the rugby field gave him the speed and he shot past them before they had chance to stir.

Racing to his car, he could hear shouts behind him and, as he fumbled with his keys, one his attackers burst out of the pub and turned towards him. Just as Matt flung open the door and tumbled inside, Carbon Copy caught hold. Matt chopped at his fingers. With a curse the man let go, giving Matt time to slam and lock the door. Carbon gave a vicious kick to the side panel. Matt shot the car into reverse and executed a screeching turn towards Warwick. In his rear-view mirror, he was pleased to see the bullies watching, helpless.

Something warm ran down his arm and without looking, he knew from the stickiness it was blood. The flash he had seen was a knife. Dismissing the injury as non-urgent, he pulled into the side of the road so that he could call control.

Even as he made the officer asking for urgent assistance call, he could hear approaching sirens. Grant must have got through to Sam after all. Relieved that help was on the way, he turned the car around and headed back to the pub, desperate to make sure Grant was alright.

Matt wasn't feeling the effects of the fight yet. It was like being on the rugby field, when all that matters is winning. You only noticed the bruises afterwards. Besides, he was worried about Grant and felt like a heel for leaving him. He tried to tell himself it had been the only way, although it didn't sit well. At least Grant would soon be in hospital and well taken care of.

Matt could see two patrol cars blocking the road and Sam's car nearby, while an ambulance was flashing towards him from the opposite direction. He drew up alongside Sam's car and jumped out.

Inside, the pub was nearly empty. Only the terrified barmaid and the older men remained. One uniformed constable was coming from the toilet corridor.

'No one through there, sir. Entry door open. Signs a couple of cars had been parked in the alley outside.'

Matt's heart sank. Surely the men couldn't have moved that fast. He turned as footsteps thumped down the stairs, pleased to see Sam.

'Seems they all ran like rats. Sorry, Matt.'

'Grant. What of Grant? He was badly injured.'

'No sign.'

'Shit.'

Matt sank down onto a bench, his mind racing. Why would they take Grant? If caught kidnapping a police officer, the stakes would be high and any judge would throw away the key. He felt tired and aware of an ache in his arm. One of the uniformed constables approached.

'Sir, we're about to put out an APB, can you give us descriptions?'

'Of course.'

Matt gave descriptions of all the men involved, while Sam and the other uniformed officers spoke to the terrified barmaid and the older men. When he had finished he sat still until Sam came over to him.

'That arm doesn't look good, Matt. You're dripping blood all over the floor. I'll get a paramedic.'

Matt would have liked to stop him, but Sam didn't give him a chance. He didn't feel like being prodded and poked for a mere flesh wound. Sam returned with a paramedic.

'Let's see what's going on then, sir.'

Matt resigned himself and allowed the man to remove his jacket. His shirtsleeve was starting to stick and Matt winced as the man tried to ease it away.

'Best we do this in the ambulance. Make it easier. From the amount of blood think it's going to need stitches too.'

'Damn, I haven't got time for this.'

Sam interrupted his conversation with the police officers and came over.

'We've got everything covered here. You get sorted and I'll catch up with you.'

'But—'

'Or should I call McRay?'

Cursing to himself, Matt allowed the paramedic to lead him to the waiting ambulance. It should be Grant they were attending to, not him.

# Chapter 58

After being stitched up in casualty, Matt had been ordered back to CID by McRay. He wanted to be out searching for Grant, but McRay was adamant. Matt couldn't settle and paced up and down McRay's office. McRay offered him whisky and Matt downed one tumbler, but refused the second.

'We need you on the intelligence side now, Matt. You saw these men, fought with them; write down everything that you can remember. I don't need to tell you how the smallest thing could make the difference. Beside, you're not fit for duty, go take a look at yourself.'

In the washroom mirror, Matt was surprised at the spreading bruise around his left eye. It didn't look pretty as the swelling was causing the lid to puff up. The cut to his right arm had been cleaned, stitched and bandaged so aside from a few other minor scrapes and scratches, Matt didn't think he was too bad. He'd come out of many a rugby match with worse.

Sitting down to write his report, he described every detail as precisely as possible, but still itched to be taking physical action. He'd got to know Grant in these last few days, found out what drove him, made him into the surly, uncommunicative man he was. Yes, he had problems, and probably shouldn't be a police officer, yet the job had done this to him and maybe, with help, he could carry on in some capacity. Otherwise, there would be nothing left but the booze.

Handing his report over to McRay, a wave of tiredness crept over him.

'How did it come to this, Matt? No shilly-shallying around now; if I'm to have your back, I need to know. This is more than Grant's drinking I take it?'

'It follows on from there, sir.'

McRay listened, only breaking in to clarify a point now and again. At the end, he stood. 'Right. Now, I'm sending you home.'

Matt was ready to protest.

'No, Matt. We've enough officers out there looking for Grant, Harper-Jones and the others. What I need is you fit for duty tomorrow. Go home and get a good night's sleep. That's an order.'

Matt knew enough not to press a point with McRay in this mood, plus he was desperate for sleep. He thought longingly of his own bed and wished, not for the first time, that Angela would disappear.

Matt drove slowly home, hardly noticing his surroundings. For once, none of the historical places he passed could offer him comfort. He thought of Grant and prayed that he was okay. By the time he reached home, he could hardly keep his eyes open.

Eppie was waiting and the door opened before he could get his key in the lock. 'Matt.' She anxiously surveyed his face while trying to find a spot to kiss.

He bent forward, putting his good arm around her and relishing in her warmth and smell. 'Looks worse than it is, really. A good night's sleep will do the trick. Do you think we could have our bed for the night?'

'I've changed the sheets already.'

'Angela?'

'Is out.'

'She won't be happy.'

'Tough.'

Matt grinned and gave her another hug.

'Are you hungry?'

'Too tired. Just a drink will do.'

'I'll bring it through. Do you need any help?'

Matt kissed her, shook his head and made his way to the bedroom. Stumbling out of his clothes, he fell onto the bed, welcoming it like an old friend. He was fast asleep by the time Eppie came in with his drink, and only stirred later at the sound of Angela's raised voice.

'I can't believe you expect me to sleep on that…that thing. Your own mother.'

'It's that or a hotel. Or a park bench for all I care. And, *Mother*, I don't know how you even dare call yourself that.'

'I was there for you all those years. You were practically grown by the time I left.'

'I was twelve.'

'There you are then.'

'I still needed you.'

'Rubbish. I'm sure your Aunt Sandra looked after you fine.'

'No. No, she didn't. I ran away. And if she is so perfect, why don't you go and stay with her?'

'Instead of my only daughter?'

'Who has no room. This is getting us nowhere. I've made up the sofa bed – would you like me to pull it out for you? Or shall I call a taxi?'

Matt didn't hear the outcome as he drifted off to sleep again with a smile on his face. He didn't even feel Eppie slide carefully in beside him, but was conscious of her when he woke the next morning. Turning to look at her, he saw her eyes were slightly puffy, as if she had been crying. As he leaned forward to kiss her, Matt remembered the angry words of last night and wondered how the argument had ended.

Memories of yesterday also flooded back, filling him with a sense of urgency. Eppie was awake now and returned his kiss.

'Are you hungry?'

'For more than food. But no time, unfortunately.'

'You'll have a shower? You can, can't you, with that?' Eppie pointed to the dressing on his arm.

'Supposed to keep it dry.'

'Right, I'll fix that. Then I'll cook you a bacon sandwich while you shower.'

By the time Eppie had secured his dressing with cling film and he was in the shower, the smell of bacon permeated the flat. He hadn't asked but the hump on the sofa bed answered the question of Angela.

Conscious of the need to eat, he hurried through the sandwich, thinking of Grant and wondering if there was any news. The sooner he was back at work now, the better. He kissed Eppie and was on his way.

# Chapter 59

Arriving at work, Matt found the place a hive of activity. He felt everyone's eyes on him as he walked down the office and tried to look confident, even though he didn't feel it. Sam was in the middle of the briefing and noticing McRay was waiting for him, Matt nodded for him to continue.

'How are you this morning, Matt?'

'Raring to go, sir.'

'Well, there has been no sighting of Grant overnight, I'm afraid. We think we have identified some of the heavies involved – the Harris brothers, Ned and Will. Known in Coventry as muscle for hire. Mug shots on your desk for you to confirm. We've alerted the West Midlands force that we're looking for them.'

'How about Harper-Jones? Grant was working on leads to him as he features in our murder enquiries.'

'Matt, I've passed all the information we have on Harper-Jones to Headquarters. Officers from the North Division are now involved in Grant's disappearance and I expect you to liaise fully with them. In the meantime, you need to concentrate on your ongoing enquiries.'

'But, sir—'

'Don't argue with me, Matt. You have enough on your plate. I'll make sure you are kept in the loop.'

Matt would have liked to protest; Grant had to be the priority as far as he was concerned, but McRay gave him no choice. He looked like he had been up all night and was never in the best of moods even without loss of sleep.

'Matt, I've had to bend the truth a little about Grant's problem, but I need to ask you confidentially. Do you think he might have compromised our investigations?'

Matt's heart sank. He'd levelled with McRay about Grant's drinking, but hadn't included his darkest thoughts that Grant may have unwittingly given away aspects of the case. He knew it was no good lying anymore. 'It had crossed my mind, sir.'

'He'd be vulnerable, given his drinking,' McRay sighed.

Matt nodded, thinking he should have been firmer with Grant, even gone ahead and got him suspended. He'd wanted to give the man a chance and had just made matters worse, not only for the case, but also for Grant. God, he hoped they found him soon.

'It's no good blaming yourself, Matt. We might have contained it, given the chance and a bit of co-operation from Grant.'

Matt did blame himself. He'd gone over and over the confrontation of last night as he drove to work, trying to figure out how things could have turned out differently. He couldn't come up with any alternative besides them both being kidnapped, or lying in a ditch somewhere, freezing to death. No one could last long in this exceptionally cold winter with temperatures dropping to minus sixteen at night. He just hoped Grant wasn't out there exposed to the elements.

'The only way to deal with this is for you to concentrate on catching Vinny James and finding his son's killer before he does.'

Matt knew McRay was right; he had to focus, get on with the job or other people could be in danger. It was no good feeling sorry for himself or Grant – he had a job to do. 'You're right, sir. I'd better get back to it.'

'Good. Keep me up to speed, Matt.'

'Yes, sir.'

Making his way to where Sam was finishing the briefing, Matt noticed a subdued air hung over the team. There was none of the usual bickering and backchat. He nodded to Sam, aware that everyone was waiting for him to speak. 'Thanks, Sam. I just wanted to reassure you all that everything possible is being done to find DI Grant.'

Someone called out. 'Can't we be involved, sir?'

'Not officially. That's down to North Division. We do have two murder enquiries running and the thought is that Grant's disappearance may be connected to these. It follows that the sooner we catch whoever is responsible in our cases, the nearer we may be to finding Grant.' Matt stopped and waited until the grumble of voices had died down. 'However, there is nothing to stop us keeping an extra sharp eye out wherever we go. Or of putting in a bit of unpaid overtime to check any area you think he might be. After all, we know our own patch best.'

There was a murmur of agreement. He knew the team would feel better if they were doing something. It seemed funny to Matt without

Grant. He even missed his drawling comments.

'Remember though, I need your full concentration on the cases we are working on. Other people are at risk and we can't afford to let them down.'

Matt nodded, conscious of the effort it took to appear as if it was business as usual.

'Want to fill me in, Sam?' he said, leading the way to his office.

'Sure, guv.'

The first thing he noticed was the mug shots for Ned and Will Harris. They matched the two tattooed men from yesterday. Now they'd identified all the men involved, except for Bruiser, surely it would only be a matter of time before they found Grant.

Mindful that he must keep to the guidelines he'd laid down for the team, he ushered Sam to the couch and sat down opposite him.

'How are you, Matt?'

'Let's concentrate on the case, Sam. I'm fine. What do we have?'

'Got a last known address for Harper-Jones, but it was before he was lifted for fraud. House was in his son's name and it was sold in 2005.'

'Location?'

'Ilmington, a village near Stratford.'

'Address for the son?'

'Seems he moved his family to America soon after his father's conviction.'

'Don't blame him. Wife or other family?'

'Haven't traced any yet.'

'North Division will be all over this, but I can't see how it would hurt to have a decent lunch break for a change. I know a nice pub in Ilmington, the Howard Arms. See if Fl...Jane is free too. We'll have a case conference. Oh, and, Sam, no one else needs to know.'

Sam grinned. 'Aye, aye, sir.'

Ilmington's Cotswold stone glowed in the winter sunshine, almost negating the fierce wind that tore at them as soon as they left the warmth of the car. Scurrying into the four-hundred-year-old Howard Arms, they were relieved to find places in front of the roaring log fire and happily took off their coats.

Attacking the menu, Matt decided on soup of the day, which was potato and leek, one of his favourites, served with crusty bread. Sam and Jane went for posh fish and chips. Although Matt was tempted, he didn't want to spoil his dinner.

While Sam went to the bar to give their order and get drinks, Matt looked around. Not many people had ventured out on such a cold day and most of the half dozen customers looked local. He was just wondering if they should only approach the staff for information on Harold Harper-Jones when Jane, who was warming her hands by the fire, spoke.

'Can we eat first?'

'Of course.'

'Only I can see you eyeing everyone up.'

'Just accessing the options. Think we'll stick to staff, unless they point us in another direction.'

'Good. I'm starving.'

Sam returned with two coffees and half a pint for himself. It was a joy to wrap one's hands around the steaming cup and Matt leant back in his seat thinking they should do this more often. The warmth from the fire made him sleepy and he stretched out his legs towards it.

Talking shop was difficult, especially when the pub began filling up, so instead they enjoyed their lunch. Thinking he had better get back on track, Matt offered to make it his treat and despite protests from Jane and Sam, headed towards the bar, glad of the chance to approach the barman. Waiting for a lull in people at the bar, he smiled at the young man.

'Hi. I'm looking for information on Harold Harper-Jones. I believe he lived around here some years ago.' Matt slid his warrant card across the counter, wanting to keep it low key. The man gave a sigh.

'Used to come in here all the time, usually with his son. Don't know much about him, except he got us to order his favourite whisky, nearly a hundred quid a bottle. No one else is going to pay that, so I've a couple of bottles going begging, if you're interested.'

Before handing Matt his receipt, the man scribbled something on it. 'That's the name of the damn stuff, in case you know anyone who'll take it off my hands.'

'I'll keep my eyes open.'

The barman turned to serve another customer. At least this was some information and had to be better than nothing. Pocketing his change, Matt started to walk back to the others but found his way blocked by a tough-looking man. Everything about him said 'copper' plus Matt remembered him from somewhere.

'Hello, Inspector Turrell. Lost your way?'

'You have the advantage?'

'DI Fraser.'

'North Division?'

'Correct. And you have been told to leave this investigation to us.'

'What investigation?'

'I'm not even going to justify that with a reply. We're doing everything we can to find your colleague.'

'As I would assume.'

Matt was aware that Sam was approaching, followed by Jane. Sam stepped to Matt's side.

'Guv?'

'It's alright, Sam. Goodbye, DI Fraser.' Pushing by so that his shoulder forced the man aside, Matt led the way out of the pub, breaking the silence only once they were in the car.

'At least we know they're on the ball.'

'Must be following up the same lead,' Jane said.

'Hope they have better luck than we did.' Sam sounded disappointed.

Matt waited until they had left Ilmington behind and were heading towards Stratford before replying. 'We didn't come away empty-handed.' Responding to their puzzled looks, he passed over the receipt.

Sam was impressed. 'So if we find somewhere stocking this whisky we could have him.'

'Correct. But we can only keep this for a couple of hours.' Both Jane and Sam looked at him. 'We can't hold back, not if it means finding Grant.' He was relieved to take their silence as agreement.

# Chapter 60

Vinny felt like pacing up and down but the narrowboat afforded him little opportunity. Passing the stove for the umpteenth time, he shot out a vicious kick. The stove shuddered, causing a pan, full to the brim, to splash down the front of Vinny's trousers. Grabbing the tea towel to wipe the worst of it away, he cursed Dan for leaving it there. Why couldn't he wash the damn thing up straight away instead of leaving it to soak like an old woman? At least he had the sense to get out of Vinny's way this morning. Vinny could see him sitting in the car, earphones in, head nodding to some unheard rhythm.

The soft purr of a car engine announced Ops's arrival. Eager for news, Vinny moved out onto the deck, only to be waved back inside by Ops as he clambered up the small bank.

Inside the cabin, Vinny burst out, 'Well?'

'Really, my friend, you are impatient. I can wait if you wish to change your trousers.'

'Forget about them. The idiot left a pan of water on the stove.'

Ops gave a sigh. 'Sometimes, Vinny, I think you forget all that Dan does for you.'

'What happened?'

'Unfortunately, I was unable to elicit full co-operation from your DI. We may have done so, but there was an interruption in the form of a DI Turrell. I believe he is a work colleague.'

'Don't know the bastard.'

'It is most comforting to know that there is at least one police inspector you are unacquainted with. However, we were forced to postpone our enquiries.'

'Gaining nothing?'

'Not entirely. I have found out who the mysterious Kathy is. She is the mother of Jack Wylde. Therefore, I cannot understand why she would have befriended young Harry, or why indeed he felt compelled to protect her.'

'She's the one, isn't she?'

'It would be unwise to jump to that conclusion.'

'You would say that.'

'I warn you, Vinny, we must move very carefully right now; no giving in to your desire for revenge until I have clarified the situation. Let me find out more.'

'I'll be waiting 'til hell freezes over while you fart about.'

'Farting about, as you so delicately put it, is not something I will be doing. As you can imagine, interfering with a police officer, or officers, is frowned upon. Therefore, I do not need to tell you that the heat is most definitely on and you would be advised to follow my lead and lie low for a while. Kathy Wylde will wait. She is not about to disappear. You will have your revenge.'

'The longer I'm stuck here, the greater chance I'll get caught.'

'Not if you are willing to listen to my advice.'

'Hasn't done me much good yet.'

'I can arrange your return to Spain, if you wish?'

Thinking of his plans for later, Vinny shook his head. 'I'll give it a couple more days.'

'Wise move. I'll be in touch later.'

Ops climbed back up the ladder and Vinny gave a vicious salute to his retreating back. The little twerp was turning out to be useless and he was glad he was taking matters into his own hands.

199

# Chapter 61

Kathy kept herself busy, trying to ignore the idea that she was in danger. Despite this, she had found herself watching the cars as they queued behind her yesterday on the way to work and once at work, she could feel herself tense whenever a stranger came into reception.

Today, with no work to distract her, it would be harder. At first, she thought she would visit Maisie, until she considered she could be taking the danger with her. Instead, she settled for baking mince pies for the dress rehearsal tonight. Next, she got together her costume, rummaging in her sewing box to find some ribbon to liven up the straw hat. Occasionally she would go to the bay window and look up and down the road, but nothing seemed amiss.

During the afternoon, Kathy got to thinking that if this Vinny person was seeking revenge for his son, maybe it was what she deserved, a sort of rough justice. But this didn't apply to Harry. He'd been trying to make up for what he had done, to get on and lead a useful life. And she liked him. The thought that she'd put him in harm's way nagged at her and she resolved to make her peace with him tonight.

She could find no solace for causing Dave's death either. From the newspaper reports and from listening to Harry, he was a disturbed young man, who had hardly been involved in Jack's death. Just like Jack, he hadn't deserved to die in such a terrible way. No amount of justification could make her feel better about that.

This isn't what she set out to do. It had all seemed so black and white at the beginning. The thought struck that maybe she would have liked Jonathan James too, if she'd given him a chance. Although, remembering his cold eyes, she didn't think so and she tried to push the thought from her mind.

Arriving at the church hall that evening, there was an air of excitement with everyone admiring each other's costumes. Taking the mince pies through to Ida in the kitchen, she glanced towards the men to see if Harry had arrived. There was no sign of him and a flutter of panic ran through her. Had Vinny caught up with him? If anything happened to him, it would be her fault. The worry caused her to spill sugar all over the counter. Ida said nothing as she helped wipe it up.

Just as rehearsal was starting, Harry arrived in a last-minute flurry, scrambling into his costume in a corner. With everyone concentrating hard making sure their performance was unsurpassed, there was no chance to talk to him until the rehearsal was over. He seemed intent on ignoring her, but she went over to him as everyone was getting out of their costumes. 'You were right.'

'About what?'

'I...I caused Dave's death.'

Harry was silent. Kathy wondered if he had heard. He shook his head and spoke in a low voice. 'No. That was me.'

'You?'

'That man in Henley Street. I told him Dave was living with his sister. If I hadn't mentioned it, he wouldn't know where to find him. It was my fault.'

Kathy had the impulse to hold him, tell him it was all because of her and her crazy need for revenge. Yet getting into an argument about who carried the greater blame wouldn't help. She patted his arm. 'We'll both be safe when the police catch Vinny James.'

'That won't be easy. The police have been looking for days. He could be anywhere – like outside right now, watching.'

The hall's large windows looked out onto the parking lot and all she could see were cars, their coating of ice glistening in the light from the hall. Harry was right – anyone could be out there. Suppressing a shudder, Kathy turned back to Harry. 'Can you stay at your gran's?'

'Couldn't put her in danger. Don't worry, I'm in a mate's room. He's gone home for Christmas. What about you?'

'I'm being careful.'

Again, Kathy thought how caring Harry was. Here he was, not only thinking about her, but worrying about his gran. She wished she could make it up to him, keep him safe. 'I'm sorry for putting you in danger, Harry.'

'It was me...us who started it off. Besides, I'm quite enjoying trying to outfox whoever is following me.'

Unexpectedly, Kathy knew what she had to do. 'I'll give myself up.'

'No. You can't.'

Amused at his reaction, Kathy smiled. 'I thought you'd be glad. It will keep you safe.'

'You mustn't do this for me.'

'It's what I need to do.' She felt lighter, more at ease, and knew she was right.

'Just wait until after the concert, please.'

Still feeling happy with her decision, Kathy nodded.

# Chapter 62

Matt arrived early and went through the usual reports, including a brief note from DI Fraser thanking him for the information about the whisky. Matt hoped some good would come of it. He was about to leave his office to start the briefing when McRay appeared. McRay often appeared miserable but as he walked towards him, Matt wondered if he was ill. The man looked like he needed a chair. His stomach constricted. This was about Grant.

McRay put a hand on his arm. 'Sorry, Matt.'

'They've found him?'

All McRay could do was nod and Matt knew it was the worst possible news.

'Where?'

'River.'

'Can I…?'

'Best not.'

'Who's handling?'

'It's still North's, Matt. And before you say anything, it's for the best.'

A surge of anger rose to flame his face. Grant was one of the team. If he and his fellow officers had been involved from the beginning, maybe they would have found him alive.

'Best for whom? Certainly not for Grant. It's too bloody late for him.'

'Matt…'

As soon as the angry words left his mouth, he regretted them. McRay was just doing his job and he would be suffering too. Matt thought of Grant's battered face and wondered what other injuries he had sustained. If he'd stayed, would the outcome be any different or would he be dead too? *If* Grant's captors hadn't moved so fast, *if* Matt could have stopped him. There were a host of ifs racing around his head, and he knew he was on a useless spiral. Nothing would change the outcome.

McRay broke into his thoughts. 'It's no good blaming yourself, Matt.'

'But I should have stopped him.'

'There is something you can do for Grant.'

'Anything.'

'You can be the one to tell his family. He has an ex-wife and daughter. I think it should be one of our team. North Division has okayed it.'

Matt stayed silent, remembering Grant talking about the loss of his family.

'Matt?'

'Yes, of course, sir. Can I go alone?'

'If that's what you want. The Chief may want to visit later and we'll send in a FLO if needed. I'll get you the details.'

'Thanks, sir.'

'Come on, let's tell the team.'

Matt followed McRay through to the main office. The room fell silent as they made their way to the front. It was as though everyone already sensed the dire news. He was glad when McRay held up his hand for silence, as he couldn't trust himself to speak and keep the emotion out of his voice.

'You will probably all realise why I want to speak to you and I'm afraid the news is bad. The body of Detective Inspector Grant was recovered from the River Leam half an hour ago.'

Matt watched the faces of his colleagues, saw the horror there, heard them gasp and hoped he wouldn't have to stand there much longer.

Luckily, McRay kept it short. 'The murder of this officer is being handled by North Division. I expect you to offer them every assistance. When we have the funeral arrangements, I know each one of you will want to attend. Grant was one of our own and we will give him a good send-off. If someone would like to start a collection, I believe Grant has a daughter soon to go to university and I'm sure she will be appreciative of your help in his name.'

McRay turned to Matt and Sam, who had come to stand at Matt's side. 'A word in your office, Matt. You too, Sam.' They moved towards Matt's office as a subdued murmur broke out. As soon as the door closed, McRay turned to Sam. 'Are you up to speed, Sam?'

'Yes, sir.'

'Good. Matt is going to give Grant's ex-wife the news. I wanted it to be one of us, rather than a stranger. Think she lives out in the Cotswolds, Matt. I'll get you those details so you can be on your way.'

McRay left and Sam turned to Matt. 'You okay, Matt? Suppose that's a daft question, isn't it?'

All Matt could do was nod. He would be glad to get out of here for a while. The drive to see Grant's wife would give him time to straighten things out in his head. McRay must have had that in mind. He sighed as Jane came in. Sympathy was not what he needed.

'We're on top of things here, Matt, so don't rush back. Oh and I'm bloody glad we didn't lose the two of you.'

He silently blessed her perception.

# Chapter 63

Matt decided to take the long way around, wanting time to steady himself and be in the right frame of mind to support Grant's family. Passing through busy Stratford-upon-Avon brought him to the edge of the Cotswolds and the market town of Moreton-in-Marsh. Thankful it wasn't market day, he managed to get through the town with little delay. The Cotswold buildings, lit by the winter sun, fought hard to cheer the day. Matt almost forgot the icy roads and bitter wind. To Matt, it always seemed as if the honey-coloured limestone retained the essence of summer. He'd read somewhere that the colour came from underwater creatures, mostly sea urchins. It was hard to imagine the whole area being underwater millions of years ago. He made a note to himself to bring Eppie to the Cotswolds, one of his favourite places in the world, a place of ancient peace. A peace he needed as he anguished over the events of the last few days.

Reaching Bourton-on-the-Water, he was grateful the shop was easy to find on the main street. Matt was able to park nearby, as apart from a few hardy Christmas shoppers, not many people were choosing to brave the icy morning. The shallow River Windrush, ambling under low bridges through the middle of the village, seemed sluggish. Matt was surprised it wasn't covered in ice.

The bowed windows of the shop were a vision. The glass ornaments on display caught and reflected the glow from Christmas lights around the window, giving Matt the feeling of being transported back to Dickens's time. Stepping inside, a welcome blast of warmth fanned over him. Matt could see no one behind the counter, but a young girl with dark brown hair turned from rearranging some vases.

'Can I help you?'

'Is it possible to speak to Mrs Procter?'

'I can get her for you.'

'If you would please.'

'May I give her your name?'

'Inspector Turrell. And I'd like a word in private, please.'

The girl's eyes widened and she smiled at him before hurrying behind the thick velvet curtain covering a doorway at the rear. While she was gone, Matt looked around, thinking how Eppie would love it here. It made him realise he hadn't even thought of Christmas presents. Still, it didn't seem right to be thinking of Christmas, given that he was delivering such bad news.

At a swish of the curtain, he turned to see the girl followed by a smartly dressed, composed woman of about forty, her dark haircut in a graceful bob and wearing a red silk blouse that complemented her colouring.

'Please come through, Inspector.'

With a nod of thanks to the girl, Matt followed Mrs Procter down a corridor piled high with cartons of stock to a tiny kitchen where more boxes filled the space. Under a window reinforced with steel mesh, she indicated a small table set with two chairs.

'Please take a seat. Can I get you a coffee, Inspector? I was just about to have one.'

'Yes, I'd like that. Thank you, Mrs Procter.'

'Lynne, please. Is this about the shoplifting? We haven't had a problem lately. It's mostly a summer thing, when the town is full of visitors.'

'No, Mrs Procter…Lynne. I work with Grant.' Matt made a conscious effort not to use the past tense. He wanted to break the news as gently as possible.

'Oh.'

She stopped filling the kettle and sat down opposite him. He could see she wasn't expecting this. Her eyes fixed on his face.

'Grant has been working on a case. Unfortunately, he got caught up in something and was attacked.'

'Richard's dead, isn't he?'

'I'm sorry. Yes. We found him today.'

'Found?'

'He'd been missing for two days.'

'Missing? Didn't you try to find him?'

Matt hesitated. This was tapping into his own guilt, but he knew he mustn't burden her with it. 'Every effort was made to find him. I'm so sorry to bring you this dreadful news.'

She was silent and Matt watched her, not sure what to expect.

Would she cry over her divorced husband? He was surprised when she spat out, 'I hated him.'

Matt waited, experience telling him there was more to come.

'I have hated him for so long. I should be laughing.' As if she wished this were true, she wiped her hand across her eyes to brush away tears. She paused to study him before asking, 'Did you know about Tom?'

'Some of it, yes.'

'It was so hard.'

'He wouldn't make it easy.'

'No. You knew him well?'

'Not until recently.'

'He always kept things to himself. I should have realised that.'

She seemed lost in her thoughts. Matt knew he should move the conversation onto a more practical level, like next of kin and funeral arrangements, but gave her the space.

'How did he...did he die?'

It was the question Matt hoped to avoid, and he paused, wondering how much to tell, before deciding on a cut-down version of the truth. 'We have no post mortem report yet, but I can tell you he got into an unequal fight and was kidnapped. He was eventually found in the River Leam so he may have drowned.'

'Was that the same fight you were in?'

Matt had forgotten his bruised eye. 'Yes.'

'But you got away?'

Matt squirmed. Even though he had gone through all of this with McRay and the super, receiving their assurances he'd acted wisely and couldn't have saved Grant, he retained the sense he should have done better. He didn't want to justify himself to Grant's widow while the doubt remained. 'Yes. To get help.' Matt paused, remembering Grant on that day. 'It didn't come in time.'

Lynne nodded and seemed about to say something when the girl from the shop came in.

'Mum?'

So, this was Grant's daughter. Matt could see the likeness now, the same hair colouring and fair complexion as her mother. He wondered how Lynne would handle this. He would need to follow her lead.

'Not now, Melli.'

Melli glanced from her mum to Matt. 'What is it? Mum?'

'We'll talk later. The inspector is just leaving.'

Matt stood in compliance, reaching for a card to pass to Lynne.

There were still things they had to discuss. As he put his card in front of her, Melli seized it.

'Warwickshire. Dad's force. What's going on? Is Dad okay?'

When Lynne declined to say anything, Matt stepped in.

'Your mum will explain. Just give her a minute.'

'Turn the sign round, Melli, please.'

At first, Matt thought she was going to refuse, and then she turned to obey. Thankful for the small breathing space, Matt turned to Lynne. 'Would you like me to tell her?'

Lynne seemed undecided.

'She'll have to know.'

'I said she could see him, before she goes to university next year. She's been badgering me for a while, and…and I've put her off. Now it's too late.'

'What's too late? Mum?'

Lynne put her head in her hands and burst into tears. Matt guided Melli to his seat and bent towards her.

'I'm afraid it's bad news, Melli. Your father has died while on duty.'

For a moment, he thought she hadn't heard or understood him. Then she sprang up and began hitting out at her mother. Matt seized her hands, letting some of the blows fall on his chest. Already their power was lessening until she put her head against him and began sobbing. Looking down at Lynne, he could see she wasn't badly hurt, except for a red mark on her left cheek. She rubbed at it in an absent-minded manner and Matt guessed she was in shock. Needing to ease the situation, he guided Melli back to the chair and turned to finish filling the kettle. They would both benefit from something sweet and hot.

By the time he placed the mugs of tea in front of them, both women's tears had dried up. Lynne was looking at her daughter, but Melli refused to return her gaze.

'I'm so sorry, Melli.'

'I should never have listened to you. He was my dad.'

'It seemed best. I—'

'For you.'

'No. For you. I couldn't let your father destroy you. Not like Tom.'

'What did you think he was going to do? Disagree with me? Did you think I'd fall apart like your precious Tom?'

'I…'

Melli turned to Matt. 'I want to see my father.'

It was a demand and her right, but Matt knew he must discourage her. He'd seen bodies recovered from the water. The bloating, the distorted features and the build-up of gases made for a smell that stayed with you for a week, with colleagues blatantly avoiding you. This might be the wrong time to have a fight with her, could make her dig her in her heels, so he chose his words carefully. 'Certainly.'

Lynne jumped up. 'No, you can't.'

Matt held up a hand to calm her and continued. 'However, I strongly advise against it. Having worked with your father, and being with him in that fight, I felt the same as you. It seemed like the right thing to do and a way to honour him. Yet, my chief inspector stopped me and I'm glad now. You may feel the same in a few days.'

'I won't.'

'Then fair enough. Give me a ring in…say in three days, and I'll arrange it.' Matt was relieved when she nodded. He turned to Lynne. 'As next of kin, you and Melli need to decide how much input you would like in the funeral. If you wish, we can arrange from our end and you can be sure we will honour our own. Just let me know.'

Lynne nodded.

'Is there someone I can call?'

'My husband will be calling in shortly, thank you.'

There was nothing left but for Matt to say his goodbyes. He was glad to step out and feel the cold on his face after the heated emotions.

# Chapter 64

Tilly waved goodbye to her friend Sarah and stepped out into the sun. True it kept hiding behind the scudding clouds, but the faint warmth felt good on her face and she needed some fresh air. She thought Nick wouldn't mind if she walked the short distance down the Parade.

She was looking forward to this afternoon: first lunch with Nick at their favourite Chinese at the bottom of the Parade, then the last scan. Her hands went to her belly and she smiled at the thought that soon their son would be born. He would probably be a Pisces, sensitive and artistic; at least that's what it said when she and Sarah had looked it up. She thought that would be lovely, but knew she'd love him whatever.

Adjusting her scarf to keep out the chill wind, Tilly began walking past the shops, aware that her walk was becoming more of a waddle. Just as she was nearing the Victorian town hall, an old car pulled up beside her. The passenger window was down and the driver leaned towards her.

'Special surprise taxi for Tilly.'

Tilly stopped. She didn't know the driver. Her first instinct was to keep going, but maybe Nick had arranged this. She knew he was worried after his meeting with Harry. She stopped and took a step forward.

'For me?'

'Yes.'

'But I didn't order a taxi.'

'No. It's a treat.'

'Oh. How lovely. Thank you.'

Tilly opened the back door and got in. As soon as she sat down the window slid up and she heard a click that told her the driver had locked all the doors. Her sister had this on her car to keep the children safe. But why would the driver need to do it for her? Maybe it was just a habit. She studied him and was sure she hadn't seen him before.

'Where are we going?'

'It's a surprise. Don't worry, we'll be there soon.'

Tilly sat back and tried to relax. The driver went to the bottom of the Parade and turned right, going past the railway station before turning left at the next roundabout. Maybe they were going onto the shopping estate where there was a Kentucky Fried Chicken. It had been one of her cravings in the beginning and she'd sent Nick out at all hours to get her some. It would be just like him to tease her with those memories.

As she watched the shopping centre pass by on the left, Tilly began to feel uneasy and leant forward. 'Please tell me where we're going?'

'Nearly there.'

'I think I'd better call Nick.'

'Don't do that.'

Before she had time to dial, he reached back and snatched the phone from her. She watched as he lowered his window and tossed it into the road.

Now she knew she was in trouble.

# Chapter 65

Kathy finished ironing her long skirt and hung it over the door while she started on the cape. She wished they could have had coloured costumes, instead of black. Still, the straw bonnet she'd adorned with coloured ribbons would liven it up. Today they had a technical rehearsal in the theatre and she'd made up her mind to try to forget about everything else and enjoy it.

She'd just put the ironing board away when the phone rang. At first, she couldn't hear the caller and had to ask them to speak up before realising it was her granddaughter, Phoebe. 'What is it, love? Slow down.'

'It's Mum. She won't come out of the bedroom. I've fed Amy and Zoe, but I'm not sure what to do.'

Kathy didn't hesitate. 'Don't worry, Phoebe, I'm coming over. I'll be there in about ten minutes. It will be alright. Okay, darling?'

'Yes.'

'Try not to worry. I'm on my way.'

Slamming down the phone, Kathy rushed about the house, threw a toothbrush and a few things in a bag, grabbed her costume and was ready to leave in under three minutes. Mrs Smart, her neighbour, was putting out a milk bottle as she scraped the ice off the car, so Kathy paused to tell her where she was going.

Not many motorists had ventured out early this Saturday morning, although this meant the ice was still fresh on the roads. Kathy daren't race, although she would have liked to; instead she kept to a steady, even pace.

Phoebe opened the door as she parked in the driveway. Close behind her were Amy and Zoe. At least they had each other and that was a blessing. Knowing she mustn't worry them, she entered with a smile.

'Right, let's get sorted here. I'm sure your mummy is just feeling a bit poorly. I'll just pop up and see if she needs anything. Do you want to come with me, Phoebe?'

Phoebe nodded. One foot on the bottom stair, Kathy turned to Amy and Zoe. 'Why don't you two go and watch the television? I'm sure Mummy won't mind, just this once.'

The two girls were uncertain and looked to Phoebe for confirmation. At her nod, they went into the lounge while Kathy followed Phoebe upstairs, keeping to the edge of the stair carpet as she was doing.

Kathy knocked softly on the door to the front bedroom. Not receiving any answer, she opened the door to find Pamela curled up on the bed. 'What's the matter, dear?'

Pam didn't answer so Kathy went to kneel beside her. She had been crying and again Kathy felt the urge to reach out and hug her, tell her everything would be alright. The barbed wire shield seemed lower and this might be the opportunity to reach her. She turned to Phoebe. 'Do you mind keeping an eye on the others, Phoebe, while Mum and I have a chat?'

Phoebe nodded and seemed glad to leave. Kathy risked reaching out to take hold of Pam's hand. 'Can you tell me what's the matter? I'm only here to help.'

Pam withdrew her hand and moved to sit up. Sitting back on her heels, Kathy waited.

'Amy fell down the stairs. And...and all I could think about was I must vacuum. I must be the worst mum in the world.'

Resisting the need to move forward and comfort her, Kathy stayed still, wondering what to say. Could this be an opportunity for getting Pam to seek help? She didn't want to spoil the chance, yet she couldn't help asking after Amy. 'Amy looked fine, did she hurt herself?'

'She cried and I couldn't go to her.'

'Why don't I go and see if she is alright and come back and tell you?'

Pam nodded and Kathy stood ready to go downstairs.

'Tell her I'm sorry and that I love her.'

'She knows that already. I won't be a minute.'

Downstairs the three girls were huddled together on the sofa watching some kid's programme. Phoebe jumped up as soon as Kathy entered.

'How's Mum?'

'She's worried about Amy falling down the stairs. Did you hurt yourself, Amy?'

Amy nodded and looking at her, Kathy thought she did seem

a little pale. 'Can you show me where it hurts?'

Standing, Amy lifted her tee shirt so that Kathy could see the spreading bruise under her left ribs. She touched it gently and stopped as Amy winced.

'Sorry, love. Does it hurt when you breathe in and out?' Again the nod and Kathy sought to remember the details of the first aid course she'd done at work. There was something about internal bleeding and damage to the spleen, but which side of the body it was on she could never remember. This needed medical input. 'Thanks, Amy. I'm sure it's fine, but just to be on the safe side, I think we'll get the doctor to check you over. Is that alright?'

'Yes, but Mummy—'

'I'll talk to Mummy and tell her what we have decided, okay?'

Phoebe put her arm around Amy to reassure her.

'Do you know where the doctor's phone number is, Phoebe?' Following Phoebe into the hallway, Kathy knew she must decide whether to tell Pam before or after calling the doctor. She'd be glad if the doctor could see Pam too, but if she didn't mention he was coming, Pam would be less likely to co-operate. By the time Phoebe found the number, she'd made up her mind.

'I'm just going to tell your mum that we're calling the doctor.' Kathy prayed that Pam would go along with the doctor coming.

She looked up anxiously as Kathy went into the bedroom. 'I've had a look at Amy and she has a nasty bruise under her ribs. I'm sure it will be alright, but I think we should have the doctor check it out.' Pam's hands flew to her face and she started to shake. 'I can ring him and ask him to come, if that's what you'd like. And I'm happy to stay and let him in.'

She didn't answer and Kathy began to wonder if she had heard. 'Pam?'

'Yes, please.'

'Fine, I'll ring him now.'

Downstairs, Kathy went into the kitchen. She wanted to talk to the doctor in private about Pam. Given the out of hours number, she spoke to a Dr Meredith, who seemed to understand the situation. Kathy hoped she would be able to get Pam onside.

# Chapter 66

All thought of Eppie's present had gone after his meeting with Lynne and Melli. Yet the High Street looked inviting with its shops full of tempting Christmas goodies and Matt hesitated. Should he take half an hour and choose something while he was thinking of it? He crossed one of the bridges towards more dazzling shops, but before he could reach them, his phone rang. 'Turrell. Yes, Sam. What's up?'

'Nick Tyler. Well, his girlfriend, Tilly. She's missing.'

'She's pregnant, isn't she?'

'Yes. Seven months.'

'Last seen?'

'Leaving Boots in Leamington Spa. She had a half day and was going to meet up with Nick for lunch, then have her last scan. She didn't arrive.'

'He's checked all the places she might be?'

'He seems to have done a pretty comprehensive job. Even rang the hospital. Now he's panicking and seems convinced it's down to whoever killed Jon and Dave.'

'You didn't mention Vinny?'

'Didn't need to. First thing he brought up. He's in a right state.'

'You know what to do, Sam. Get the ball rolling and I'll be back as soon as possible.'

Giving up all thoughts of Christmas shopping, Matt hurried to his car, praying Tilly hadn't fallen into Vinny's hands. He had already shown himself to be a vicious, hardened criminal.

The traffic was light, so Matt made it to the M40 motorway in good time, only having a minor hold-up trying to get past a tractor laden with bales of winter feed.

Arriving back at CID, Sam met Matt as he walked into the office.

'Had some luck with the CCTV. Shows Tilly getting into a dark green car just outside the town hall.'

'Dark green? Old Escort?'

'Could be.'

'Similar to the car at Jonathan's funeral. If it is, then Vinny has her.' Everyone stopped to listen. This was the very worst news. Vinny's handiwork, displayed on the incident board, reminded them of his capacity for violence. Tilly, a pregnant, defenceless woman, wouldn't stand a chance. They had to find her, and fast.

'Any more sightings?'

'Last seen heading down the Parade and onto the Old Warwick Road, before going down Europa Way. Picked up briefly on the M40. As no further sighting further on, we believe he took the Stratford exit. From there he had several options. I managed to get a patrol car to the Longbridge Island and another on the A46 pretty quick, in case they made the bypass. I've alerted West Midlands and West Mercia. Only one man seen in the vehicle, beside Tilly – no ID yet.'

'Tilly's mobile?'

'We've picked up a signal on Europa Way. It's now stationary. We think it's been thrown from the vehicle. Fl...Jane and uniform are searching now.'

'Well done, Sam. You okay to co-ordinate from here while I catch up with Jane?'

'I'm fine. Oh and local television will put out an appeal at 6.30 pm.'

'Good. Let Jane know I'm on my way.'

'Will do.'

Leamington was busy with Christmas shoppers and Matt wished he had a blue light to ease his way down the Parade. Once he'd turned onto the Old Warwick Road, it became easier and soon he reached Europa Way where he could see the flashing lights of the patrol car. He drew up in front and Jane came forward to hand him an evidence bag containing a mobile phone.

'Present for you, Matt. Obviously thrown from the car.'

'Damn. That cuts out one avenue in finding her.'

'Afraid so.'

'We've got the M40 and A46 well covered so while we're waiting for news, think I'll take a look at the Acorn. Don't think they would be stupid enough to use it again, but you never know. Do you want to follow me?'

'Okay. How about uniform?'

'Tell them to keep watch. Patrol from here to the A46.'

Matt left her talking to the uniform officers and drove to the

Golden Acorn. Parking outside, he shivered at the memories the place held. Forensics had gone over the upstairs room but found little except finger marks that matched the Harris brothers and Harold Harper-Jones. However, although the barman had been questioned, he had been released. Jane was only a minute behind Matt and by then he'd calmed down, rationalizing that it was only a building.

Jane hurried him on. 'Come on then.'

Inside matched his nightmares. Even the old men sat in the same place, although the rest of the pub was empty. The floor was still tacky and the barmaid remained nervous. He wondered if she was the only member of staff in the place. Taking the lead, Jane went to speak to her.

'DI Turrell and DC Meadows.' She held up her warrant card and then produced a picture of Tilly.

'Have you seen this young woman today?'

The barmaid gave a shake of her head. Jane looked at her intently and moved away to question the old men. Matt stepped forward to the barmaid and raised his eyes to the stairs. She shook her head. Jane joined him as he turned away.

'No one's seen her, guv. Did you want to look anywhere else?'

'Let's not waste time. I'm sure we won't find anything here. Let's check in, see if there have been any sightings.'

# Chapter 67

Tilly watched her phone bounce into the gutter, then began tugging frantically at the door with no success. How could she have been so stupid? Nick would be waiting for her, all her favourites ordered, and he would be getting worried. She felt like crying but knew it wouldn't do any good. Maybe she could open the window and shout for help. With her eye on the driver, she reached for the handle only to find it immovable. Sliding over to the driver's side, she tried again with no luck. Feeling the baby kick increased her panic. She had to survive for his sake. What would happen if she hit the driver? There was a risk this would make them crash but she considered the risk worth it. Using all her strength, she punched the back of his head. He laughed.

'That will do you no good. I'd sit back if I were you.'

Where was he taking her? They were taking the slip road onto the M40 and then the exit road to Stratford before going onto the A46 towards Coventry. After that, with panic setting in, Tilly lost track. Nick would never be able to find her this far away. She sat back, hands over her belly, trying to calm herself and think. After about twenty minutes, they went under an aqueduct before turning immediately left into a pub car park. The pub was busy with the lunchtime trade and for a moment, Tilly became hopeful until the driver went past the parked cars and drew up beside the canal where the narrowboats moored.

The driver parked and clicked open the doors. 'Here we are.'

Tilly held back.

'Let's get you into the warm. He only wants to talk.'

Moving with as much speed as she could muster, Tilly shot across to the other door intending to make a run for it, but the man moved faster and grabbed her arm before she had gone two steps.

'None of that. Or he won't be pleased.'

He pulled her up the grassy bank, leading her to one of the

smallest boats and pushed her onto the deck. 'Go down into the cabin,' he ordered.

Tilly had no option but to do as she was told. Inside it was dim and she stumbled down the last few steps. Someone caught her roughly and pressed her down on to a small bench. The man towered over her and his raw sweat made her want to heave. Now her eyes were becoming used to the dimness she recognised him.

'Mr James.'

'Yes, I'm glad you know me, saves the introductions. How about my boy, Jonathan, do you remember him?'

'Of course.'

He bent over her, arms on the table.

'Yet you couldn't be bothered to go to his funeral, could you?'

'I couldn't get there – don't drive.'

'You didn't care for him at all, did you? Just leading him on, weren't you?'

'No.'

Tilly backed away, but Vinny came closer; his hand reached out to grasp a handful of her hair to pull her towards him.

'I see your type all the time. Little users. Well now you are going to help me, and my boy, by telling me all you know. You see, I'm going to enjoy making whoever killed him pay, and pay big. This is where you come in. You're going to tell me all about his so-called mates.'

'I don't know them, not anymore.'

'Oh you'll have to do better than that, girlie. You wouldn't want anything to happen to that little worm in your belly now, would you?'

He dropped his hand to caress her abdomen. The very touch of him made her want to retch. Tilly tried to push his hand away but couldn't.

'Whose is it? Young Nick's? Now he's certainly in my sights. Getting his life back together, consorting with Jon's girl. Maybe he wanted to get rid of the competition. He's definitely someone I should look closely at. And his mate, Harry. Maybe they did it together?'

'No. Please, let me go.'

'You know. I'm sure of it.'

'I don't know anything, honest.'

'Oh, you'll have to do better...or this little bastard...'

His hand pressed deep and she felt her baby kick against it. She had to make him stop. It burst out: 'Harry knows.'

'What?'

'Who did it.'

Tilly squirmed as his fingers bit into her belly. She had to make him get off her. 'Please.'

'Who killed my boy? Tell me, you stupid bitch or I'll rip this brat from you with my bare hands.'

'It was Kathy Wylde.'

At last, Vinny stood back.

Hearing footsteps on the deck, Tilly opened her mouth to scream. Vinny clapped his hand over her mouth, forcing her head back against the bulkhead. The man from the car shot down the steps into the cabin. He had a look of urgency about him.

'He's here. Says you're to let her go. Right now.'

'Calm down. I give the orders.'

'He says if you don't, he'll phone the police himself.'

'He can say what he likes. I'm paying him. Here, stay with her. I'll sort him out. Keep her quiet.'

Vinny left and Tilly wanted to wipe away the touch of him. Instead, she took a deep breath and tried to think. She had to get out of here. This man didn't seem frightening at all after Vinny. Trying for a smile, she faced him. He seemed embarrassed and turned his head away. This gave her a chance to look around, try to find a way out or a weapon. There was a heavy black frying pan on the little stove. She noted that as a possibility, if she could get a swing in this tiny place. Aside from that, there was nothing. Attempting to get her jumble of thoughts in order, she remembered watching the narrowboats when she was small and was sure most of them had two entrances.

From outside came the sound of voices raised in anger. She shifted slightly and tried to see but only caught a glimpse of two pairs of legs. 'Please can I go to the toilet?'

The man looked at her as if she had asked to go to the moon. 'Can't you wait?'

'No. I'm pregnant.'

The man glanced outside. 'I guess it can't hurt. There, on the left. And remember, I'll be right outside.'

'Thank you.' Giving the man a shy smile, Tilly squeezed past him into the narrow corridor. He followed her. The cubicle was small, especially with her baby bulge. The tiny window offered no way of escape. She hadn't thought the man would follow and stand outside. How could she get rid of him?

'I'm sorry, but there doesn't seem to be any toilet paper.' Ear pressed to the door, she prayed he would go to look for some. There was a pause and she could almost hear his brain ticking, then the slow thud of his footsteps moving back into the cabin.

Knowing she would only have seconds, Tilly slid open the door and turned away from the cabin towards the rear of the boat, waiting for the shout telling her to stop. She came to the end of the corridor and opened the door. Inside a double bed filled most of the cabin and she looked about frantically for a way out, stopping when she heard heated voices. Looking out one of the windows, she realised she was closer here to the two men and sank down out of sight. She couldn't see the other man as Vinny was in the way, but his voice sounded more refined.

'I cannot tolerate this constant disobedience. You have carelessly put my associates and me in danger. Despite offering you my help '

'At a price.'

'Despite offering you my expert advice, you choose to ignore it. I've passed at least two patrol cars in this area. The police will be tracking the Escort and could be here at any minute.'

'That's it?'

'Besides putting me at risk, I cannot countenance the kidnapping of a young, pregnant woman.'

'Ever the gentleman. What about the cop? The one you bumped off. It was on the news.'

'That was an unfortunate occurrence and not planned.'

'Try telling the cops that. You're forgetting what you owe me?'

'Not by any means.'

'If I get caught, I'll take you down with me.'

'That wouldn't be wise. If that happened, I may be forced to appropriate certain funds you have entrusted to my care.'

'You filthy sodding crook. I should wring your rotten neck.'

'You certainly have that choice, but it might be wiser to let me get you out of your immediate dilemma, thereby reducing the risk to both of us. I am willing to arrange return to your safe haven, as this would protect both of us. However, if I am to do this safely, it might take a little time. For now, I have arranged a safe house where you will stay until I can arrange to get you back to Spain. If you agree, I will gladly refund your fee, taking out only my costs.'

'Big deal.'

'I'll take that as a yes. Fetch your things and lock the girl in – that will give us a head start. Dan knows what to do with the boat.'

Tilly couldn't hear much after that as the men moved away, but she saw Vinny's legs moving back towards the boat and looked around for somewhere to hide. There was nowhere and for a moment, she felt like crying. She could hear the man who had brought her here still rummaging about in cupboards. What would they do with her? Realising that she may have to fight her way out, she picked up a large glass ashtray from beside the bed and stood trembling by the door. The smell of stubbed-out cigarettes was close to her nose and she didn't know how long she could hold it at the ready.

Tilly could hear a mumbled conversation. Then the engine started up and there was a loud clang. For what seemed a long time she held the ashtray aloft, before putting it down and listening to the silence before gathering the courage to open the door a crack. There was no sign of life and she crept out to make sure, checking the bathroom on the way.

Weak with relief, she sat down by the table, wondering why the little cabin looked different before realising that the doors out to the deck were closed. Jumping up she tried to open them, but they wouldn't budge. She had to get out of here before the men returned. It was then she heard the trickle of water.

# Chapter 68

After leaving the Golden Acorn, Matt picked up PC Charlie Baker and set off for the A46 where a dark green Escort had been seen taking the Warwick exit. From there the Escort may have gone into Warwick or turned left to Henley-in-Arden. With the help of all available patrol cars, Jane would check the Warwick side while Matt took the route towards Henley.

Charlie reminded him of the presenter on *Crimewatch* but Matt couldn't waste time thinking about that now; he was thankful that he was quiet and intense as he wanted to concentrate on finding Tilly.

They raced towards the A46 bypass but once they reached the road to Henley, Matt slowed down, looking for any sign of the green car and woefully aware of the hundreds of places it could have turned off. Reaching the traffic lights at Henley, Matt decided to turn left towards Stratford. By the time they reached Wootton Wawen, Matt was convinced they didn't stand a chance in hell of finding Tilly. Then, just past the Navigation Inn, Charlie called out.

'Sir, there's a green car there, further back.'

Matt put on the turn signal, ignoring the motorist who sounded his horn at his late decision, and turned into the disused forecourt of a gas station. He could see the Escort now and it looked like the car that had been at the crematorium. Pulling up to block the Escort, he jumped out, shouting to Charlie as he did. 'Good work, Constable. Let everyone know we've found it.'

The car was empty and, holding his breath, he moved to open the boot, praying that it would be empty. It was locked, and with frustration building, he called to Charlie. 'Find something to open this.'

Charlie went to the boot of Matt's car and came over with a tyre lever, applying pressure until it sprang open. They both sighed in relief at the empty space.

'She could be around here somewhere or they might have just

switched to another car. Let's get SOCO onto those tyre tracks and have a good look around.' Matt started back towards the pub, leaving Charlie to check out the canal. He'd only gone a few yards when Charlie called out.

'Sir, over here.'

Recognising the urgency in his voice, Matt ran to join him, finding him standing beside a narrowboat, one of several moored along the canal. But this boat looked different from the others, lower in the water and listing to one side.

'I thought I heard someone inside.'

'Call the fire brigade. I'll check it out.'

The boat was listing away from him so Matt couldn't see anything through the windows. Taking off his heavy coat and jacket, he stepped onto the sloping deck only to find himself skidding down the icy deck towards the water. Grasping onto the tiller, he managed to right himself and began to drag himself up to the cabin doors.

'Tilly, are you there?' Listening, all he could hear was the gurgling water. 'Tilly!'

There was a faint voice from inside. 'Help me.'

'Coming. Don't worry, we'll get you out of there. Charlie, the tyre lever.'

Tugging frantically at the frozen lock made his fingers bleed. Matt stood back to get the balance for a kick, but found himself in another sickening slide down the slippery deck. Scrabbling madly for something to hold onto, he fought against the shock of the arctic water before managing to lock his fingers around the deck rail.

Hauling himself up, he saw Charlie's anxious face; he'd taken off his heavy gear and was ready to come after Matt. For a moment, Matt wanted to laugh at his relief, then seeing the rope in his hands, to cheer for such a practical PC.

'Tie this around you, sir.'

The rope landed at Matt's feet and he risked letting go with one hand to catch it. Fumbling with deadened fingers, it was difficult knotting the rope around himself, as he daren't let go with both hands. The boat was now on its side and, after tying the rope, he manoeuvred his way to the top where he could see through the murky panes down into the cabin. The water was pouring in. He couldn't see Tilly and knew he had to act fast. The quickest way in would be through the window. He shouted just in case.

'Stay back, Tilly!'

One kick shattered the window and Matt plunged through feet first, ignoring the jagged pieces that tore into him. He seemed to have landed on something that kept him out of the deepest water. Adjusting to the gloom, he glanced around, relieved to see a pair of terrified eyes looking back at him just above the waterline opposite.

'Thank God. Tilly, I want you to reach out and grasp my arm. You're safe now and we'll soon have you out of here.'

Tilly nodded and stretched out her arm. Although he had spoken to reassure her, Matt was far from certain that they would both get out alive. It would only take a sudden settling of the boat and they could both be lost, yet he knew the calmer Tilly remained the easier it would be.

'Great, I've got you. I'm going to pull you towards me, tie a rope around you and get you out through the window, okay?' There was no time to wait and Matt pulled hard and felt her bump into his side. He shifted sideways so she could find a footing beside him, but she began to sink and panicking, pulled him down. Covered in the icy, muddy water, Matt fought to control his fear as he grabbed her under the shoulders and pushed her upward. Breaking water, he was relieved to see that she held firmly on to the window ledge.

Untying the rope, he slipped it around her. Tying it seemed to take an inordinate amount of time but finally it was secure. Tilly was limp and he wasn't sure how much she would be able to help. As he knocked the worst of the broken glass out of the way, he shouted for Charlie to pull while trying to encourage her. 'Once you are out of this window, Tilly, you are going to be fine – my colleague is at the end of the rope. I'm going to help from this end.'

He wasn't sure how much she took in, as her lips were blue and her eyes unfocused. Taking a deep breath, he dived into deeper water to push her from behind, forgetting all modesty. She finally cleared the window frame and he surfaced to see Charlie reaching out to receive her.

The panic over, he felt tired and would have given anything to shut his eyes. He could hear Charlie shouting and the sound of emergency vehicles arriving, but they all seemed far away and nothing to do with him. Then he felt something hit him sharply across the face. Puzzled, he realised it was the rope and knew he must rouse himself and make an effort. Imagining Eppie, he conjured up reserves from somewhere and clung on, easing himself out of the window. Warm hands reached out to help and soon he was sprawled, shivering violently, on the towpath.

As a firefighter put a foil blanket around him, he sat up, turning to watch the boat give a final gurgle and sink.

Charlie knelt beside him. 'Tilly's on her way to hospital, sir. They think she's going to be alright.'

'Thank God.'

'There's another ambulance coming for you. Should be here any minute.'

'I haven't got time.'

'You'd better listen to him, Matt.'

Matt looked up to see Jane standing by the firefighter.

'I'll be fine. Help me up.'

'This is what he's like, Ethan.'

Matt was surprised to hear her addressing the man in such a familiar way. Ethan crouched down beside him.

'This is serious, mate. You need to listen. Your core temperature is bound to be low after taking a dip in that. If you go racing around now, you could bring on a heart attack. Believe me, I've seen it happen. Whatever is going on, it's just not worth it.'

'Matt, please go and get checked out,' Jane added.

Ethan handed Matt a plastic cup filled with hot chocolate. He took it gratefully, glad of the warmth. Besieged from all sides, Matt gave in, conscious that it made sense. While they were fussing over him, Vinny was getting further away. An ambulance pulled up behind them. 'Okay, okay. Maybe I'll catch up with Tilly while I'm there.'

Jane sighed and looked up at Ethan, who to Matt seemed enormous in all his gear.

# Chapter 69

Vinny crouched low so that the dense hedge hid him. Just three more houses to go and he would be home. Not that it was his home anymore but he had something to collect and had a few choice things to say to Mary.

He had waited until dusk before leaving the safe house provided by Ops and had planned his route with care. Not much had changed since he'd left, except the occasional new garden shed, complete with padlock, and the height of some of the hedges, intended to hide the occupants from their neighbours. He was grateful that people insisted on privacy as they offered him greater cover.

Moving on, he stopped to peer through number six's ten-foot monstrosity, cursing as the thorns caught his jacket. As he pulled himself free, he caught a flash of yellow and froze and watched as the patrol car slowed in front of Mary's. He'd guessed the bastards would be keeping an eye on the place. Looking at his watch, he noted the time, five past five, and estimated their next pass would be around six o'clock. Mary should be home soon, and he aimed to be safely inside by then.

Reaching his own backyard, he squeezed through the broken fence and flattened himself against the rear of the shed. It had grown more decrepit in his absence and he hoped Mary hadn't felt the need to follow her neighbours' examples and protect the rusting tools and old paint tins with a lock. The house was in darkness and he needed to find what he came for before she arrived home. The first thing she would do is turn on the kitchen light and the shed was directly in its path.

Slipping around to the front of the shed, he was relieved that all was as he left it. Opening the door, he held his breath at its grinding squeak and crept inside. The smell of earth, paraffin and paint was comforting and he paused to let it wash over him, not daring to turn on the light, even if it still worked, as that would give him away. Instead, he began to feel amongst the debris, freezing when he heard footsteps approaching. However, it was only the next-door neighbour, who obligingly turned on a bedroom light that allowed a faint glow to penetrate the grimy window.

In the glimmer, Vinny could see the petrol tin tucked in next to the old lawnmower. Picking it up, he was relieved when the weight reassured him it was still there. The rusting false bottom fell to pieces as he pushed against it, allowing the package to fall into his hand. Eagerly fumbling with the oilcloth, he savoured the cold metal and a surge of power rushed through him. The cops wouldn't expect this and it shifted the balance in his favour. It would need a good oiling but he could do that in the comfort of the house. Stuffing the gun, ammunition and oil into his pockets he left the shed, needing to get into position before Mary came home.

By the time he heard her footsteps crunching on the icy path, his legs were cramping and he was shuddering with cold. It was rubbish collection day tomorrow and if Mary followed her usual practice, she would enter the house through the back door, put down her bag and take the bin out to the street, leaving him time to slip into the house. He relished confronting her about all her failings.

# Chapter 70

Minus his wet clothes and wrapped in warm blankets, Matt still shivered as he gave in to the administrations of the male nurse. He'd been here a lot in the last few days and all he wanted was to stop shivering and get out.

As he lay back and tried to relax, he caught a glimpse of Charlie hovering outside, but before he could call out, a female doctor entered and picked up his chart.

'I understand you're a bit of a hero, Detective Inspector Turrell.'

'No way.'

'Well I hope you don't take dips into frozen water for fun. Our main concern is your core temperature. You've been very lucky and have only suffered mild hypothermia. However, your temperature is below normal so we'll need to bring it back up slowly and need to keep an eye on you for a bit before we let you go. My colleague will be setting up a drip and an oxygen mask. And although that wound is healing nicely, I think we'd better give you antibiotic cover. There are some nasty things in that canal. Do you have any questions?'

'How soon can I get out of here?'

'I would like to keep an eye on you overnight and assess you in the morning. Then it will depend how stable you are.'

'No chance of making it home tonight?'

'It wouldn't be wise.'

Matt sighed, feeling like he was wasting his time. The doctor interrupted his thoughts.

'Look, I go off duty hopefully at ten. How about I come back and give you the once-over before then? I might be able to discharge you, if you promise to rest. Best I can offer.'

'I'd really appreciate that. Thanks. Is the PC outside?'

'The one pacing like an expectant father?'

'That'll be him. Could I have a word?'

'I'll send him in.'

When the doctor had gone, Matt let the nurse insert a cannula in his arm ready for the drip and fasten the oxygen mask around his face. Charlie came in looking worried.

'Sir.'

'Worse than it looks. I'll need you to let DS Withers, Sam, know how things are here. I may not be out until morning. Could you also phone my wife, taking care not to scare her? I'll give you the details.'

'No problem, sir.'

'Have we heard how Tilly Rowlands is doing?'

'No, except she went to ICU. I'll find out and report back, sir.'

'After what we went through, I'd drop the sir. Make it Matt or guv, unless the higher ranks are around.'

'Thanks, s...guv.'

After giving Charlie Eppie's details, Matt allowed his eyes to close as the warmth began to spread through him. He had no idea how long he dozed, but woke up to find Jane standing by his side.

'Hi, Matt, how are you feeling?'

'Ready to get out of here. What time is it?'

'Nearly nine.'

'Bloody hell.' Matt made a move to get up, forgetting his attachments.

'Hey, hold on.'

'Have we caught Vinny James yet?'

'No, but, Matt, we're doing everything possible. It won't be long. There's nothing more you or anyone else can do.'

Matt sank back and noticed one of his old jogging suits on the bedside chair.

'Eppie's been?'

'Yes. She was here when I arrived. I sent her to get a coffee. Oh and the latest update regarding Tilly is that she is stable but has been moved to the labour ward.'

'But the baby's not due yet.'

'Matt, she's in the right place, thanks to you, so stop worrying.'

'Is Nick with her? We should have a word with him.'

'If you think I'm going in there to drag him out, I won't do it.'

Despite himself, Matt laughed. Jane was back on form. This led him to wondering about the fireman. What had she called him? He couldn't help asking.

'So who's your pet fireman?'

Jane sighed as if expecting the question. 'We're seeing each other. He was in physio the same time as me, and, well, we just got on. He makes me laugh.'

For a moment, Matt felt jealous. 'I'm glad.'

'Thanks. You'll like Ethan.'

'He's why – your nickname?'

'Yes, he didn't like it.'

'Fair enough.'

Any further discussion stopped when Eppie arrived, followed by the doctor, who checked him over and said he could go home if he promised to rest. Eppie reassured her he would and Matt couldn't scramble into his clothes fast enough.

# Chapter 71

As soon as Mary began trundling the bin to the pavement, Vinny crept forward, knowing he only had seconds to get inside the house. He was relieved that she had left the back door unlocked and crept inside, letting the warmth sweep over him as he stretched his legs. Everything must look normal and he didn't want to alert the patrol car. It would be best to let Mary settle in for a cosy evening thinking she was safe. Deciding to hide in Jon's room, he made his way through the dark hallway and upstairs to the back bedroom.

Inside reminded him of Jon, all teenage sweat and secrets. He fought a wave of sadness by balling his hands into fists. If only the lad had listened to him, leant on his wisdom, he'd have taught him how to take care of himself, how to deal with the likes of Jack Wylde.

Sighing, he took the gun, oil and bullets out of his pockets and dropped them on the bed. Although he daren't turn on a light, the gun was an old friend and he could clean it in the semi-dark while listening to the noises below. He heard Mary go into the living room, turn on the television and pull the curtains before turning on the hall light. This allowed a narrow beam to pass under the door of Jon's room.

By the time the wonderful aroma of Mary's stew drifted up the stairs, the gun was fully oiled and loaded and Vinny realised how hungry he was. Wondering if he should stroll down and surprise her, he checked his watch, saw it was nearly seven o'clock and time for the patrol car to pass. He'd wait another half hour and interrupt *Coronation Street*, one of her favourite soaps. That would feel good.

Hearing the familiar signature tune, he tiptoed down the stairs and slowly opened the door to the lounge. She didn't see him at first but when she turned, Vinny relished the look of horror on her face.

'Mary.'

'You can't be here. They're looking for you.' She glanced towards the window.

'But I am here, and no, it's not time for the patrol car. I thought we could have a cosy evening in. You are my wife, after all.'

She seemed to be recovering and stood. 'I'm not your wife and I've nothing to say to you.'

'Oh yes you have. I want to know what happened to Jon.'

'You turned him into a bully. That's what got him killed.'

Vinny hit out with the flat of his hand, knocking her back onto the sofa. At first, he thought he had knocked her out, but then she rallied and drew herself to the far end without taking her eyes off him.

'You'd have turned him into a mummy's boy.'

'He was never that. Didn't stand a chance with you around. Neither of us did.'

'He needed discipline, just like you.'

'He needed love.'

'Twaddle.'

'You wanted him to be like you, nothing else mattered.'

'I wanted him to be a man. To be able to stand up for himself. That's what men do.'

'He was a boy. Just a boy. My boy.'

Mary began to cry. Vinny knew from experience she wouldn't be fit for anything if he allowed her to carry on. 'We can talk later. Now get me some dinner. And don't try anything.' Vinny pulled back his jacket to show the gun tucked into his trousers.

Wiping her eyes, Mary stood, giddy from the blow, to move warily past him into the kitchen. Vinny followed. As he guessed, there was plenty of stew left. Mary always made it last a few days. He gobbled it up, wiping around the plate with a chunk of bread. It was years since he'd enjoyed a good English stew and it mellowed his mood. Once he'd finished, he ordered Mary to find some booze, knowing there was usually something in the house around Christmas. He just hoped it wasn't sherry or some other women's rubbish. She brought out a bottle of decent whisky, explaining it was a gift for someone at work. He'd rather have a beer, but this was better than nothing and he snatched the bottle out of her hand, before ordering her back into the lounge. She chose to sit in a chair by the fire, leaving him to sprawl on the sofa. A red mark highlighted her cheekbone.

'Why have you come?'

'I told you, I want to know how my boy came to be murdered. No one is going to do that and get away with it. Not even you.'

'You're crazy if you think I wanted this to happen.'

'You should have controlled him.'

'That was impossible after what you turned him into.'

Vinny put down the whisky bottle and took out the gun, moving across to Mary and waving it in her face. 'I'm not listening to this.' He grabbed her arm, pulling her up. 'You can sit over here with me. A husband has needs.'

As he pushed her down on the sofa, he watched her shudder and laughed. He sat down and pulled her close, one arm around her shoulder dropping down to her breast, making sure that his fingernails bit into the soft flesh. She stayed rigid, like a mouse playing dead with a cat. Slowly moving the gun around her face to end at her lips, he chuckled.

'Now you are going to tell me everything.' He was pleased to hear the tremor in her voice.

'I don't know who killed Jon.'

'I'm not asking that. I know who killed him. I'll deal with her later.'

She seemed bemused. 'Her?'

'Yes, another stupid bitch, Kathy Wylde.'

'Oh my God.'

'And I wouldn't be surprised if his friend Harry didn't have something to do with it. But don't you worry, I'm going to sort them both out.'

Vinny laid the gun on his lap and reached for the whisky bottle. This silly cow couldn't tell him much, but he may as well enjoy himself while he was here. She was no match for the young senoritas who came willingly to his bed, lured by expensive gifts, but her reluctance was turning him on. He could feel himself getting hard and decided to continue upstairs.

First, he made her go through her normal night-time routine, just in case the patrol car noticed anything different. Coming to the hall, she hesitated by the light switch, so he leaned forward and snapped it off. Pushing the gun into her back, he forced her upstairs, conscious he'd have to be out of here before dawn. Thanks to Dan and his parting gift, he knew where to find both Kathy Wylde and Harry. And they were next.

# Chapter 72

Vinny turned up the collar of his old workman's coat. He'd hoped never to wear it again but for now it was a godsend, as it would make him look like just another worker setting off on an early shift.

Before dawn, he'd rummaged in the hall cupboard looking for his winter fleece and found this coat with its fluorescent bands. It reminded him of when he worked as a lackey on the council's gritting team, before he'd realised that working for a living was a mug's game. Together with his old lunchbox, it made the perfect disguise. The gun fitted easily into the lunchbox and fumbling in the dark kitchen, he managed to put together a ham sandwich that fitted neatly on top.

There was no sound from Mary, but he'd expected that. Silly cow had turned awkward. He supposed it was because he'd not been there to keep her in line. Vinny did what was necessary. Not that he intended to see her again, but a man had to keep control over what was his.

Peering out through a gap in the curtains, he watched the patrol car pass. Now he could slip out of the house by the back door, past the shed and go through the hedge. Safely in the next street, he headed into town, intending to catch the first bus to Stratford. Despite the walk to the top of the Parade warming him, he was glad of the heavy coat and turned up the collar to protect against the chill.

Although a couple of police cars passed by, they only gave him a fleeting glance and Vinny congratulated himself on his disguise. By the time he reached the bus stop he still had twenty minutes to wait. He didn't fancy standing on show for that length of time so crossed to a nearby all-night petrol station that had a coffee machine. The coffee warmed his hands and by the time he got back, he was relieved to see two other men waiting. He grunted a greeting and leaned back against the wall.

The bus arrived late and with the coffee finished and the cold seeping into his boots, he was glad to enter into its warmth, opting for upstairs where he could keep an eye out for cops. Heading out of Leamington towards Warwick, the houses and streets showed white in a thick hoar frost and coming to open fields, it looked like snow had fallen.

The journey meandered through numerous villages and the icy roads slowed their progress. More than once Vinny had felt the wheels lose their grip and begin to slide, causing him to clutch the seat in front and hold his breath.

By the time they arrived at the bottom of Bridge Street in Stratford, he was glad to get off. He was delighted to find the McDonald's right by the bus stop had just opened and decided to treat himself to breakfast while thinking over what he intended to do to Kathy Wylde.

# Chapter 73

The call came at five thirty when Matt was in a deep sleep dreaming of being in a snowy landscape from which he couldn't escape. The call could only mean trouble, so he snatched up his phone and went into the bathroom, blinking as he turned on the light. 'Turrell.'

'Sorry to disturb you, sir. Mary James has been taken to University Hospital after being found beaten. She is asking for you. Doctor says her condition is critical, otherwise I wouldn't have disturbed you.'

'That's fine. You did the right thing. I'll get there ASAP, and thanks.'

Matt dressed as quietly as possible, not wanting to wake Eppie, who would try to stop him going. He decided to risk putting the kettle on for a cup of instant coffee, just to make sure he was fully awake, even though the bump on the sofa bed tossed and moaned.

Less than ten minutes later, he was turning onto the A46 heading to Coventry, glad of the almost deserted roads but wishing they weren't so arctic. Only a short time later he pulled up at the emergency entrance of University Hospital, Coventry, parked and left his card on the dashboard.

Inside, the department looked busy and knowing he couldn't afford to wait in the queue this time, he went straight to the front to show his warrant card. The rest of the queue eyed him with distaste while the receptionist put up a finger indicating he should wait while she dialled a number. He tried to wait without looking impatient and was finally directed along a corridor to the right.

Matt's long strides took him along the corridor at speed. When a doctor stepped out of a room to his left, he flashed his warrant card at the man. 'Mary James?'

'This way.'

'How is...?'

'She's taken a terrific beating, Inspector. If she hadn't been asking for you, I would specify no visitors.'

'Chances?'

'Not good. If you know of any family?'

'There is a brother. I believe he lives up north. We'll try to contact him. Aside from that, no one else, except for the bastard who did this to her.'

The doctor nodded. 'She's in here. Please try to keep it short. I'll be back in a minute.'

'Of course.'

The doctor moved away, leaving Matt at the door to a single room. Dreading what lay behind it and berating himself for not forcing McRay into providing better protection, he pushed open the door. Lying in the bed, Mary James looked smaller. Her right arm was immobilised in one of those temporary plasters and he hardly recognised her face. Both eyes were swollen red and black with bruises and every inch of her face was covered in a similar pattern. A host of tubes led to the machines that surrounded her. Burning anger rose at the thought anyone could do this to a defenceless woman.

Not sure if she was awake, he tiptoed to the bedside.

'Mary.'

There was no response so Matt looked for a spot without a bruise and found one on her left hand. He touched it softly.

'Mary. Mrs James, it's Inspector Turrell.'

Matt thought her eyes fluttered slightly but it was hard to see with the swelling. He leaned in towards her. 'Mary.' Her hand moved under his.

'Inspector.' Her voice was little above a whisper.

'I'm here, Mary.'

'Vinny.'

'He did this to you?'

Her voice was faint and he only just managed to hear her. 'Yes.'

Matt swore to himself he would make Vinny James pay for both Mary and Dave, somehow, sometime. He bent forward as Mary spoke again.

'He knows.'

'What does he know, Mary?'

Mary gave a long sigh and it was obvious to Matt that her strength was failing. He became aware that the doctor was standing on the opposite side of the bed. 'I think you had better wrap it up, Inspector.'

'One more question. She is trying to tell me something.'

'Just one then.'

Matt went as close to Mary as possible. 'What does Vinny know, Mary?'

'Who killed my boy.'

'Who was it?' Matt had to ask despite the glare from the doctor.

Matt bent close as Mary murmured, 'Kathy…Harry.'

'You really have to stop now, Inspector.'

'Of course.' Matt turned to Mary. 'I'll sort it all out. You just get well and I'll come back and tell you all about it.'

Matt couldn't tell if she had heard so brushed her hand again, frightened in case his touch hurt her. There was no response. Matt turned to the doctor. 'Anything she needs. Keep me informed, please.'

He handed over his card and left, glad to be out in the corridor and ashamed of a tear that threatened. Mary James hadn't had much of a life and she didn't deserve it to end like this. Pushing down the sadness, he found it replaced with anger and the desperate need for action.

# Chapter 74

By the time the rest of the team arrived, Matt had been hard at work for over an hour. Mary James's brother was on his way from Sheffield. The hunt for Vinny James had intensified and his picture had been circulated to all surrounding forces, ports and airports. The owner of the narrowboat, a Joe Richard, would need a visit. SOCO had not been able to find any distinctive tyre tracks that hadn't been trampled by the emergency vehicles. Uniform teams searching for Kathy and Harry were having no luck and Matt hoped they weren't already in Vinny's clutches. He felt impatient and wanted to be doing something active, but with tiredness threatening to overtake him, he took a break and called Eppie. She answered straight away and he guessed she had been anxious, so he tried to dispel her fears without giving any details of what was going on.

'Hope I didn't wake you.'

'Hey, you needed the sleep more than me.'

'Way it goes.'

'Must be serious?'

Matt chose his words carefully. 'Yes, but hopefully moving towards closure.'

'That would be good.'

'Must go. Team starting to arrive.'

'Matt, please take care.' She paused. 'Oh, I'm sorry, that sounds like we're in one of those old westerns, doesn't it?'

Despite himself, Matt laughed. 'Sure does, partner. Don't worry, I'll see you soon back at the ranch. But I may not make the concert, so say sorry to your mum and Ida.'

'If I didn't know you better, I'd say you planned this, Sheriff Turrell.'

'Definitely not. Scout's honour.'

Jane was the first to arrive, bringing with her the delicious smell of bacon baps and drinkable coffee. Sam followed soon after. Their presence and the welcome breakfast re-energised Matt and once again, he gave silent thanks for such a great team. He outlined what had been set in place and together they went over their plan of action. Sam would visit the owner of the narrowboat, and then try to track down Harry, while Matt and Jane went to look for Kathy.

The roads remained treacherous, the few cars cautious, provoking Matt's sense of urgency and making him glad that Jane was driving.

'Relax, Matt. It won't help if we end up in a ditch.'

'Sorry, didn't realise it showed.'

'Try taking a deep breath, and let it out slowly through your mouth. I learnt that in hospital. Seems to work for me.'

Matt did as she suggested and felt his muscles begin to unclench. It had been a pig of a week, with one thing after the other. No time to think about Grant and the issues around his death, issues he'd pushed to the back of his mind. No one blamed him but he still questioned his decision to leave Grant and seek help. How would it have turned out if he had stayed? Would he have ended up dead alongside Grant? He thought of Eppie and shivered.

Jane glanced at him. 'We've got through worse than this.'

He nodded, thinking of Mary. She probably wouldn't get through what Vinny had done to her. 'I don't want that bastard to harm any-one else.'

'We'll get him.'

Although Matt agreed, he was feeling far from certain and breathed a sigh of relief when they pulled into Kathy's driveway. No lights were visible in the house. Matt jumped out of the car as soon as Jane eased it to a stop. Before he rang the bell, Matt put his ear to the door but could hear nothing. Jane joined him.

'I'll check the back.'

Matt waited until she had gone along the side passage before ringing to hear the sound reverberate through the house. He rang again while glancing at his watch. Eight fifteen – there was a chance that Kathy Wylde was still asleep but he doubted that, as uniform had called earlier and also received no answer.

A man came out of the house next door, car keys in his hand, stopping when he saw Matt. 'Can I help you?'

'You may be able to, sir. I am Detective Inspector Turrell.' Matt paused to show his warrant card. 'We are concerned for the safety of Mrs Wylde. Can you tell me when you last saw her?'

'You need my wife, officer. I'll just ask her.' He stopped before going back indoors. 'Although I did hear a couple of other people at her door earlier on, she could have left with one of them.'

'Two different callers. At different times?'

'Yes.'

'Can you recall the time of those callers?'

'First one was early, before the alarm clock went off, so about seven fifteen. The second about fifteen minutes later.'

'Do you know if the door was answered on either of those occasions?'

'Couldn't say, officer, I don't make a habit of listening to my neighbours' comings and goings.'

'Of course not, sir.'

Matt's mind was racing. Vinny must have been the caller at seven fifteen, as the patrol car reported no answer at seven thirty. Was Kathy lying inside, beaten like Mary or worse? He had to get in there.

# Chapter 75

Sam drove through the countryside towards Kineton, heading for the Richards' farm. Passing Compton Verney art gallery on the right, he knew he wasn't far away. He'd heard that the grounds of Compton Verney had been designed by Capability Brown and decided to take a look in the spring. Maybe Clare would enjoy it. Their first date had gone well but he was keeping the information to himself to avoid the inevitable ribbing.

Finding the Richards' farm, he turned onto a winding dirt track leading through fields of wintergreens. He guessed sprouts as he could see pickers in the distance. Coming to some outbuildings next to a redbrick farmhouse, he parked in the muddy yard and headed for the house.

A voice called him back. 'In here.'

Sam changed direction and headed towards one of the outbuildings, hoping it didn't contain any cows. Since finding himself alone and terrified in the middle of a herd on a school trip, he'd been careful not to put himself in that situation again.

Adjusting his eyes after leaving the brightness outside, he looked around, surprised to see rows and rows of theatrical costumes.

'You from the Snitterfield Players? I'll have your costumes ready in about ten minutes.' The speaker, a woman of about sixty adorned with a tape measure and many pins, came from behind one of the rails, arms full of costumes that she dumped on a long wooden table.

Sam stepped forward to introduce himself. 'DS Withers. Sorry to interrupt but I'm looking for a Mr Joe Richard.'

'Someone rang. This about the boat?'

'Yes, that's right.'

'Well, you're out of luck. I tried to tell them he wasn't here. Here, hold that against yourself will you, love. You're about five ten, aren't you?' She thrust a vivid pink flounced dress at him, leaving Sam little choice. 'Pantomime season, always a nightmare,' she explained while she checked the length.

Handing the dress back to her, he attempted to get back to the agenda. 'Mr Richard?'

'Father-in-law. He's away with the darts team. Lives and breathes for it now he's retired.'

'Would your husband know anything about the *Daisy Lou*?'

'Doubt it. It was Joe's. Although he didn't have much to do with it either.'

'So you don't know who rented it?'

'Didn't know anyone had. This is my sideline. Keeps me more than busy.' She turned to a notebook and made a tick against the pink dress before putting it to one side.

'Is your husband around?'

'Gone to Cheltenham. Looking at some heifers.'

'When is Joe back?'

'Couple of days. You can leave a message?'

Seeing she was looking from him to a garish bonnet, Sam backed away, holding out his card. 'If you could ask either your husband or father-in-law to call me, I'd be grateful. It is urgent.'

'Will do. You couldn't just—'

Sam missed the rest as he made his escape.

# Chapter 76

While Matt stood imagining the damage Vinny could do, Jane came back.

'All secure back there, Matt. Any luck?' Matt shook his head.

The neighbour turned to re-enter his house. 'I'll just get my wife, officer. She may be able to tell you more.'

'Thank you.'

'I'm pretty sure Vinny has been here, about fifteen minutes before uniform. We may have to break in. Let's just see what the neighbour says.'

From next door, a woman in her late fifties appeared, tying a fluffy blue dressing gown around her and followed by her husband.

'Mrs Smart, officer. What is happening? Is Kathy alright?'

'There is nothing wrong as far as we know, ma'am, but we would like to establish that she is not at home. Do you know if she is away at the moment?'

'She usually tells me. We have her key and she has ours, just so we can keep an eye on things.'

'We really need to have a word with Mrs Wylde. Would it be possible for you to come inside with us, just to make sure she's not there?'

The woman looked to her husband as if seeking his permission. He nodded and she went to go back inside. 'I'll just get the key.'

Matt reckoned once they had established that Kathy wasn't inside, they'd head to Pam's. They should be able to get there in less than ten minutes, although he thought it was unlikely she would be there at this hour.

Mrs Smart returned to open the door and went to step inside. Matt stopped her and indicated she let them go first, just in case. Entering someone's home always felt like an invasion of privacy to Matt. Adding to this was the dread of what they might find and he suggested Mrs Smart remain in the hallway.

Matt was relieved downstairs was as he remembered, minus the smell of baking. Trying to take his mind off what they might find, he reflected on what a difference it made.

Full of foreboding, Matt took a deep breath and led the way upstairs. Finding each room empty, a surge of relief swept over him and it took a moment before he could gain control and go down to thank Mrs Smart.

'She did go to her daughter-in-law's yesterday, Inspector. There was some problem with one of the little ones. It would be very unusual but she could have stayed over.'

Matt nodded, hoping this was the answer. Pam's home was the other side of the river, across the Clopton Bridge, but what Matt thought would be a short journey took nearly half an hour. Two minor prangs caused by the road conditions held them up and had Matt cursing. With no way around, there was nothing to do but wait while the damaged cars moved to the side of the road so that drivers could exchange details.

Arriving at Pam's, he was disappointed when he couldn't see Kathy's car, either in the driveway or on the road. 'Think you'd be best to tackle this one, Jane.'

She nodded. 'I didn't have much luck last time though.'

'Give it a try.' He watched as she approached the door. There appeared to be no response, but then he saw her bend down talking to someone through the letterbox, before scribbling something on the back of her card and pushing it through.

Returning to the car, she explained. 'Sorry. Granny has left. I've said we need to speak to her urgently. Hopefully the message will be passed on.'

'Damn.' As he wondered what to do next, his phone rang. Hoping it wasn't bad news, he put it on speaker. 'Turrell.'

'Thought you'd want to know, sir, Tilly Rowlands is asking to speak to you.'

'Thanks, Wendy. Has she had the baby?'

'Sorry, sir, they didn't say.'

'Don't worry. We're drawing a blank here, so I'll head over there.'

# Chapter 77

Although Dr Meredith was not worried about Amy, Kathy made regular checks on her throughout the night, only managing to doze in-between. At 6 am, she gave up trying to sleep, made herself a cup of coffee and watched the dawn begin to lighten the morning into brilliant clear light.

These cold, crisp days were her favourite. She and Bill loved to go for a walk down by the river, mingling with the dog walkers and joggers. They would wander along, past the bandstand, admiring Holy Trinity Church from the opposite side of the Avon, before passing the weir and crossing Lucy's Mill Bridge to walk back through the old town. Sighing at the memories, she shook herself into action, hoping that Pam had retained her resolve overnight. Dr Meredith had said it was important for Pam to realise the children needed her as this would encourage her to work towards recovery.

Amy woke saying she was hungry and after checking she didn't have a temperature and wasn't in any pain, Kathy cooked the girls a treat of pancakes with some maple syrup she'd found in the back of a cupboard. They were Jack's favourite and the girls wolfed them down. While they washed up, she took a cup of tea up to Pam, surprised to find her up and dressed. 'Amy is fine this morning. How are you, Pam?'

'Frightened, Kathy. I'm frightened.'

Again, Kathy felt the urge to hold her, tell her it would be alright. Instead, she grasped her hands. 'It won't be easy, but your girls are worth it.'

Pam nodded and sank onto the bed. Kathy sat beside her. 'It's okay to be scared.'

'What if I can't do it?'

'You won't be on your own. There will be help every step of the way.' Even as she said the words, Kathy hoped they were true. Dr Meredith said she would do her best, but there were long waiting lists for psychological services. 'Let's see what the doctor says today, shall we?'

If the doctor's visit went well, Kathy made up her mind she'd do the concert tonight. It would provide a good memory for her last night of freedom. First, she'd collect Pam's prescription and stock the cupboards, freezer and fridge with plenty of easy meals and Christmas goodies.

Town was crowded with Christmas shoppers and it took Kathy nearly half an hour to reach the Maybird Centre. Clopton Bridge proved to be a bottleneck with traffic backed up along the Banbury and Shipston Roads. Phoebe and Zoe had come along so they could choose things they liked and were excited at the unexpected outing.

An hour and a half later, Kathy manoeuvred the heavy trolley into a checkout queue that stretched halfway down one of the aisles. Phoebe and Zoe were enjoying themselves and it was brilliant to spend time with them. After wondering what Pam would say, Kathy had given way and let them choose a small artificial Christmas tree and decorations.

At Pam's, Phoebe helped put the groceries away. Amy came into the kitchen and pulled at her skirt. Kathy bent down to hear her soft voice. 'What is it, Amy?'

'A lady came. Said I was to give you this.'

Taking the card, Kathy's stomach somersaulted. 'Thank you, Amy.' The card was from DC Jane Meadows, the one who had visited her with DI Turrell. Were they on to her already? There was a note on the card asking Kathy to get in touch as soon as possible. Well, they could wait. She tucked the card in her bag and set about preparing lunch.

Dr Meredith arrived mid-afternoon. Kathy hung back as the doctor ushered Amy into the lounge. Pam hesitated, until Kathy indicated she should follow.

Moving into the kitchen, Kathy sat at the kitchen table, helping Phoebe work out menus. Phoebe wanted to take over and do everything until Kathy tried to explain that she should be her mum's helper, as this would be more of a help to her. She displayed a practical quality that reminded Kathy of Jack.

As Dr Meredith left, Kathy went to let her out. 'Mrs Wylde has given me permission to bring you up to speed. Amy is fine, there are no worries on that score. Did you collect Mrs Wylde's prescription?'

'Yes.'

'That should give her some support. I've stressed she must take the tablets regularly. I've also managed to call in a favour or two and I'm hopeful there will be a place on a cognitive behavioural course starting in the New Year. These are hard to come by, so she mustn't waste it.'

'I'll encourage her, but I may not be around as much as I would like.'

Although Dr Meredith gave her a quizzing look, she didn't ask why. 'Just do what you can.'

'Thank you, Dr Meredith.'

After the doctor had left, Kathy realised she was going to be late for the theatre.

# Chapter 78

Vinny had arrived at Kathy's house at seven fifteen but there was no response to his pressing of the bell. Checking that no one was watching, he looked around the back, but could find no means of entry except for putting a brick through a window. In case she was a heavy sleeper, he decided to stick around, but needed to do this without arousing suspicion. Spotting a crew from the water board setting up a little way down the road, he strolled towards them.

'Hi, mate. Cold enough for you?'

'Bollocks and frozen come to mind.'

'Know the feeling. My mate's always bloody late, supposed to pick me up at seven fifteen. Mind if I wait in the cab?'

'Sure, help yourself.'

'Thanks.'

From his seat in the water board lorry, Vinny watched as fifteen minutes later a patrol car called at the house, followed soon after by an unmarked police car that pulled into the driveway of Kathy's house. The tall detective he'd seen at Jon's funeral rang the bell while his colleague, a tasty blonde, went around the back. He was pleased to see the cop got no response either. Then the neighbour came out, followed soon afterwards by his wife, who took the cops into the house.

The detectives drove away, and he wished he knew where they were headed. If only he had a car, he would have followed them. Deciding he'd be better off seeking out Harry, he climbed out of the warm cab. Chances are he'd still be at college. Vinny knew from experience how family and friends preferred you to be somewhere else after you got on the wrong side of the law. He called to the workers. 'Thanks, mate. Think the bugger's forgotten me, so I'm off home.'

One of the workers called back, 'Don't blame you. Wish I could do the same.'

With a wave of his hand, Vinny snuggled down into his coat and headed for the college. He missed having Dan to boss around, but the little rat scuttled after Ops. At least he'd left the parting gift of where to find Kathy and Harry, no doubt to keep him sweet in case the chance of a berth in Spain came up again. Ops, blast him, had withdrawn all his help, except the offer of getting him back to Spain and Vinny figured that was only to be rid of him. The pickup was ten thirty tonight, giving Vinny only a few hours left to avenge his son. The thought motivated him and he increased his stride while trying to figure out a way of getting into the college and at Harry. Passing a newsagent, the Christmas display gave him an idea and he went in to buy a large tin of Quality Street before continuing.

Vinny checked out the accommodation block from the main road. The college was bound to have security but he couldn't see any sign. Moving to the entrance, he could see it needed a code. He waited until a giggling group of Chinese girls came out.

Holding the tin of chocolates, he explained he was Harry's uncle and he wanted to surprise him with a Christmas treat. There was some conferring between the students, none of which he could understand, before one pointed to the second floor.

'Number forty-two.'

Vinny thanked them with a smile while holding the door open. As soon as they left, he bounded up the stairs. Hearing nothing from Harry's room, he decided to take a look now he was here. The door was no problem and he picked the lock in record time. Inside it was smaller than his last prison cell with little more than a bed and a desk. Disappointed, he placed the tin on the desk, next to a flyer for something called Open House dated this evening. Underneath was a musical score for *The Pirates of Penzance*. Harry might not be in his room, but he knew where he would be tonight.

Vinny heard footsteps in the corridor and stood still. The steps stopped outside and Vinny cursed, knowing the door was unlocked. He moved to stand behind the door, fingering the gun in his pocket. If this was some friend of Harry's then he should be able to fob them off with his story of delivering a Christmas present. Someone knocked and he heard the key in the lock.

'Harry, its DS Withers.'

Blast. What were the bloody police doing here? Vinny withdrew the gun and waited, watching the handle turn. Would the bastard be alone? If he stayed hidden behind the door, maybe he would give the room a quick glance, realise Harry wasn't there and bugger off.

'Harry?'

The cop took two steps into the room and began to turn. Vinny raised the butt of the gun and aimed for the head, striking hard so that the man crashed to the floor. Kicking his legs out of the way, Vinny hurried to shut the door.

Looking down at him, he wondered what to do next. Cops were like rats: where you found one, another one would be around, maybe waiting outside or in the corridor. He bent down to turn the man over, causing him to moan. Vinny waited in case he was coming round, prepared to strike again, but he appeared to be out cold, so he rifled through his pockets, taking his mobile phone and warrant card.

With another kick to the torso, Vinny turned to leave, catching his toe against something metal. Bending to pick it up, he saw it was the key to the room. Even better, he'd lock the bastard in.

# Chapter 79

The maternity ward had its own special smell above the usual hospital odours of disinfectant. Matt guessed it was something to do with the babies – maybe milk or powder. He asked for Tilly Rowlands at reception and a nurse took him to a small ward. Before they entered, Matt asked, 'Is Miss Rowlands alright?' The picture of Mary James still preoccupied him and he needed to be prepared.

'See for yourself.' The nurse held open the door and moved to one side. Matt entered, relieved to see Tilly sitting up in bed smiling. She didn't look like a woman who'd just lost her baby.

'Inspector.' Tilly reached out to him. 'I've had a little boy.'

Matt moved to sit beside her, feeling out of his depth. 'I'm so pleased. Is he doing well?'

'He's fine. They said he was protected from the cold inside me. He's in an incubator as he's early. Nick's with him.'

'I'm so relieved. Didn't think either of us was going to make it at one point.'

'Thank you for saving our lives.'

'Just wish we could have got there sooner so you didn't have to go through that.'

'Have you caught him yet?'

'No, but we're getting closer.'

'He's out to get Harry and that man's mother...the one...I thought I'd better tell you.'

'Thank you. Do you feel up to giving us more details about what happened? It could help us apprehend Mr James. I could send a female officer if you'd prefer it.' From the look on her face, it was as if Matt had physically struck her. He glanced at the nurse for help.

'Maybe later, Inspector.'

'That's fine. At least we are aware of Mr James's plans.'

'I'm glad. I wouldn't want anyone else to go through what...'

Tilly began to cry and Matt could see how fragile she really was. He was at a loss and was relieved when the nurse spoke.

'Now, now, you're worrying the inspector. He'd never guess you have a wonderful little boy, now, would he?'

'I'm sorry.'

Matt stood, hoping to escape. 'No need, you've been through a lot.'

Through her tears, Tilly struggled to speak. 'I wanted to ask you something.'

'Yes.'

'Can we name the baby after you?'

It came as a complete shock to Matt and he sat down again. The nurse laughed. 'But you don't even know my name.'

'Someone said it was Matt, Matthew, and we both like that. Please say yes. It would be our way of thanking you.'

'She's very determined, Inspector. I would just give in.'

'Well, yes, of course. I'd be honoured.'

Matt walked out of the ward in a daze, thinking of the tiny baby boy now stuck with his name. He couldn't wait to tell Eppie.

# Chapter 80

This was the day. Harry woke feeling both excited and scared about the coming performance to reopen the RSC theatre. At the dress rehearsal yesterday they'd worked on the magnificent thrust stage. That was such a thrill. They must have the best sound system and today he hoped to get a look at it, betting they wouldn't have to wave a piece of tin to create thunder.

He couldn't help thinking of Kathy and wondering if she'd make it today. According to Ida, one of her grandchildren had been ill yesterday. And would she really hand herself in after the concert? It would take the pressure off the rest of them, yet she was only in this position because of what they did, and he couldn't decide what he wanted. When she'd said she liked him, despite his involvement in the death of her son, he'd been shocked. Not many people in Harry's life were so accepting; his parents, for example. Maybe he wasn't all bad. On the down days, that would be good to remember.

Despite their differences, he liked Kathy. The anger he'd felt over Dave's death had gone, yet Tilly and her baby were another thing. Nick would never forgive him if they didn't pull through and he'd been on edge ever since hearing of Tilly's ordeal. Maybe if she and the baby were both alright, Nick would forgive him for putting them in danger.

Harry decided he would talk to Kathy today, try to change her mind. She was only giving herself up so they would be out of danger. How could she do that after the pain they had caused? On the twelve o'clock news, he'd seen a warning about Vinny James. Maybe he would be caught soon and Kathy would reconsider handing herself in.

Glancing at his watch, he began to get ready, intending to treat himself to a late lunch at McDonald's before heading to the theatre. Showered and ready to go and with his costume over his arm, he left his friend's room on the ground floor and waited near the entrance so he could leave with a group of students heading into town. Reaching the American fountain in Rother Street, he glanced around and not seeing anyone suspicious, left the group to make his way down Bridge Street.

After a Big Mac and fries, Harry headed the short distance along Waterside to the theatre and joined the G&S group waiting to be led backstage. Harry looked around for Kathy but couldn't see her. He tried to get close to Ida but as the group compressed into the narrow passages and corridors backstage, it was impossible.

Entering the Swan Theatre, their guide explained this is where they were to stay until their time to perform. The G&S group settled themselves in the stalls, a few rows back from the stage, and began to get into their costumes. Some of the women, including Ida, opted to change in the toilets so Harry still couldn't ask her about Kathy.

As he changed, he wondered if Vinny had caught up with her and hoped this wasn't the reason she was late.

# Chapter 81

Sam struggled to sit up, holding his head and fighting the need to throw up. Grasping the waste paper basket, he heaved into it and leaned back against the desk, head spinning. How long had he been unconscious? It was now two twenty so it couldn't be that long. He tried to think back and could remember entering the room, but after that, it went hazy. There had been someone behind the door who'd hit him over the head. From the brief glimpse, Sam couldn't be sure if it had been Vinny James, but odds on it would be him. He must let Matt know.

Reaching for his phone, he couldn't find it, even after crawling around in case it had fallen out of his pocket. Struggling to his feet and holding onto the desk to steady himself, he managed the few steps to the door. Tugging at the handle, he couldn't comprehend why it wouldn't open. He remembered security giving him a key but he'd found the door open. Where was the key? Searching the floor again caused searing pain to shoot through his head and he stopped, realising the door must be locked from the outside. Now he was in trouble. Banging on the door, despite the pain it caused, brought no response so he sat on the edge of the desk to contemplate his situation.

Surely security would wonder why he hadn't returned, but then the man had been busy directing some workmen when Sam arrived. Deciding he might be better attracting attention via the window, he moved towards it. The movement made him throw up again and he took the basket with him, glad it wasn't an open weave design. Looking out at the empty car park, he didn't bother opening the window, deciding the door was his only chance.

Searching through the desk drawers brought forth a Swiss penknife. Opening the various implements, he wondered if he would be able to pick the lock with any of them. Feeling unsteady, he dragged the chair to the door and sat down to concentrate on the lock.

# Chapter 82

Stamping his feet in an effort to keep warm, Vinny watched as people carrying costumes walked up the steps to enter the Swan Theatre. Ten minutes later, he was beginning to feel uneasy and his toes were turning to ice. By now, Mary could have called the police and although it was only a domestic, it would increase the surveillance for him. The last thing he needed was to be standing here on the street corner.

Kathy and Harry were probably already inside and that is where he needed to be. He fingered the gun, now tucked into his belt; the cold metal gave him comfort. As long as he had his friend, no one could stop him. He was thankful that the police in England didn't carry guns.

Walking up the steps of the Swan Theatre, he could see a bar to his left. It was surprisingly quiet considering all the people he'd seen entering. Following the chatter of voices, he found himself in a wide space that led to the main theatre. It was full of excited people. Hating crowds, he wanted to push people out of the way, but instead forced himself to smile and nod.

The crowd thinned and he became aware that some of the people were disappearing through an opening in the shiny wall. As he watched, a panel slid open and a young woman with a clipboard took some of the people through the gap. The group kept close together and when the last one had entered, the opening disappeared. Seeing this performance repeated, Vinny realised if he wanted to get in, he needed to attach himself to a group. Taking off his coat, he moved next to an elderly man, leaned against the wall and smiled. 'Exciting, isn't it?'

'Yes, and such a privilege. We'll be testing out the whole theatre, you know?'

'Hope we get it right.'

'I'm sure we will after all those rehearsals.' The man squinted at him. 'I don't think I know you, young man.'

Vinny extended his hand. 'John. Helen's husband.'

Shifting his costume and bag to the other hand, the man shook his hand.

'Here, let me take those.' Vinny lifted the costume and bag from him and smiled.

'Thank you. They were starting to feel like lead.'

'No problem.'

The panel opened and his group surged forward. Vinny stayed at the end, close to the man, holding the costume like a badge. Everyone was excited and eager to get inside and no one turned to see or question him. Their guide led them through the backstage area where the height and space seemed enormous, then into a darker, smaller area where the only light came from an electronic board that flashed in various colours. Although their leader warned them to be careful, coming from the bright into the dark, they still bumped into each other.

Exiting into a corridor with lockers and toilets, she paused. 'Hello, has everyone caught up?'

Vinny stayed close to the elderly man as some of the group glanced around. He held his breath and was relieved when no one ousted him as an imposter.

The guide continued. 'With such a large group of performers, we have given the use of the dressing rooms upstairs to the youngsters. You, together with the other adult groups, will change in the Swan Theatre. Just find yourself a space in the audience section and stay together. Toilets are on your left in this corridor.'

Following her, the group slowed to turn right into a dim, narrow corridor, before going up a few steps and disappearing. Stumbling along at the end of the queue, Vinny heard gasps of delight from those in front. Wondering what it was all about, he stepped through the opening and was horrified to find himself standing on a large stage surrounded by tiered galleries that glared down on him with empty black eyes.

Feeling exposed, he thrust the costume and bag at the old man. 'Here, mate, got to go to the loo,' he said before shooting back down the steps into the welcome dimness.

# Chapter 83

Leaving the hospital still feeling bemused, Matt headed back to CID to reunite with Jane and check on progress. He was in the middle of telling her about Tilly's decision when a call came in from PC Baker.

'Hello, Charlie.'

'Sir, I'm here at the minor injuries unit in Stratford with DS Withers. He's been struck on the back of the head. We found him in Harry's room at the college. I've sealed off the room and left my colleague on guard in case you want to get forensics to take a look.'

'Well done, Charlie. How's Sam?'

'He's seen the nurse and is waiting for the doctor. They are talking about possible concussion.'

'Okay. I'll be there soon. Can you stay with him 'til then?'

'Yes, sir.'

'Thanks.' Matt brought Jane up to speed and alerted all units to concentrate on the Stratford area. Both Kathy and Harry would be at the concert tonight and he was praying that Vinny hadn't acquired that knowledge.

While he went to check on Sam, Matt sent Jane to look at Harry's room to see if they needed forensics. She'd then continue the search for Kathy and meet them at the theatre later.

The minor injuries unit at Stratford Hospital was at one end of the two-storey building. PC Baker was pacing in the corridor as Matt entered. 'How is he?'

'Says he's fine. The doctor's with him.'

'Good. Rescuing members of CID is becoming a habit, Charlie. Think we'll have to make you one of our own.' From Charlie's grin, it was obvious he liked this idea. 'Tell me how you found Sam?'

'We'd been making regular calls at the college in case Harry or Vinny showed up there. On our last call, the security man was in a fit about the key to Harry's room. Seems a detective had borrowed it and not brought it back. We went to investigate, thinking it might be Vinny. DS Withers was locked in, so we got him out.'

'Any sign of Vinny James?'

'Not in the immediate vicinity.'

'Well, at least we can concentrate on Stratford now.' The small waiting room was full so Matt and Charlie remained in the corridor. Matt felt like he'd spent the last week in and out of hospitals and hoped this would be his last visit for a long time. He moved forward as the consulting room door opened and Sam came out with the doctor.

'I'd advise rest for at least twenty-four hours and it would be better if you were not on your own tonight.'

'Thank you, Doctor.'

Matt stepped forward. 'No work today then, Sam?'

'I'm fine, raring to go. You heard what the doc said.'

The doctor turned back. 'Although DI Withers sustained a blow to the head, there are no signs of concussion, no vomiting or loss of consciousness. But he would be wise to rest.'

'Thank you, Doctor.' Matt followed Sam, who was already striding out of the department. 'Rest, he said. Are you deaf, Sam?'

'I've got a hard head. Stop worrying, Matt. I'll rest when the bastard is caught.'

Still arguing, they caught up with Charlie. Sam stopped to thank him. 'Thanks, I owe you one.'

'It was nothing.'

'Listen to him, Matt. He only broke down the door. My lock-picking skills were getting me nowhere.'

Matt was about to answer when his phone rang. 'Turrell.'

It was Jane. 'How's Sam?'

'He'll live.'

'Good, was a bit worried. Did he tell you he vomited?'

'No, he didn't.' Matt turned to look at Sam, who was avoiding eye contact.

Jane continued. 'Anyway, I've had a quick look around Harry's room and I don't think there will be anything of use. But there is a poster here for the concert tonight, together with a musical score, so chances are Vinny is clued up about that.'

'Damn. I was hoping they might be safe there.'

'It was in clear view on the desk. Do you want me to head down to the theatre?'

'Just make a quick check at Pamela Wylde's in case Kathy has gone back there. I'd rather catch her before she runs into Vinny. If she's not there, then head on to the theatre. We'll swing by her house just in case she's there.'

'See you at the theatre, Matt.'

Matt ended the call and glanced at Sam, trying to decide whether to send him home. He did look pale and the news that he had been sick, when he'd obviously told the doctor otherwise, was worrying. 'You were sick?'

'Nothing much, probably the hamburger I snatched on the way over.'

'Then why didn't you mention it to the doctor?'

'Come on, Matt. You know what they're like. Got to cover their backs.'

'Just as I have.'

'I don't want to miss out on catching up with Vinny. You've got to admit, *you* didn't follow the doctor's advice, Matt.'

Despite himself, Matt laughed. 'Suppose not. But you've got to promise me, any feeling queasy or anything at all, you have to tell me.'

'Will do.'

'Right, Charlie, if you get back on patrol, we'll swing by Kathy Wylde's house and then head to the theatre.'

# Chapter 84

The taxi dropped Kathy at the Swan entrance and as she climbed up the steps she wondered if they would let her in. They'd had strict instructions to arrive on time, meet on the walkway, and to stay in their groups. She wasn't surprised to find the walkway empty.

The only sign of life was at the other end, towards the main theatre, where a young man was setting out items in the shop. He scratched his head at her dilemma but thought it best if she went to the stage door at the rear of the Swan Theatre.

Thanking him, she went back outside, walking around behind the Swan to the stage door. Pressing the buzzer, she explained how she had missed the call time for her group and held her breath, wondering if they would let her in. She could see through the glass doors, the woman consulting a list before pressing the release for Kathy to enter.

Told to take a seat and wait, Kathy suddenly felt very excited. At last, she was breathing in the rarefied air inhaled by some of the most famous actors in the world.

It felt like ages as Kathy sat waiting, clutching her costume, before someone came to escort her to the Swan Theatre, where she was thankful to see the rest of the G&S group.

Ida called out to her. 'Over here, Kathy. I've saved a place next to me.'

Making her way along the row, stepping over bags and clothing, Kathy was grateful to sit down. Now all she had to worry about was the performance. 'Thanks, Ida. Had a bit of a problem with young Amy.'

'Oh dear. I hope everything is alright now. Harry was getting concerned.'

'Yes, all sorted.'

'I can show you where the ladies' toilet is if you want to change there?'

'Just give me a minute, thanks, Ida.' She wanted to sit and take in her surroundings; watch the other groups, the individuals posing for pictures on the stage or up in the galleries that framed the stage in a semi-circle. Excited chatter came from every corner. This was a once-in-a-lifetime opportunity. Some people were eating sandwiches or passing along cakes. She'd planned to bring some mince pies, but hadn't had the chance to bake. Still, there seemed an abundance on offer and she selected a cupcake from a plastic container before passing it on.

Ida went to have her photo taken and Harry came over to sit beside her. 'Glad you're safe.'

'You too. We're protected in here, so let's forget about Vinny James and just enjoy ourselves, shall we?'

Harry nodded. 'Are you still going...?'

'Only way to keep you safe.'

Before Harry could reply, Ida gestured for Kathy to join her on the stage, so fishing out her camera, she asked Harry if he would take a photo for her. Climbing the steps to join Ida, she felt self-conscious, experiencing for the first time what it would be like standing here with the audience looking up, waiting for her to perform. A prickle of stage fright began to build in the pit of her stomach.

Taking her camera from Harry, she and Ida returned to their seats. Harry stood awkwardly by and she sensed he had something on his mind. Guessing he would be trying to persuade her not to give herself up, Kathy ignored him and moved back to her seat.

Ida spoke. 'Did you hear that Tilly Rowlands has been attacked? They're still waiting to see if her baby will be alright.'

Despite the heavy blanket of guilt that threatened to suffocate her, she managed to mumble a vague reply to Ida. Looking up to catch Harry's eye, she guessed this is what was bothering him. Before she could say anything else, there was a swirl of excitement as Greg Doran entered to wish them well. Kathy was glad of the interruption as it enabled her to get her thoughts in order.

She watched as Angela bounced onto the stage, determined to be first in line for a photo with Greg Doran. Ida and several of the others went to join her. Kathy beckoned to Harry. 'You knew about Tilly?'

Harry nodded, shamefaced. 'She'll be okay. I'm waiting for Nick to ring me back.'

'Why didn't you tell me?'

'Thought it might make you...you know.'

'Give myself up?'

'Yes.'

Kathy paused. 'I've already decided to do that.'

'I don't want you to.'

'Why?'

'It doesn't seem fair.'

'It seems fair to me. I expected you to pay for what you had done, so why shouldn't I?'

'But, I like you.'

'What difference does that make?' Suddenly angry, Kathy jumped up, needing to get away. Taking her camera, she'd take some pictures, give herself some time and space to think.

# Chapter 85

Taking a moment to adjust his eyes, Vinny slid further behind the stage into the shadows. From his glimpse inside the theatre, he'd seen groups of people, some in costumes, scattered about the audience area, mostly in the stalls, and he was beginning to realise his task wasn't going to be easy. Kathy and Harry would also be in costume and so harder to pick out. Harry shouldn't be a problem, but despite a photo of Kathy, thanks to Dan, he wasn't so sure he'd recognise her. He needed to be somewhere where he could observe and single them out. Those dark galleries where he could look down on the assembled groups offered the best vantage point, if he could figure out how to get there.

Vinny turned left, jumping as he caught a glimpse of himself in a mirror surrounded by lights, just like in the movies. Further on, he came to a corresponding entrance leading to the stage but he didn't intend to go there again. Instead, he cautiously opened a door to the right and was relieved to find this led to the ground floor gallery. From here, he could see the steps leading up to the next gallery and, walking as if he had every right to be there, he strolled over to them. Upstairs he chose a seat to the right of the stage in the second row and sat back to watch.

It took him a while to spot Harry but once he'd identified the right group, it was easy to pick out Kathy. The photo was recent and showed her curly brown hair. Looking down on her, she didn't look like a murderess at all, sitting there talking to Harry, but then you could never tell. Now all he had to do was get her alone. He'd noticed pairs of women going off to the left and guessed they were heading to the loo with the women sticking to that silly habit of going in twos. Kathy would be sure to follow the pattern eventually and this would give him better odds, so he moved around to the other side of the gallery to wait.

Behind him was a door marked fire escape, and it crossed his mind that he could shoot her from here and be through that door before anyone realised what was happening. But he knew from experience that he was hopeless at hitting a target from this far away and that it would be a one-shot opportunity. Plus, he wanted to be close, to look into her eyes, and make sure she knew why she was going to die.

Keeping an eye on Kathy and Harry, he saw her snatch a camera from Harry and move away to take pictures. Maybe if he were patient, she would come to him. Hearing footsteps coming up the stairs, he leaned over the balcony and pretended to be drinking in the view. The footsteps belonged to a couple dressed in what he guessed were medieval costumes. Both had cameras and were intent on capturing every angle of the theatre. Vinny nodded to them and they passed by without comment. Breathing a sigh of relief, he wished Kathy would do the same and fall in with his plan.

# Chapter 86

There was no reply at Kathy's house and they'd heard from Jane that she'd no luck at Pamela's either. Matt and Sam were about to leave when Mrs Smart, Kathy's neighbour, came out to ask if they had any news of Kathy. Out of courtesy, they stopped to reassure her, despite itching to leave. When his phone rang, Matt left Sam talking to her and moved away, hoping he'd get the point and follow.

'Turrell.'

'A man answering Vinny James's description has been spotted outside the Royal Shakespeare Theatre, sir.'

'Thanks, Wendy. At what time?'

'It was about an hour ago, but has only just been reported.'

At last, they had a sighting. 'Direct all units there and warn DC Meadows. We're on our way.' Giving a shout to Sam, Matt was in the car and ready to go in seconds.

Traffic on Waterside was heavy with people heading towards the RST. The theatre wasn't officially open yet and Matt guessed that folk intended to get a first look at the changes.

He heard Sam sighing beside him. 'Don't they ever look in their rear-view mirrors?'

'Certainly doesn't look like it.' Matt gave up struggling and pulled up on the pavement behind a patrol car, ignoring the annoyed glances of the pedestrians. Leaving Sam to follow, he ran up the steps to the main theatre, noticing through the glass foyer that it was already crowded. A buzz of excitement met him as the theatregoers explored the alterations. Matt wondered if Eppie had arrived yet and hoped he wouldn't run into her – there was no time for explanations and he didn't want to worry her. He felt reassured to see PC Baker and his partner moving amongst the crowd.

Spotting a programme seller, he asked for the manager. The man hesitated so Matt hurried him. 'Whoever is in charge, please. Now.'

The man finally moved, leading them towards the ticket desk. Pushing in front of a queue of people, Matt asked one of the girls there to get the manager. She looked as if she was going to ask questions before complying, so Matt stepped close and held out his badge and she went into the back office.

In what seemed an age, she returned followed by a tall man.

'I'm the front of house manager. How can I help?'

'We have reason to believe that this gentleman,' Matt paused while Sam showed Vinny James's photo, 'may have entered the theatre and is intending to harm one of the cast.'

'Well, there would be no way he could get backstage. We have rigid security in place.'

'Nevertheless, we would like to take a look. It could mean saving someone's life.'

'Very well, follow me.'

The manager led them into the theatre and turned left to go down a curving corridor with many entrances to the stalls, through which Matt could see the stage that came right out into the audience. At last, they reached a door leading backstage and Matt could see some of the performers already gathering in the large open space to the left of the stage area. Nervous chatter rose from the group. Matt glanced over them but couldn't pick out anyone he knew. Presumably, Kathy and Harry would be waiting with their group. Following the manager, they entered a corridor, and after passing the Green Room, stopped at the stage door while he tapped a code into the door pad.

Matt and Sam followed as he crossed the room to address the woman behind the desk. 'Paula, could you explain to these gentlemen our security measures for today? There is concern that an unauthorised person may have been able to gain access.'

Paula explained. 'Normally entry would be through the stage door, where everyone is required to sign in and I always have a list of who is expected. But today, with so many people involved, we are bringing them in one group at a time from the front walkway. I don't see how anyone could add themselves to a group without the rest of the group being aware.'

'Thank you, Paula. Does that help, Inspector?'

Matt, despite seething with impatience, thanked Paula, before turning to the manager. 'I need to see where the performers are.'

The man looked as if he hoped the matter had been settled, but didn't challenge Matt's authority and led them back into the corridor.

'The adult performers are changing in the Swan Theatre.' He led them back into the corridor and pointed to a door. 'If you go through this door you will be in the auditorium.'

'Thank you. Could you take my sergeant to the walkway – we'll need to check out the security there.'

As the manager left with Sam, Matt paused to answer his phone, surprised to hear McRay's voice. 'Matt, apparently Vinny James has a gun. This information came from Mrs James, who has just died. I've called out Armed Response. You are to pull back.'

Even as he listened to McRay, Matt could hear screams from inside the Swan. 'Sorry, sir, the signal is not good here.'

'Don't try that one, Matt.'

'It sounds like it's kicking off here, sir.'

'The order is the same. Matt '

People began pouring out of the door as Matt flicked off his phone and pushed his way through.

# Chapter 87

Kathy wished Harry would stop trying to persuade her. After getting it all so wrong, she needed to pay for what she had done and giving herself up was the only way. It would be too easy to let Harry talk her out of it, especially now Pam needed her. She realised she had been thinking in black and white and life wasn't like that. Harry had opened her eyes and proved people could change. Maybe in time he would forgive her. As for the others, like Dave and his family, never mind Tilly and her baby, she couldn't bear to think about them. Needing to be on her own for a while, she decided to get some photos from up in the gallery. Seeing Angela mount the stairs to the left, she took those on the right.

Everything looked so different from up here. Kathy had only been to the Swan a couple of times as Bill wasn't much of a theatregoer. Moving close to the edge, she managed to get some good shots looking down at the stage before continuing around.

Mid-gallery, she met Angela and stopped to acknowledge her. Carrying on, Kathy knew she ought to go and get changed, but reasoned there was plenty of time as they weren't on 'til the end of the first act. She'd just time for a few more shots.

She sensed him first as the threat spread around her. There was no escape.

'Kathy Wylde.'

Taking her time, she turned, not wanting him to know she was terrified. He didn't look like his picture, but then a picture couldn't portray the sense of evil. His eyes were blue and cold like Jonathan's while the bitter line of his mouth betrayed his real nature.

'Yes. I'm Kathy Wylde.'

'You killed my boy.'

'And he murdered mine.'

'He shouldn't have got in the lad's way.'

'But he's dead all the same.'

'As you'll be in a minute, bitch.' Vinny reached out and grasped her arm, pulling her towards him and thrusting his face into hers.

His eyes gleamed and she realised he was enjoying himself. Trying to turn her head away, his grimace widened as he pushed her back against the seats, tightening his grip on her arm.

Dominating always gave Vinny a thrill and he delighted in having control. If only he had the time, he'd make this bloody cow suffer like Mary and take his revenge slowly. He twisted her arm and watched as her face contorted in pain. Laughing, he raised the gun to prod into her neck. The terror in her eyes excited him and he wondered what she feared most. He would love to have fun exploring how to bring her to a quivering wreck begging for mercy, but right now, he needed to finish the job and get out. Realising what was to come, she began struggling and kicking and he chuckled at her efforts. When she began to scream, he hit her hard across the face. The scream changed to a whimper.

Realising someone was approaching from behind, he let her fall to the floor and spun around, gun at the ready.

'Let her go. It was me.'

'Harry. Some friend. You'd stick up for this murdering cow, instead of my son. Get out of my way.' Vinny swung his arm to deliver a vicious blow that sent Harry staggering towards the balcony rail. The opportunity was too good to miss and he was there in seconds. Dazed from the blow, it was easy to lift him, watch him fall. The thud was rewarding and glancing down, he could see Harry's still figure on the ramp leading from the stage.

Every face was looking up at him. Someone started to scream. But no one could stop him now and he turned to look for the bitch. She was crawling away behind the seats. Her efforts were pitiful and he sniggered as he strode forward to stand over her. Reaching down to grasp her by the hair, he dragged her up to face him.

# Chapter 88

Matt, confronted by a medieval knight and several other costumed characters, struggled to get through them and into the theatre. Once in the lower gallery, he saw that every exit was jammed with people in a panic to get out. From where he stood, he noticed a still figure lying at the edge of the stage. From this angle it looked like Harry and he was relieved to see Sam pushing his way through the crowds to reach him. A movement on the balcony above caught Matt's eye and he searched for a way up. Finding the steps, he took them at speed.

Reaching the top he stood with his back to the wall listening. In the comparative quiet, he thought about what he was doing. He had every right to back off, follow orders and keep himself safe. Eppie would want that. If Vinny was here alone, he would be happy to do just that, but it looked like he'd already attacked Harry. Matt needed to find Kathy before she ended up like Mary. He couldn't deal with his emotions around Mary now and pushed her from his mind, except to hope she had been mistaken about the gun.

A faint scuffling attracted his attention further around the gallery. Matt crept forward, hugging the wall.

'Police. Come out with your hands up. You're surrounded.'

A dark figure emerged from between the seats, dragging a smaller shape with him. Eyes adjusting to the dimness, Matt could see it was Kathy. 'This isn't going to help you, Vinny.'

'Nor you, bastard.'

As Vinny swung Kathy around, Matt caught the glint of gunmetal. Bloody hell, so it was true. Armed Response should deal with this, but it was too late now. Vinny was levelling the gun on him. Kathy appeared dazed and Matt could make out a mark across her cheek. Anger surged and he struggled to press it down in case it interfered with his judgement. He'd seen enough of Vinny's handiwork. Loudly, so that Sam would hear, he called out as he moved forwards. 'Put the gun down.'

Vinny laughed and moved backwards, dragging Kathy with him. 'You'll have to do better than that.'

Vinny gave a quick glance around and Matt realised he was edging towards the fire exit. If he reached it, he would kill Kathy and make a bid to escape. Matt took two steps forward.

'Stay back.'

The gun straightened again and he stopped, held up his hands. 'The building is surrounded. Give yourself up now.'

'Not 'til I've sorted her out.'

Matt edged closer. 'What good will that do?'

'My boy will be avenged.'

'And get you a life sentence.'

Vinny laughed and aimed the gun at Matt's heart. 'Then I'd better make it worthwhile.'

Matt could see Vinny's hand tensing.

Although concentrating on the gun, Matt was aware of a figure edging along the top row of seats behind Vinny. Angela! What on earth was the stupid woman trying to do? That was all he needed. There was no way he could signal her to go back without giving her away.

Kathy suddenly cried out, 'No!' Taking advantage of Vinny's attention on Matt, Kathy twisted out of his hold and flung herself on his gun arm.

At the same time, Angela hurled something that caught Vinny on the side of the head. It did little to distract him, but Matt used the moment to fling himself forward. The force threw them both to the floor. Desperate for possession of the weapon, Matt clung to Vinny's gun arm with both hands. Vinny used his free hand to gouge at Matt's face. As they twisted and turned, Matt felt Vinny's hand tighten on the trigger. He bent his head as far back as possible as the shot blasted across his face.

# Chapter 89

Eppie wished Matt could be in the empty seat next to her and hoped whatever he was working on would soon be finished. She tried to discount the small voice that suspected he might be using work to get out of coming to the Open House with her.

The buzz from the audience as they looked around the new theatre quietened as the curtain went up. The commentator introduced the first act, a lively dance routine from a local youngsters' group, and everyone settled down to enjoy the show. The thrust stage meant that the performers were right amongst the audience and Eppie decided she liked it.

After the applause, there was a long break and people began talking amongst themselves until the commentator came back on the stage.

'Well, ladies and gentlemen, we did say this was a test evening and unfortunately we seem to have hit a small technical problem and we have to ask that you retire to the lobby while we fix this. The staff are waiting to help anyone in need of assistance. Thank you for your cooperation.'

There was a collective sigh amongst the spectators but they took it in good part and began to filter out. Eppie rose to join them and soon realised this was more than a minor technical fault. The lobby was full with uniformed police who were ushering the crowd out onto the wintery Bancroft Gardens. She was glad she had kept her coat with her and pitied those who had checked them in.

Pausing to offer her scarf to an elderly woman, she moved as close to Waterside as she could only to find the road filled with police cars and cordoned off. What worried her even more was the arrival of two ambulances. Matt was bound to be at the heart of whatever was going on.

The ambulances stopped outside the Swan and she tried to get closer to watch as a stretcher was brought out. Pushing her way through the crowd, frantic in case it was Matt, she sighed with relief, until she took another look and realised it was Harry. He appeared unconscious and she wondered what had happened to him. The paramedics loaded the stretcher into one of the waiting ambulances and it sped away using lights and sirens. She had to find out if Matt was alright.

There was talk amongst the crowd of a gunshot. Matt wouldn't stand a chance against that. Images of Matt already dead, lying covered in a coat or a sheet, swept through her head.

# Chapter 90

The blast from the shot sheared across his eyes so he couldn't see or hear. Knowing Vinny would be suffering the same effect, Matt tightened his hold on Vinny's arm, knocking it against the rear of the seats to loosen his grip. Vinny brought up his left arm to push Matt's head away. With a tremendous effort, Matt managed to roll Vinny over and pin him to the floor.

Powder residue blackened Vinny's face and he guessed he looked the same. At least his eyes were clearing. Matt daren't let go of Vinny's gun arm. How long could they go on like this? They were evenly matched and each as determined as the other. Taking a chance, Matt released his right hand to land a punch on Vinny's jaw. Although Vinny tried to move his head, it caught him squarely and his eyes flickered. In case he was faking, Matt hit him again with renewed force and felt Vinny's fingers loosen on the gun. He snatched it away, sliding it along the gallery and out of reach.

Staggering to his feet, Matt was relieved to see Sam and Jane racing around the gallery, followed by several uniform police. He nodded towards Vinny in disgust.

'Caution him and get him out of my sight. The gun's along there somewhere.'

With the adrenalin evaporating, Matt let the weariness overtake him and went to the balcony rail, needing to get his breath and compose himself. Below, Harry was being taken out on a stretcher attended by paramedics. At least he was still alive.

Kathy. He had forgotten about Kathy. And Angela. Without them, he would be dead. Angela was talking to a PC further round the gallery. Kathy sat in the seats to his left, also looking down at Harry. She appeared forlorn. Matt knew it was his duty to arrest her and wished it could be otherwise. He moved to collapse into the seat next to her.

'Thanks.'

She nodded towards Harry. 'It doesn't make up for him, or the others.'

'No. Maybe not.'

'I couldn't let him hurt you too.'

'I'm very grateful. It took a lot of courage.'

She turned towards him and he could see Vinny's handiwork. He should get the paramedics to check her out.

'You know what I need to do?'

'Yes.'

'I'm sorry.' She nodded and he helped her down from the seats while quietly cautioning her and formally making the arrest.

'What happens now?'

'Let's get you checked over by the paramedics, and then if you're fit enough, DC Meadows will take you to the station and book you in. You'll be interviewed later and can make a statement if you want to.'

'Can I ask one thing?'

'Yes.'

'Could someone tell Pam? Oh, and let me know how Harry is doing?'

'Certainly.'

Jane came forward to take her arm. Matt put up a hand to delay her. 'Thanks again, Kathy. You saved my life.'

She gave a brief nod before Jane led her away. Matt sat down on one of the nearest seats and beckoned to Sam, noting how pale he still looked. Before Sam could reach him, a paramedic arrived and began placing wet dressings on his face and eyes. Not wanting a fuss, Matt would have liked to push the man away. Instead, he gave in and tried to speak to Sam through the gauze. 'How's Harry?'

'Broken arm and collar bone, not sure yet about internal injuries. He should be alright. They'll let us know.'

'Good. Now you can go home.' From the look on Sam's face, Matt could tell he wasn't expecting this.

'Never mind me, I'm feeling fine. *You* should go home. Jane and I can handle this. She's just texted to say Eppie is outside wondering what the hell has happened to you. Best you put her mind at rest. You can pick up the pieces and debrief in the morning. Besides, McRay is on his way.'

Matt had the impulse to laugh. 'Someone's ready to take their inspector exams.'

# Chapter 91

When she saw Jane escorting a woman towards the remaining ambulance, Eppie shouted out. At first, she thought Jane hadn't heard. The paramedic began opening the doors and she shouted again. On the steps of the ambulance, Jane turned, searching the crowds. Eppie waved frantically and pushed forward. Jane saw her and hesitated, said something to the paramedic and came towards her.

Reaching the police tape, Jane grasped her hands. 'He's okay. Don't worry. The danger is over. Look, must go, have a prisoner. I'll let Sam know you're here and get someone to take you in.'

She hurried back to the ambulance, pausing only to direct a woman PC in her direction. Eppie breathed a sigh of relief, aware that tears were streaming down her face. A quick wipe of her eyes and she went towards the PC who held up the tape and waved her through.

'If you would follow me, Mrs Turrell.'

'Thank you.' Eppie followed the PC into the Swan Theatre and Sam came to meet her.

'Hello, Mrs Turrell. Please take your husband home.'

'He is alright, isn't he?'

'He's fine. Just looks like a chimney sweep, that's all.' At Eppie's anxious look, he clarified. 'The paramedic says he's fine, no permanent damage. But he's done enough for today and I can't make him see that.'

'And you imagine he's going to listen to me?'

Sam smiled. 'It's the only chance.'

'Suppose it's worth a try. But, Sam Withers, if I get grief for the next month, I'll come back to you.'

Laughing, Sam led her up to the first gallery. Eppie was too worried to take in her surroundings. Seeing Matt, she was relieved to see him looking more or less normal, just a grimy redness across his nose and eyes. She waited until he had finished talking to the uniform officers, before moving to his side, making sure not to embarrass him with the hug she needed.

'Eppie.'

As he turned, she could see how tired he looked. The week hadn't been easy: besides the fight, he'd suffered hypothermia, plus the loss of a colleague. She could see why Sam was concerned. He was running on automatic pilot.

'Matt?'

He put out his arm to draw her in. 'I'm fine. Don't worry.'

'Can you come home?'

'There's a lot to do.'

'Sam and Jane can cope. You've trained them well.'

'Come on, guv, it's all paperwork and the boring stuff. Just take a break, get something to eat. One of us will report in every hour.'

Eppie could see Matt was weakening and applied the final incentive. 'Steak and kidney pie, followed by apple and blackberry crumble.'

Matt grinned and gave in gracefully. 'Give me five minutes.'

Eppie waited until he had gone to speak to the manager before high-fiving Sam. She was sure, when she got Matt home, fed and relaxed, he would see the sense of getting some rest. Angela was the last thing on her mind so she was shocked to see her walking round the gallery in the company of a PC. Eppie thought she looked rather pleased with herself.

'You have a lot to thank me for, young lady. I've just saved your husband's life.'

'You? How?'

'Oh just a well-aimed bottle of water. All those years playing tennis finally paid off.'

'Mum, you're making this up.'

'No, she's telling the truth.'

Eppie turned to find Matt behind her. He stepped forward to shake her mother's hand while she watched, shocked out of all speech.

'Thank you, Angela. You were a bit foolhardy, but what you did certainly helped the situation. Do you want a lift home?'

'No, thank you. I have to go and make a statement and then Derek will be waiting. Don't wait up.'

Angela went off with the PC and just when Eppie thought Matt was ready to leave, he turned back to talk to Sam. 'Don't forget you're supposed to have someone with you tonight.'

Sam grinned. 'I've got that well covered, guv.'

'Clare?'

'Spot on.'

'Good for you.'

Giving a tug on his arm, Eppie led him away before he could think of anything else to worry about.

# Chapter 92

It was a replica of her son's funeral: the same elderly neighbours, the vicar, Mary's brother and himself, this time on his own. The rest of the team were getting ready to say farewell to Grant, whose funeral was later today. Matt needed to be here for Mary. He'd tortured himself going over what he could have done to bring about a different outcome, to keep her safe. With everyone's head bowed in prayer, he asked for her forgiveness.

Shaking her brother's hand afterwards, Matt was at a loss to know what to say beyond the usual platitudes. As they moved out to where the flowers were on display, he was glad that he had sent a wreath that helped augment the sparse contributions. Not knowing anyone and keeping a note of the time, Matt stayed for ten minutes before making his excuses and leaving to make his way to St Mary's Church in Warwick and Grant's funeral. He'd heard from Lynne that she and Melli were attending and he wanted to be there to greet and look after them.

By the time he arrived, the top brass were already beginning to assemble. Briefly acknowledging them, he went to stand in the doorway of the church. With over a thousand years of worship, St Mary's held a unique atmosphere, as if spirits from those thousand years lingered to comfort those in the present day. Not that Matt felt any spirit could console him today. Taking a deep breath, he moved back outside to wait for Lynne.

'Inspector Turrell.'

Matt turned to find DI Fraser. 'Inspector Fraser.'

'A sad day.'

Hardly trusting himself to speak, Matt replied, 'Yes.'

'We did do our best, you know?'

'Pity it wasn't good enough.' As soon as the words were out of his mouth, Matt regretted them, knowing how it felt when an investigation failed to save a life. He tried to soften the impact. 'It was probably too late before you became involved.'

'Maybe.'

'Any luck with Harper-Jones?'

'Not yet, although we did get close thanks to your whisky tip-off. He's a cunning old bastard.'

'That's for sure.'

It was a relief when the cortège arrived accompanied by two motorcycle outriders. He waited as the Chief Super helped Lynne and Melli out of the funeral car. Matt thought they both looked overwhelmed and hesitated as to whether he should step forwards. Lynne solved the problem by moving to greet him.

'Inspector Turrell, I'm so glad you are here. Would you mind escorting us?'

Matt glanced at the super, not wanting to tread on his toes, and received a nod to continue. As they paused for the coffin to be unloaded, Matt sought for something to say. Melli stood pale and quiet, appearing to be in a world of her own. Following the coffin up the aisle, Matt chose to sit next to Lynne, hoping that having someone else to support would take his mind off the fact that Grant was dead and this was the final goodbye.

Lynne remained dry-eyed throughout and didn't seem to need his support. As always with funerals, the music brought feelings to the surface and Melli burst into tears at the start of the first hymn and cried throughout. The super had come prepared and offered his hankie while Lynne held her hand. Matt hoped this indicated their relationship was back on track.

As the service continued, he risked glancing round to see stony-faced colleagues, including Jane and Sam, successfully burying their feelings and turned back to concentrate on the elaborate carved pulpit. When at last it was over, Matt sensed the relief of the whole congregation.

Outside, as Lynne received condolences from the top brass, Melli dried her eyes and approached him. 'Inspector Turrell, can I talk to you?'

'Of course. What's on your mind, Melli?'

'I want to join the force, here in Warwickshire, like Dad.'

'Aren't you going to university?'

'Not now.'

Matt paused. This sounded like some sort of grief reaction and he didn't want to encourage her, even though it echoed his own choices. He was aware of Lynne's anxious glances towards them and guessed she was aware of Melli's decision. Choosing his words carefully, he led Melli away from the crowd. 'This may not be a good time to make such an important decision.'

'That's what Mum says.'

'And she's right, Melli. You would be better getting your degree and then, if you still want to join the force, it would give you more choices.'

'Dad worked his way up. I want to do the same.'

'Things have changed so much since your dad and even I joined. The advance in technology alone calls for better-educated officers. And yes, there are advantages to working your way up, but if you were my daughter, I would recommend getting your degree first.' Matt realised this was the first time he could understand where his dad was coming from. Could he have been right after all?

Lynne approached. 'I hope you are not encouraging her, Inspector Turrell.'

'Of course he isn't. No one understands.' Melli began to flounce away.

Matt reached out to stop her. 'Hang on. I have an idea. You have nine months until you go to university. How about you keep your options open until then and, if you're still keen, sometime next year I'll try to get you a few days' work experience.'

'You'd do that?'

'Can't promise I'll be able to swing it, but I'll ask.'

'No tricks?'

He wanted to laugh, already seeing an astute mind that someday could make an ideal member of the force. 'None at all. I'll send you some information meanwhile.'

'Okay.'

'Thanks.' Lynne touched his arm as she followed Melli back towards the cars.

Matt wondered what Grant would have made of his offer. Maybe he wouldn't thank him.

# Chapter 93

It was Christmas Eve and the lights from the Christmas tree bestowed a shimmer on the room, softening the corners and giving it a snug, inviting feel. For the first time, Matt felt the charm of the tree. He drew Eppie onto his knee, enjoying the feel of her body as she relaxed against him. 'Alone at last.'

'Not for long. Mum should be back soon.'

'That's where you're wrong.'

Eppie sat up straight and turned to look at him. 'What are you up to, Matt? You've had that look all day.'

'Your mother is at this moment enjoying a welcome drink…'

'You found somewhere?'

'Yes.'

'Where?'

'Heath End Spa.'

'Oh.'

Eppie looked worried and, given the memories of the place, Matt thought it wasn't surprising. He tried to reassure her. 'Hey. Clive Draper is in custody. They don't breed serial killers there.'

'No. Of course not. It's just… I can still see… Promise you'll never take me there.'

'I've got no intention.'

'Was she pleased?'

'Couldn't get out of here fast enough.'

'Did you tell her it was—'

'No way. Anyway, I don't intend to spend Christmas talking about your mother, Mrs Turrell.' He pulled her close and indulged in a long kiss.

# Also by JJ Franklin

## Urge to Kill

### The first DI Matt Turrell investigation

*Matt shivered at the odd mix of images. It was almost as if they had the copper's nightmare to deal with – a child's murder. Except this was no innocent child but a young woman; he would guess around twenty-two and with everything to live for. Though it was obvious she was a woman, the bows in her hair, her pink party dress and white ankle socks said she was a little girl.*

Detective Inspector Matt Turrell returns from honeymoon to face the most bizarre and dangerous case of his career after the body of a woman is found at a luxury spa near Stratford-upon-Avon. However, struggling within the confines of his new marriage, and haunted by a past mistake, Matt finds it difficult to concentrate.

Killer Clive Draper is a clever, ambiguous character whose motives and personality are not beyond empathy. Empowered by his first kill, Clive uses his charm to draw further victims into his net. Seeing Matt as his mortal enemy, he uses his charisma to lure Matt's new wife into his snare.

With the danger coming ever closer to home, Matt finds himself drawn into a deadly duel, where he must put his own life on the line and where the stakes have never been higher.

*Urge to Kill* is the first in a series of novels featuring DI Matt Turrell of the Warwickshire Police. It is a rich psychological thriller with great character development of both the detective and the murderer. The reader quickly becomes engaged in the epic battle between these two men. The book is set within the historic district of Stratford-upon-Avon.